"YOU'RE LYING IN YOUR TEETH, MISS BOLTWOOD.

We'll have the truth now, if you please."

"I didn't steal anything, if that's what you think!"

"No, I didn't think it was money you were after, and I am wearing my diamond stud. So, what was it brought you here? I would like to conclude it was a social visit merely."

Her tongue touched her lips as she tried to calculate what actual danger she was in. Under her father's roof, he couldn't do anything to her. "This is the last place I'd come to for agreeable company!" she said sassily.

He looked over his shoulder to the locked door, and advanced from the desk to where she stood, placing himself squarely between her and the door. "You're not home free yet, my girl."

"You will not quite dare to *murder* me in my own home," she replied. But she knew he was capable of anything. . . .

Also by Jennie Gallant:

LADY HATHAWAY'S HOUSE PARTY

THE MOONLESS NIGHT

Jennie Gallant

FAWCETT COVENTRY • NEW YORK

THE MOONLESS NIGHT

Published by Fawcett Coventry Books, a unit of CBS Publications, the Consumer Publishing Division of CBS Inc.

ISBN: 0-449-50040-3

Printed in the United States of America

First Fawcett Coventry printing: April 1980

10 9 8 7 6 5 4 3 2 1

1

Bolt Hall sat perched on the rock cliffs of southern England overlooking the gray Atlantic, somewhat resembling a toad preparing to take a plunge into a pond. So it had sat, not greatly changed since the late fifteenth century. With its squat solid body, gray and ugly, further disfigured by an awkward combination of round and square towers, its only beauty was its dramatic location. Below it the rock fell away sheer to the sea. On the west side of the promontory a sheep or a nimble-footed person could find sufficient foothold to descend down the scarp to a dock below. There was a bay here, with a river debouching into the sea. Several yachts danced at anchor at the dock, lending a holiday liveliness to the scene. The brisk breezes caught the sails of one that was preparing to take a run westward to Plymouth.

There was considerable running down to Plymouth in this July of 1815. By boat, carriage, horse, or shank's mare, the whole countryside was bent on reaching Plymouth, where Napoleon Bonaparte was imprisoned aboard the British frigate *Bellerophon*, not more than a mile from shore, after surrendering himself to the British. The neighborhood pastime of late was endeavoring to get a glimpse of this monster before he was hauled off into oblivion. But the yacht of Sir Henry Boltwood, the proud owner of Bolt Hall, was not so frivolously occupied. It was, to the chagrin of Sir Henry's son David, being overhauled for the much more important task of capturing Boney when he tried to escape.

"If that ain't just like Papa, to be having the keel scraped and painted when I might any moment have to go dashing to Captain Maitland's aid," David lamented to his sister, who stood with him on the cliff that was their front lawn.

Marie smiled in commiseration. "There are any number of other ships you can use in that case, Dave," she comforted him. "You must see there are seven yachts at the wharf, ready to form a flotilla and go after General Bonaparte should he manage to flee Captain Maitland."

"Yes, but *I* won't be the captain if it's Sinclair's yacht takes the lead. Besides, ours is the best in the neighborhood. You know Papa must always be first in everything. The *Fury* could beat them all in a race. How I'd love to have a crack at Boney," he said wistfully.

A college boy still, he had not been permitted to have the more formal crack that joining the army would have allowed. No, what must *he* do while Wellington chased Bonaparte across Europe but have his nose stuck into a book of Greek poetry, learning useless stuff at Oxford. That the nose was more likely to have been stuck into a tankard of ale was no consolation either. His life had been wasted, and now the last chance for glory was being similarly thrown away because Papa had decided to have the keel scraped and painted. In his mind's eye he stood at the helm of a frigate, wearing an admiral's uniform, one eye covered by a black patch like Nelson, and possibly an arm in a sling, if it wouldn't impede his activities too much. There was an heroic gleam in his brown eyes, a noble expression on his youthful countenance, and a hard candy stuck into his cheek to ruin the whole of his pose as he stood looking out to sea.

"I don't suppose he'll really try to escape," Marie mentioned. She was young too, but not so young as David, and not so much given to heroism. Twenty last birthday, she considered herself a lady now, and tried to behave like one. From having roamed the rocks, the roads and the sea with her brother for as long as she could remember, she occasionally lapsed into behaving like a gentleman. She was aided in her efforts by two very high sticklers, however, her father and his sister, Biddy Boltwood, who was her chaperone.

"What, not try to escape and Plymouth full of cutthroat Frenchies come for no other reason than to give him a hand? I swear the place is overrun with them. I don't know what Liverpool is about, to be letting them run loose at a time like this. They ought to be everyone locked up till Napoleon is packed off somewhere safe."

Marie recognized the echo of her father in this speech, and asked, "Who would rescue him in that case?"

"He'd rescue himself," was the unhesitating answer. "He is up to anything. You can't think a mere shipful of British sailors a match for the Emperor?"

"I don't suppose a thing more exciting will happen than that he will be transferred to a different ship, and taken away in a week or so. I wonder where they'll take him."

David bridled at this down-to-earth suggestion, but as he happened to have overheard his father discuss this point with Mr. Sinclair, he answered. "There is talk of Saint Helena. It's an island out in the middle of the ocean somewhere—Africa, I think, is the closest land to it."

"Pity," she said, shaking her head sadly, as she looked down at the yachts ready for, and their owners all craving, a little excitement.

David did not share her pessimism. He felt in his bones he would do battle with Boney yet, and to be prepared, he scampered down the rocks to harry the painters into getting the keel of *Fury* finished up. In a pinch, he could ride to sea in a boat with wet paint.

Marie took one last hopeful look out to sea, where the *Bellerophon* was well beyond her view, but to know it was out there, off Plymouth, with Napoleon Bonaparte in a cabin lent a new charm to the same waves she had been viewing all her life. Like David, she had a feeling something should come of the Emperor's proximity. With her, it was not a chase or a rescue that figured so prominently as a vague feeling of romance. Napoleon was surely a magnet that would draw famous, interesting and eligible persons to Plymouth, where she could meet them. Of all the hordes who were there and still swarming in every day, there must be *one* amongst them willing to fall in love with her.

Deprived of her brother's company, she turned and went into the Hall, to find her father sprawled out on a chaise lounge, his left arm exposed with three leeches, their oblong bodies engrossed, clinging to it. Biddy was bleeding him again. "Say what you will, these speckled leeches are not so effective as a good Hungarian green leech," she was saying, for perhaps the sixth time that afternoon, and the sixtieth at least that month. "Here, I believe this fellow is ready to come off," she added, lifting the largest by the tail.

"He's still in," Sir Henry informed her with a wince.

"So he is," she agreed, and settled back to wait, too wise in the way of leeches to remove one by force, and risk leaving its teeth in the arm to cause mischief.

"Mr. Hennessy wants some of our leeches, Henry," she went on. Biddy kept a leech reservoir, and had accomplished what was beyond so many of her fellow quacks, had coerced her leeches into propagating. She raised the best leeches in England, she allowed modestly. The south of Europe of course gave a better leech, but during the Napoleonic wars, she had been the main source of clean leeches in the country, and was as proud of it as if it were thoroughbred horses she raised. She guaranteed half an ounce at a draw if the flesh were well cleaned before applying, and if the leech had been aired, and if, of course, you didn't skint by trying to use the same leech before the requisite four months were up between applications.

Her appearance was plain in the extreme—a tall, gaunt, thin-faced lady of perhaps fifty years. Her fortune was small and her accomplishments few, but she had created for herself an amusing oasis in the desert of life with her leeches. The oasis was gradually enlarging to include other branches of medicine as well. An embrocation, a posset or a pill was not beyond her, and while she had not yet got into the setting of bones, she was beginning to tamper with internal disorders.

"Where is David?" Sir Henry asked, looking up from under his beetle brows, his lips assuming their customary sullen line. It was the remark he most often addressed to his daughter. He had a housekeeper and nurse in Biddy, a son and heir in David, and an unnecessary nuisance in Marie, though he did not by any means dislike her. Merely he had been so grievously disappointed when his wife's first pledge of her love had been a female that he could never quite forgive either of them.

"Out at the dock hurrying the painters on, Papa," she told him, knowing he would be pleased at his son's interest in the preparations for Boney's capture.

"I'm surprised he isn't gone into Plymouth to rub elbows with every hedgebird and commoner in the place, and come home with a cold," Biddy adjured, keeping a sharp eye on her leeches. One fell off, and she hefted it with a professional hand, informing her patient it was not less than half an ounce in this one.

"I have to go into town myself," Sir Henry displeased his strict sister by saying.

"Henry, you must rest an hour after leeching," she warned him. "Your blood will be thinned. You must have a lie-down and a cup of posset." Henry was her older brother and the owner of Bolt Hall—a more important person altogether than Miss Boltwood, but she had a strong personality and the power of her cures to add to her authority. She was seldom talked down by Henry.

"Yes, yes, I'll have my posset, but I must go into Plymouth before dinner. David will want to come along." David and

Sir Henry got on famously. It was no idle boast that David would like to go along. He idolized his father nearly as much as the father idolized himself.

"Parish board business," Sir Henry announced importantly. This conveyed to the intimates that Sir Henry was about to pester the directors of this unimportant body into yet another meeting to discuss "the situation." The area had many matters demanding attention—schools, hospitals, the roads—all were in need of improvement, but Sir Henry's pet hobby-horse was none of these. The indelicate "situation," never put into words before Marie, dealt with the problem of bastard children fathered outside the parish being foisted on the rate-payers of Plymouth for care and maintenance. There had been an alarming increase in this nefarious business of late. An increase of one hundred percent, in fact, from one child to two.

Marie heaved a weary sigh at the sameness and dullness of life, when she had so hoped that Napoleon's coming amongst them might make things livelier. But nothing was changed for *them*. Oh, the neighbors had their yachts docked at Bolt Hall, and came more often to discuss with her father plans for stopping any escape; she went every day with David to Plymouth to rub shoulders with the commoners and hedgebirds, but she had expected more. It seemed every house in the neighborhood but their own was bursting at the joints with visitors. With the half of London run down to Plymouth to get a look at Boney, it seemed a pity no one had come to them. But between her father's poor health and irritable nerves, he did not encourage company. She had envisioned parties and routs, too, but they hadn't been asked to one. The thing was, each large home had so many guests that they made up their own party in the evenings, and the Boltwoods were out of it. How she longed for company—some interesting gentlemen, preferably, though even a lady would have been a welcome addition.

"What are you in the hips about?" Biddy asked sharply, examining her niece's face in hopes of discovering another patient.

"Nothing."

"You look peaky to me."

"I'm fine, Auntie."

"I'll mix you up a paregoric draught," Biddy declared, scanning her store of provisions—oil of cinnamon, a drop of linseed oil, aloes . . .

This threat had the immediate effect of getting Miss Boltwood to her feet and out the door.

David was just returning from the dock when she reached the cliff. "I've just had a capital idea," he said, excitement lending a brilliant hue to his rosy cheeks.

"Father wants you to wait till he's had his posset and go to Plymouth with him," she answered, having a fair notion his capital idea was another jaunt into the city.

"That ain't it. I'm going to put up a telescope at Bolt Point," he informed her.

"What for?"

"To see *Bellerophon* of course. The point is half a mile closer to Plymouth than the Hall. It juts a good quarter of a mile into the ocean, and is a mile high," he exaggerated wildly. "It will give us a dandy view of the ship, much better than we can get from the cliff here, where you can't see a thing if it's the least bit hazy, and it always is. What an excellent thing it will be for the watchmen."

This sounded a great and unnecessary extravagance to Miss Boltwood, but she thought David just might talk their father into it. No trouble was too great for the owner of Bolt Hall. He took his duty seriously. For several centuries the Hall had stood on guard against invaders, and on occasion had spewed out invaders of its own. The siege of Calais had had men and ships supplied from Bolt Hall. Here the Royalist garrison had camped and eventually fallen during the Civil War; it had been active during the Spanish Secession wars, and more recently when Bonaparte had his flotilla readying at Boulogne to attack, one hundred ships, ninety-five of them fairly useless, had stood at the ready to repulse him. And now again, with the menace of one deposed general floating at their doorstep, Sir Henry was readying his private forces to defend England. Oh yes, he would agree to the telescope.

David dashed into the Hall to interrupt the taking of the posset, to his aunt's dismay, but he never minded old Biddy. He had soon talked his father into being thrilled with the idea. "I wonder it wasn't thought of before. An excellent notion. You are as long-headed as they come. A chip off the old block, heh heh."

Long before the hour's rest was up, the pair of them were driving into Plymouth to purchase a powerful telescope to be erected at Bolt's Point, where men would be on duty from dawn to dark, looking out to sea, when they should be cutting hay and picking vegetables. Boltwood's army was comprised entirely of Sir Henry's own fieldhands.

Marie went along with them for something to do. It was hard getting the days in at Bolt Hall, and any diversion was welcome, particularly a diversion that featured so many strangers, many of them wearing the scarlet tunic and shako of the army lately stationed at Plymouth, and many more wearing the more familiar blue tunic of the navy. Accompanied by a father who looked considerably like a dragon, and a dashing gentleman who might have been a beau for all a stranger knew, she had very little entertainment other than looking at the young men. They greeted her with respect and reserve. She didn't get so much as a nod from any of them.

David, who went to Plymouth with no thought of romance, had his mind jolted in that direction by the appearance of Madame Monet. This intriguing foreigner had reached Plymouth the week previously, when Bonaparte had been at Tor Bay. She was a French lady of doubtful background and uncertain years, though Biddy said certainly she was not under thirty. In any case, she wore the remnants of a handsome, lively face, and managed her eyes better than Bonaparte managed an army. She was a subject of consuming interest to the younger Bolts. David of course assumed she was a spy, come here for the purpose of freeing her lover, Napoleon. Marie would have liked to share this view, but had had dinned into her ears by Biddy that "the creature" was here for a quite different purpose, to land Sir Henry. As Madame's forward behavior tended to support this claim, Marie was forced to put some faith in it.

On this occasion, Madame Monet wore her golden curls pinned up under a wide-brimmed bonnet of peacock blue, her full frame encased in a gown of similar color, and in her hand she carried a parasol to ward off the sun. Her eyes widened with interest as she spotted the Boltwood party, and she was soon rushing towards them, having scraped an acquaintance first with David—not difficult to achieve—and soon enlarged it to include the whole ménage.

"Sir Henry—*enchantée* to see you!" she smiled, revealing a set of teeth in good repair. "I had fear the humid weather would unsettle you." She offered her hand, which Sir Henry accepted with diffidence. He was no stranger to the theory that Madame had designs on him, and while he was not averse to the sympathy of a pretty woman, he did not wish to make it a permanent feature in his life, so treated her with reserve.

"It takes its toll," he admitted stoically.

"Ah, but you are pale like a ghost," she complimented him.

"I have been leeched," he informed her, and was congratulated on this wisdom.

"How do the preparations go on at Bolt Hall?" she asked, knowing what subjects were pleasing to him.

David slid a knowing glance to his sister. *Here is what she is really after,* it said. She was told about the telescope, and expressed such an interest in it that David had to interfere before she got herself invited up to the Point for a demonstration by his father. If anyone took her, it would be himself.

"Any news on the quay today?" David asked, to change the subject.

"A rumor for every hour, each proved untrue in its turn. They have turned three hundred customers away at the inn where I stay, and raise the rates every day. They are trying to put an *actress* into my room with me! *Mon Dieu,* how I wish I had some acquaintances in the neighborhood to stay with. To be jostled and crowded by commoners is not at all *comme il faut,* not what I am accustomed to."

"You would be wise to leave," Sir Henry told her, his tough old heart completely in league with anyone who disliked a too close propinquity to commoners.

"But where to go?" she asked pathetically, hitting him with the full force of her large eyes, hinting at unshed tears. "Do you have many guests at Bolt Hall?" she asked next, making her aim quite clear.

The question went unanswered. "I meant leave the neighborhood entirely," Sir Henry explained. "This is no place for a lady."

"I plan to return to France as soon as that Corsican villain is sent away," she explained at once. "There I have many friends. My husband's home, the Château de Ferville, was requisitioned by Napoleon, you must know. Hundreds of his soldiers desecrating its priceless walls. The Gobelin tapestries thrown on the floor for blankets or rugs. The paintings used for target practice, the silverplate for tools, and the *meubles, sans prix,* thrown into the grate for firewood. The only thing I managed to rescue was the Monet sapphires, worth a small fortune of course, and a few smaller jewels that I pawn from

12

day to day to pay for the inn. I fear for my sapphires, at that inn with poor locks. But I always take them with me when I go out. I have them on me now, but it is impossible to show them to you," she explained, patting her bosom to show their resting place. "I shall stay and see with my own eyes he is deported. They should kill him."

This tale of awful behavior struck a responsive cord with Sir Henry, who was always happy to hear ill of a foreigner. To hear repeated his own theory that Napoleon ought to be killed went down even better. "Ought to be drawn and quartered," he agreed.

"You should set up a petition to that effect. Mine would be amongst the signatures," she told him, having heard in the streets of his fondness for a petition.

Somehow the idea of petitioning the Emperor's death had not occurred to him. In truth, little did occur to him till it occurred first to another who told him of it. The notion appealed strongly to him at once. To be heading up another committee, dashing about from one illustrious home to another spouting off his ideas, having his name in the papers—it would have the parish board beat all hollow for distinction. They'd write it up in London. He thought of his racked constitution, hardly kept on his pegs by the ministrations of his sister, and wondered if he were up to it. But standing in the sweltering sun talking to a foreigner he was not up to, and soon was taking his leave.

"Do you have many guests at Bolt Hall?" Madame repeated, just before he got away.

"We are not set up for company at the Hall," he answered.

She blinked her big blue eyes to hear a huge mansion, a castle really in all but name, with close to forty bedchambers and as many servants, was incapable of taking a single guest.

"Is no one at all with you?" she asked, stunned.

"No, no one. Good day, Madame," Sir Henry said, bowed formally, and left. David cast one last suspicious glance at Madame, torn by the conflicting desires of keeping the spy out in the cold and getting her to Bolt Hall, where he could keep a sharper eye on her, and possibly be compelled, in the line of duty of course, to make love to her.

"You see what she's up to," he said to his father. "She wants to get into Bolt Hall to interfere with our preparations. I don't doubt she's in league with the set that plans to free Boney."

Marie had mixed emotions. Madame was vulgar of course,

and she had not the least desire to acquire her for a stepmother, but men followed in Madame's wake in shoals. With this French *fleur* in the saloon, it would not long be empty of men. She placed little reliance on the story that Madame was in on the scheme, if there even was one.

There was no doubt allowed in the matter of the scheme's existence so far as the men were concerned. The preparations at the Hall, the assembled yachts, the painting of the keel, the new telescope—all were founded on this hypothesis, and it was long established as fact. No man could call himself Sir Henry's friend at such a time if he did not subscribe to the theory, and by talking it over with the converted it had gone beyond dispute that there was such a plot, but of so secretive and insidious a nature that they had not yet discovered anything about it.

2

In a small, out-of-the-way corner within the labyrinth that is Whitehall, there is one office whose door bears no brass plaque, whose inhabitants, and they are only two, are not officially listed in the records of the Admiralty, to which department they are assigned. It would be easy to imagine the elderly gentleman who presides over his one employee there as a king's pensioner, given a corner to grow old in in payment for some minor service to his country in times gone by. His nearest neighbor within the building, a very junior liaison man for the naval supplies department, smiles on him with great condescension and pity, and thanks his stars that *he* has an uncle who is married to a lady who is connected with Melville, First Lord of the Admiralty, or he too might end up in such obscurity. The young liaison officer is not personally acquainted with his tenuous connection: Lord Melville, does not, in fact, recognize him when he sees him several times a month, come into this backwater of the building.

Had he been at his door any time during the past four days he might, however, have recognized the Foreign Secretary, Lord Castlereagh, for he had been presented to him at a ball once, and he would have recognized the Lord Chancellor of England, Lord Eldon, as every public servant knew him and his nasty temper. The Chancellor of the Exchequer, Lord Vansittart, went in unrecognized, along with sundry less exalted personages attached to the Lords Commissioners of the Admiralty. The Prime Minister had not been to call, but it was not unknown for that elderly gentleman to meet with him in cabinet at Downing Street.

The traffic to and from the little office was not always heavy; sometimes no one came for days in a row, but recently there had been many comings and goings, ever since Napoleon had escaped from Elba, but more especially since he had been defeated at Waterloo. Between June nineteenth and twenty-second, Sir George had not been home at all. As chief of Admiralty Intelligence, he had been greatly occupied to discover the movements of Napoleon, and more importantly, his plans.

So efficient was Sir George's operation that he knew within a hundred guineas how much property the lately deposed Emperor had amassed for his escape, including his stepdaughter Queen Hortense's farewell gift of her diamond necklace, exchanged for his wedding ring. Gold, silverplate, books—all were inventoried. One could not but respect a man who worried about his books with his neck stretched so far out. He knew how many of his followers were with him at Rochefort —sixty-four, including Fouché and of course his loyal valet, Marchand. Knew as well that Rochefort, the most easily blockaded port in all of France, had been chosen by Fouché and Savary. With such friends, Boney had no need of enemies. He'd be dead by now if that pair had their way. The precise options open to Bonaparte were known, along with the persons who had proposed them, and the reasons why they had been rejected. Captain Philibert was for taking him to America in style and openly, but the safe conduct had not come through. Fat chance! Las Cases and his set were for smuggling him to America by means of a plan devised by Admiral Martin, a veteran seadog. Slip him onto the frigate *Bayadère*, anchored in the Gironde, and hence across the sea to America. Yet another loyal follower, Besson, offered to run the English blockade and smuggle him to America with a cargo of cognac, hiding him in a cask if searched. But the Emperor—funny how one went on considering him an Emperor still—was too proud for that. His brother Joseph's offer to pose as the Emperor at Aix while Napoleon made good his escape was likewise rejected. Faithful—he had a certain style, an integrity. He was not for saving himself at the cost of his friends and family.

Returning to Paris with Louis XVIII already in power was out. The solution found, foolish as it sounded, was to come to England, the oldest and most hated of his enemies. Here, in this bastion of personal freedom, he hoped to go free, and he would be disappointed. Thought he would set himself up as an English squire as his brother had been permitted to do in Worcestershire. But Lucien and Napoleon were two very different articles. If one thought for a moment Liverpool and Eldon would allow it, an accident might be arranged, but there was no danger. The English government officials were as one in not wanting him. Not one bloody toe would he set on English soil. Plymouth Harbor—that's as close as he would get to England's shores, and it was too close for comfort!

There was a tap at the door of Sir George FitzHugh's oak-paneled office, and a tall young gentleman strolled in, nodded without smiling, and possessed himself of the stiffly uncomfortable settee lately used as Sir George's bed. He threw one leg over the other, stretched his arms along the settee's back and said in a bored voice, "Well, Fitz, let's have it. You haven't summoned me here . . ."

"*Invited,* my friend," Fitz corrected.

"True, the message was worded as an invitation, but somehow you know, when one of your demmed clerks pulls me by the elbow as I strut down Bond Street—I *wish* you would ask him not to pull at one's jacket—and shouts 'Urgent,' one feels the invitation to be—ah, peremptory."

"Did he do so? Well I'm very sorry about the jacket, but the deuce of it is, it's a bit of a rush affair this time."

The gentleman gazed at a mote of dust on his Hessians and frowned. Receiving no further intelligence from his informer, he finally raised his dark eyes. "Do go on, Fitz," he invited.

"Yes, a rush affair. Very hush hush you know," he continued in a low voice, his blue eyes peering about the room, as though the walls might have ears. Satisfying himself at length that he had only the one hearer, he announced in a voice of strained solemnity, "It's Boney, you see."

The guest jerked to attention. "He hasn't got away!" he asked, in a voice much too loud to please Fitz. He was told

16

by a finger to Sir George's lips that his tone was to be lowered.

"Not yet," Fitz answered in a significant tone. "But I have received word from a reliable source that plans are afoot to free him."

Every muscle of the listener's body was tense now, his glance trained on the speaker, and his head bent forward the better to hear the low words. No further words were forthcoming, however, and he thought a moment before speaking. "This is impossible," he said. "Napoleon is on a British ship in British waters, surrounded by Holsham's navy. His army is defeated—he could not return to France if he did escape. He knows what happened to Ney. He gave himself up to England freely. You alarm yourself for nothing, Fitz. This is a bag of moonshine someone has delivered you."

"Hear me!" Fitz interrupted, raising a finger. "I told you my source was reliable. He has just made a trip to Plymouth, and tells me the place is rife with Frenchmen. You may imagine for what purpose."

"But the French émigrés are adamantly against Napoleon, surely. They would not help him escape. They will be preparing to return to France and make their bows to the Bourbon king."

"No, no, you misunderstand me. I don't speak of the noble families who fled the Revolution, though to be sure that was twenty-five years ago now, and there might be some younger sons with views different from their parents. They have seen Napoleon take on nearly the whole of Europe and come perilously close to conquering it. Hero worship. They might be happy enough to throw in their lot with Napoleon—but then this is hardly the time for it, when he is finished. I speak of quite a different sort of Frenchman, however. After Bonaparte's escape from Elba some think him a superman, and believe he will one day go back and be Emperor again."

"The Congress of Vienna expressly forbid . . ."

"Deuce take it, *I* know he's done for. At least—well there's no saying with Boney. The crowd will spit on him when he's down but only let him get a leg over his white horse with his three-cornered hat on his head and they're ready to bend the knee to him again. He has something."

"A certain *je ne sais quoi*," the gentleman agreed.

"Eh?"

"He has a certain something, true. But still, how do they,

these French upstarts, think to remove him from Maitland's ship, with half the navy standing by?"

"It ain't standing by. It's loitering around France and strung out ready to blockade him if he tries to run for America. There are only three ships actually on guard—the *Daphne,* the *Slaney* and the *Myrmidon.* But they don't mean to run him through the blockade. He had that chance with Besson and passed it up."

"What then, get him to England proper? He'd like that well enough."

"Aye, to become an English squire like his brother. We kept a close watch on him at Thorngrove, eh lad? You made an admirable footman."

"And sometimes gardener, Fitz. You forget my dual role."

"I forget nothing. However, I believe Napoleon has something else in mind now. He asked us for the safe conduct to America you recall, and he still means to get there. Knowing the seas are guarded closely at this time, he has in mind to hide out in either England or Ireland for half a year or so till the heat cools down, then go on a fishing vessel or some such thing. The Irish would be happy enough to give him a hand to spite us. They don't love us, you know. There are rumors the Ribbon Society is re-forming, likely for this very reason. Our government is determined to get him well beyond reach this time and incarcerate him. While that man walks free, Europe is not safe. He has been shedding blood these twenty years, and it must be ended. Well then, you see the position. He is on Captain Maitland's ship, the *Bellerophon,* with a few of his own men. Since the end of June he has known he was coming to England. With the General's known ingenuity and attention to detail, it is absurd to think he has not been funneling money, men, and very likely arms, too, into England. These Frenchmen hanging around the wharf are not necessarily the penniless wanderers they seem to be. They might very well be trained soldiers and sailors. Bonaparte was known to have gathered his friends and chattels around him at Rochefort. If he made no arrangements himself, his faithful followers would have forseen the need of their help. Yes, the coast of England is crawling with Frenchmen bent on rescuing their Emperor."

"Yes, I see an undesirable situation exists. With Napoleon it is wise to take no chances. What, though, is it exactly you would have me do?"

"Get down to Plymouth at once. Keep that sharp nose of

yours to the ground; use your ears to hear what you can, and keep in close touch with me. You'll take that valet and groom of yours with you, I expect. Send one of them to me immediately if you hear anything, and if the matter is urgent—well, I don't have to tell the Fox how to proceed to thwart a mutual enemy."

"Can't imagine why you stuck me with that demmed silly name. It's not as though I were cursed with a red thatch, and have not, I hope, a vulpine phiz."

"Alphabetical. You were my sixth assistant. You're now number one. Chapworth and Dillen and the others are either dead or retired. Oh, speaking of retirement, you're to put up with Sir Henry Boltwood at Bolt Hall."

The Fox's face fell. "Not that rum touch who used to be at the Admiralty some several eons ago, ordering up woolen undershirts for Wellington's men sweltering in Spain?"

"The same," Fitz replied, with a mute rolling of the eyes that told his caller he shared this view of Sir Henry.

"Ah well, into every life some rain must fall. This promises to be a deluge. Does he know why I'm going?"

"He knows what he must. I had to give him a hint to explain billeting you on him. His place is always the rallying point at Plymouth for any trouble. You will meet everyone there, and there are yachts in plentiful supply should your work take you out to sea."

"Couldn't I put up at an inn, and hire a ship?"

"Full. And you know Boltwood, so your going will not appear unusual."

"Precisely, I know him, and it must follow as the night the day that I not wish to be a guest under his roof."

"The inn is chockful, and old Boltwood for all his prosy and missish ways knows everyone in the neighborhood. He'll be useful for contacts. Has a nubile daughter, I might add."

"Did you think to inquire whether the *cellars* at the inn are full, too?", the Fox asked with a sneer that was intended for a smile.

Fitz laughed lightly. "That I didn't, but if you are too stifled with Sir Henry you might wangle a short visit to some other homes. You'll be in touch with Admiral Keith in charge of the naval station in Plymouth and he'll put any of his lads you require at your disposal. Rig up some story for the others to account for your being there. The old lad doesn't entertain if he can help it."

"He does not *entertain* at all, even if he has company."

"The daughter might do as an excuse. You could make out you are interested in her."

The Fox shook his head. "A footman, a gardener or a gypsy I could simulate. A suitor to Sir Henry Boltwood's daughter is a role well beyond my poor capabilities. Leave it to me, Fitz. I did not come down in the last rain. Now, is there anything else?"

"One more tidbit. I've been saving the best for the last. What would you say if I told you Cicero is squatting down Plymouth way?"

"Ah—now there is a definite lead!" the Fox replied, smiling. "I have been itching to lock horns with Cicero. Missed out on all the fun in Vienna when Cicero led your boys a merry chase. But if it is Cicero who is to be watched, all your fine talk of the French admiring Bonaparte is chaff. Plain old money is what motivates Cicero."

"And the rest of the world, by and large. These chaps who call themselves patriots only have an eye to self-advancement under a new régime. You must by all means keep a sharp eye on Cicero."

The Fox felt a tingle of excitement and an impatience to be into his curricle. "Very well. I can leave within the hour. I'll keep in touch."

He arose to a height of six feet, straightened his exquisitely-cut jacket with a hunch of his shoulders, and lifted his curled beaver and malacca cane from the settee.

Sir George, glancing at the elegant creature before him, found it hard to believe he was interested in anything but the cut of his coat. Having some familiarity with the Fox's past exploits, however, he was not deceived by his bored smile and air of ennui. Fitz's army was not quite the scum of the earth, as Wellington had seen fit to describe his, but there was scum aplenty in it. But he had need of all manner of recruits, and an impeccable gentleman such as the Fox had access to places and persons denied to ordinary mortals, as in this case for instance.

The Fox performed a little salaam, turned and left, walking at a lazy gait that did not for an instant fool FitzHugh as to his recruit's eagerness for the job. When Sir George's clerk entered the room a moment later, he was surprised to find his superior chuckling into his collar.

"Good news, Sir George?" he ventured to inquire.

"Good fun, Chipworth. Good fun. I wish I could go to Plymouth myself to see the Fox mix it up with Sir Henry

Boltwood." He shook his head in regret, and picked up a memo from Lord Bathurst, outlining the place of exile planned for Napoleon, frowning at the name of Hudson Lowe chosen as guardian.

3

Sir Henry sat at his polished mahogany desk admiring the trophies of a hardly illustrious career of five years duration with the Admiralty. His wife's demise in 1808 had coincided with the departure of the fleet from Bolt Hall, and to find purpose in a meaningless existence, he had volunteered his services to king and country to help fight the menace of Napoleon Bonaparte. A corner had been found for him in the Admiralty, where it was thought (wrongly) that he could do little harm dispatching supplies to Wellington in the Peninsula. He had caused the Iron Duke more woe than the rest of all the body politic together, dispatching guns without ammunition, winter uniforms for summer campaign, and fruit from his orangery, perfectly ripe when it left England's shore, putrid before it was a week at sea. Wellington had managed to get him transferred to the office in charge of shipping goods to Canada to fight the Yankees, where his first act was to unload a cargo of much needed weapons and place in its stead hundreds of barrels of fresh water, to go to a country whose surface was largely composed of freshwater lakes and rivers. It was this carrying of coals to Newcastle that had led to his slightly premature retirement.

He was politely told that Bolt Hall was of more strategic importance to England than having such an accomplished supplies master, and sent home. But no one wished to hurt the old boy's feelings. The Prince of Wales had given him not only an ivory miniature of himself, presently framed and propped in a stand that allowed it to tilt up and down, but had knighted him as well. Plain Mr. Henry Boltwood had been raised to Sir Henry Boltwood, K.B.E., retiring to Bolt Hall covered in laurels, and Wellington had been allowed to get on with winning the war. Lord Liverpool, too, had been pressed into tendering his thanks, for the chap had taken no pay after all, and came up with a certificate of merit, hung on the wall of the study. Bathurst had given him a very ugly inkwell with hammered gold lid that he wished to be rid of, and Sir Henry had had a little plaque made up at his own expense to go with it. He was well pleased with all these tokens of success, and spent what time his poor health allowed sitting at his desk, admiring them and explaining their significance to callers.

To spend more time in his study, he had accepted a post on the board of directors of the local parish board, and was further adding to his glory at the moment by wording up the petition demanding execution for General Bonaparte, when his mail was brought in. A smile formed on his thin lips when he saw the crest of the Admiralty on one long envelope. They were asking his opinion about what to do with Boney, he thought complacently. They'd know his opinion well enough when Bathurst got his letter! With a respect bordering on reverence, he slit the envelope open, taking care not to rip into the seal. The crested envelopes made dandy book markers in books he never read but left sitting occasionally on his desk. The smile turned to amazement as he read down the page. "Dear sir: We seek your help in a matter of vital importance to the security of this country. We are aware of a plot to free General Bonaparte and ask your generosity in housing a special agent we are sending down to oversee this matter . . ." He read on, his heart beating tumultuously. There was much in it to please him, but the demand for complete secrecy sat poorly. Then, too, there was a certain insistence that the agent was to be master of the whole that discomfited him to no small degree. *He* was Sir Henry Boltwood, in charge of scotching Napoleon's plans, and for Lord Melville to speak of Sir Henry "tendering aid," to another skated precariously close to being an insult. He considered the matter for full twenty minutes before picking up his quill and penning a reply. It was in the affirmative, of course—one could not refuse to do his bit when his country needed him, and as to "tendering aid," there was nothing actually said of the fleet. He would remain in charge of the fleet, the captain of the ship that would put Boney in chains prior to drawing and quartering him. His reflections were not so far removed from those of his young son as he sat, pen in hand, staring at the Prince Regent's likeness.

It was a busy morning for him. The letter from Melville answered, he jotted one off to Bathurst asking what he thought of the notion of a petition demanding execution. He was so sure of a positive answer that he went ahead and drew it up, putting his own signature at the top of the page—Sir Henry Boltwood, K.B.E., in an impressive scrawl. He then dashed off to get Biddy, David and Marie to add theirs. He was so busy trotting from house to house amassing signatures and dropping the crested envelope and oblique hints as to an important missive from the Admiralty that he didn't spend a second overseeing the installation of the powerful telescope at Bolt's Point, thus saving David a great deal of annoyance.

The whole family was pleasantly occupied throughout the day, Marie with David, Sir Henry with his letters and his petition, and Biddy with preparing a room for a mysterious guest. She half thought from Sir Henry's air of importance the Prince Regent himself was coming to put up with them, and was thrilled at having a royal patient to see to, such a lovely invalidish one, too. The Prince's love of being bled was legendary. She had her plumpest leeches picked out, ready for royal blood.

The younger Boltwoods had no intimation they were to entertain company, and the young lady at least was delighted to find a fashionable gentleman sitting in the saloon when she came down to dinner. Had she known, she would have taken more pains with her toilette, but the caller did not seem to find anything amiss with her dark hair, bound back with silk primroses, her large brown eyes, sparkling with excitement to be at last doing some entertaining, nor even her gown, not quite in the highest kick of fashion, but stylish. The unwarranted treat of having company lent a high color to her cheeks.

Only Biddy was disappointed. No prince, not even an invalid. The young gentleman, Mr. Benson, looked remarkably robust. Not that he was a big, stout ruddy-faced man. They were good patients for leeching. This one was elegant rather than large. Hardy, but lean and athletic, with a pair of broad shoulders tapering to a narrow waist. He was thirtyish, dark and good looking. Sir Henry presented him as a family connection on his wife's side.

"My daughter is said to resemble her mama," he pointed out, the assumption being that Mr. Benson would have known the mother.

"You must have had a very pretty wife, Sir Henry," Mr. Benson replied, destroying that illusion.

"So, you are come to get a peek at the Corsican," Sir Henry went on, then explained to the family. "I finished up with my petition in Plymouth, and found Mr. Benson there, with no place to rest his head for the night, for the inns are full to the rafters."

Biddy knew this was nonsense, for she had been told specifically to turn out the gold suite, but naturally she said nothing. The gentleman said, "Very kind of you to give me rack and manger."

"I am happy to do it. Everyone is putting up guests these days. You would not be at all comfortable at the inn—my wife's cousin, after all. What do they say of Bonaparte in London?"

"There is a spirit of optimism that we have caged the lion at last. This will be the end of him. Saint Helena is spoken of as a place of exile."

"Exile! It is execution he wants. We saw how ineffective exile was at Elba. He'll be back at our throats with another army within a twelvemonth if he isn't executed. I have a petition going around. I have been in touch with Bathurst about it. You will want to add your name to the list."

"Yes, certainly," the man said, looking surprised. He was handed the sheet, and said as he wrote, "There is no talk in London of executing him, actually. A closer watch must be kept on him than was done at Elba of course, but it is exile only that is discussed. After all, he *did* give himself up voluntarily to Captain Maitland, and asked for mercy in his Themistocles-letter to the Prince Regent."

"As to that," Sir Henry began, assuming his customary scowl, "it was an impertinence on the Corsican's part to write such a missive. 'I come, like Themistocles, to throw myself on the *hospitality* of the British people.' Hospitality, mind you, not mercy. And to put himself under the protection of our laws, as though he were a British subject, and not a damned—ah, dashed prisoner of war."

"Still, in common courtesy it was expected the Prince of Wales might at least have answered the letter. It was a gratuitous insult to ignore it," Benson answered reasonably.

To suggest his beloved Prince Regent, the First Gentleman of Europe, was lacking in courtesy roused Sir Henry to wrath. "We'll give him a taste of English hospitality. Chains and the rack is what he wants! If it were me in charge of the man, he would be hanged like a common felon."

"Let us hope your petition proves effective, Sir Henry," Mr. Benson said, handing it back to him, "but I think myself that he is a very uncommon felon."

Marie, examining their visitor closely, thought she discerned a trace of amusement on the stranger's face, a touch of laughter hiding in the dark eyes. She wondered why he was with them. A connection of Mama's, of course, but not a close connection. He didn't even know what she had looked like. She supposed that he must have a yacht that was to be kept at Bolt Hall. Nothing else would account for such magnanimity on Papa's part. A yacht, at such a time, was better than charity for covering a multitude of sins. She put this question to him.

"No, I am not a sailor at all," he told her. "I would like to hire a boat and go out for a look at him, though, if I could get a crew together."

"Save your blunt. I'll take you," David told him. "As soon as the keel is dry. We have just had it painted. We have seven ships resting at the dock this minute, ready to thwart any escape plans Boney may have."

"Had a hundred when Napoleon had his flotilla readying at Boulogne," Sir Henry added.

"What, do you think he will try to escape?" Mr. Benson asked, startled.

"Certainly he will," Sir Henry told him. "It was at the back of his mind when he gave himself up. He little thought they would anchor him off Bolt Hall. If he were half as clever as everyone says he is, he would have known it. I daresay Plymouth was chosen with Bolt Hall in mind." He then went on to give a detailed history of Bolt Hall, till his listener's eyes were glazed. "But he won't get away. I'll take you down to the docks tomorrow and show you the ships, and the winch and chain."

"Winch and chain?" Mr. Benson inquired, in some confusion.

"It is too difficult to explain. It must be seen. I'll show it to you myself tomorrow. You will be interested to see it. Ingenious contraption. Bonaparte will have no hope of landing with my winch and chain to stop him," Sir Henry finished up, with a sage nod.

They went in to dinner, the talk being on the same subject as before the meal—Napoleon. When the ladies retired to the saloon, Marie said to her aunt, "I wonder why Papa asked Mr. Benson to stay with us. He hasn't a ship."

"Don't look a gift horse in the mouth," Biddy told her bluntly. "He is family, a well-born, well-to-do gentleman, with a nice little property of his own in Devon. Oakhurst, it is called. I expect Henry asked him to give you a chance to attach him. He has mentioned Benson to me before as a possible *parti* for you. It's high time you were married, Marie."

"Oh, is *that* why he is here?" she asked, smiling with pleasure. The matter of finding a husband for Marie was frequently discussed in the family. At twenty, she was not only ripe but becoming a little passé in the view of some. Her mother had been married at eighteen, and three-quarters of her own friends of the same age were married. There was not felt by the young lady herself to be any urgency in the matter. With a naval station at Plymouth, there was always such a gratifying surfeit of gentlemen at all the balls that one could not feel quite an ape-leader; still, younger sons making their way in the navy were not considered eligible for Miss Boltwood of Bolt Hall by either her father or her aunt. It was not a uniform they wanted, but a jacket by Weston, similar to that worn by Mr. Benson. Marie, always partial to a uniform, began to perceive that a black jacket, too, could lend distinction, when worn by a gentleman of the cut of their guest.

When the men returned to the saloon after their port, she felt some little hopes that she had incited Mr. Benson to admiration. He took up a seat beside her and began some conversation regarding her life, the very spirit of it showing her he was sensitive, considerate. "A pity your father had to leave London at just the time you were to have been presented," he mentioned. "I looked forward to meeting you."

Unfortunately, Biddy decided to reply for her. "Sir Henry should never have gone to London," she said. "It ruined his health forever. His lungs, his heart—they have never been the same since."

Benson acknowledged this irrelevance with a nod, then looked to Marie. "I was sorry to leave, but of course my father's health must come first," she replied.

"I had thought he was quite recovered. He looks well," Mr. Benson made the dreadful error of saying next, and was soon being treated to a list of his ailments, and in more length, their cures. He listened patiently to all this, but when she entered upon a pandect of healthful laws that ought to be followed by everyone, the patience began to wear thin. Changing tack, Biddy asked him if he had had that little cyst on his cheek examined professionally. Mr. Benson had a small mole at the outer side of his left cheek. Marie had just been thinking how attractive it was.

"No, it is nothing. I have had it forever," he said in a dismissing way, then looked hopefully to the younger Miss Boltwood for rescue.

She tried gamely to wrest him from Biddy's clutches, knowing nothing would be more likely to send their visitor looking elsewhere for a bed than one of Biddy's lectures. "We have just had a telescope put up on Bolt's Point today," she said. "Perhaps you would like to go up and have a look at it tomorrow."

"I would like to go this evening," he said at once, glancing to the windows, where it was far from dark. They kept country hours, dining at five. "Is it very far?"

"No, only half a mile away," she answered, and was on the verge of offering to point out the route, as it was visible from the garden, and the garden seemed a good spot to get Mr. Benson to herself for a moment.

"You won't want to go out with dark coming on," Biddy told him. "We get a nasty damp wind here on the coast."

"I am not at all troubled by dampness," he said, quite curtly, and looked to Marie. "Which direction is it?"

"It's just half a mile west of the Hall, towards Plymouth," Biddy informed him. "David will likely be going, if you care to see it in the dark."

"It won't be dark for an hour," Marie pointed out. Mr. Benson arose without further ado and offered her his arm.

They made good their escape into the garden. "I really *had* hoped to meet you in London, you know," he said, not even looking westwards towards the Point.

She was curious to know why he had never called on them, and was soon hearing the reason. "I was only intermittently in town. I travel about a good deal, but if I had any notion I had so attractive a connection I should have made a point to call. In fact, Sir Henry had most particularly asked me to do so just before he left town, but I had to go to Vienna for the Congress around that time, and when I returned, you had left."

"Papa had a severe attack of gout and retired," she remarked, knowing little of his shenanigans at the Admiralty.

Mr. Benson, a little better acquainted with Sir Henry's

career, said, "However, there is more than one place for us to become friends, and I was much gratified at your father's kind offer."

"Do you plan to make a long visit, Mr. Benson?" she asked.

His eyes lingered on her face and he smiled a very nice smile. "I hope Bonaparte is in no hurry to get himself rescued," he answered.

In confusion, she pointed out the path to Bolt's Point, and they returned to the saloon.

Sir Henry came to join them, suggesting a little music. Marie was flattered to see that Mr. Benson stopped all talk of going to the Point that evening when she went to the pianoforte. He sat listening with apparent pleasure while she played and David sang. This was the pastime till tea was served, after which there was no entertainment at all. Their young guest, an international traveler and Londoner, was shown to his chamber before ten o'clock. The ladies also retired, while David went down for a look by moonlight at the *Fury*, to touch its keel with his finger, and find the finger come away covered with paint. It being still far from late and the night being fine, he took his mount and rode into the inn at Plymouth for some more shoulder-rubbing with undesirables, and some elbow-bending with the same.

4

When Marie felt an arm being rudely jostled, she thought it must be morning. But as she rubbed her eyes, she saw it was pitch-dark in her chamber, and her rouser was not Biddy hauling her out for a brisk turn in the garden before breakfast as she occasionally did when she could not sleep herself, but David. She could smell the ale on his breath, and realized as she became more alert that he had been drinking more than he should, though he was not foxed.

"Wake up! Wake up," he was saying in an excited voice.

"What is it? What is the matter?" she asked, her own excitement rising at his unexpected call.

He busied himself with lighting her candle as she got out of bed and struggled into a robe. His eyes, she saw, were flashing, and the high spirits were not caused by an excess of ale as happened occasionally, but something more serious. "You'll never guess what!" he whispered. "There's *spies*, right here at Bolt Hall."

"David, what do you mean?" she asked, her heart accelerating with sheer delight.

"I heard 'em, and saw 'em, too."

"Who are they?"

"I don't know."

"You saw them, you said."

"Saw the tops of their heads. I rattled in to the inn for a couple of wets with the fellows, and didn't feel like sleeping when I got back. I went out on the balcony off my room to blow a cloud, and that's when I noticed them. There's a full moon and I saw them as clear as if it were daylight. They were standing beneath me, half under the balcony so I couldn't get much of a look at them, and they were talking up rescuing Boney, just as we knew someone would."

"Wonderful!" she breathed, her own eyes shining like stars. Not that she wished to see the Corsican freed, of course, but that there would actually be an attempt was certainly a welcome piece of intelligence. She had never half believed it. "What did they say?"

"Couldn't hear every word. They were whispering. Two of them. One said something about spending a sprat to catch a mackerel, and I took them for a couple of fishermen, but then the other answered something like, 'Yes, for putting up ten thousand pounds we stand to make a hundred thousand. Not a bad day's work.' And the other laughed and said, '*Night's* work. We won't tackle it in broad daylight. Some quiet moonless night it'll be, eh, mate?' I figured they were thieves—a hundred thousand pounds, how would anybody make such a sum honestly? But then I twigged to it it was Boney they were talking about, of course. So I stepped on my cigar to hide the smell of the smoke and crouched as close to the railing as I could get and cocked my ears sharp. Then the first one went on to say that the biggest joke of it all was doing it from Bolt's Hall, right under the old boy's nose. Papa, you see."

"Who can it be?"

"I don't know. Let me tell you the rest—the best part. They went on talking, saying not much of any account but enough to give the show away. Then one of them said, 'Handy having the money right here. Wouldn't Henry stare if he knew there was ten thousand pounds in gold sitting on his doorstep the whole time;' Then they went on to argue a bit about it not being handy but a demmed nuisance to try to get ahold of such a sum in a hurry, and he wondered what Cicero was thinking of, to make him do it. One of them put up the whole sum. And the other said that if Cicero said ten thousand was needed, then ten thousand was needed, right enough, for there wasn't a better brain in Europe than Cicero's."

"Who is Cicero?"

"It ain't Cicero the old Roman scholar they meant. It's a code name is what it is for the ringleader, so they don't have to use his real name. Cicero is certainly the fellow in charge of the whole—they said enough to make that clear. Gad, but I'd love to discover him. I decided to nip down to the saloon and sneak outdoors and circle around to get a peek at them, but when I got there, they'd gone. Not a trace of them. I went outside and looked all around, right down to the dock, but there wasn't a mouse stirring."

"You have *no idea* who it was?"

"Just an idea one of them wore a uniform. There was something glittering in the moonlight, and I think it was brass buttons. Not big brass buttons like some of the chaps wear at school, you know, but two rows of smaller brass buttons, like a soldier or sailor—an officer, I mean."

"You didn't recognize the voices?"

"No, they were whispering the whole time. It changes the timbre of the voice. I couldn't tell a thing but that they were men. Oh *Englishmen*, not foreigners as I thought it would be when I first tumbled to it they were spies."

"Are you sure it was Bonaparte they were talking about? Did they use his name?"

"No, they never used a single name except Cicero, but they talked of 'rescuing him' and a hundred thousand pounds reward—they might have mentioned the *Bellerophon*. Who else could it possibly be, in Plymouth at such a time? There are no famous criminals on the loose. What should I do?"

She sat thinking what course to take, but before she came up with an idea, David had reached his own conclusion. "I must tell Papa," he decided.

Marie was aware of a dull return to earth. It was of course the proper thing to do. Their father was in charge of all operations at Bolt Hall, but it was somehow an anti-climax to this incipient adventure to go dragging Papa into it, to write a letter off to London, and set up a petition, when what she really desired was to be listening at keyholes, lurking about the shadows late at night, following dangerous suspects, and capturing the spies.

"I'll let you know what he says," David said, already walking to the door.

"You won't rouse him out of bed!" she asked, horrified.

"Deuce take it, this is an *emergency!*" he told her, and went to do just that.

He was back within ten minutes, crestfallen. "He already knew," he said.

"He knew that and didn't tell us!"

"Had orders to keep mum. Heard all about it from the Admiralty yesterday. That is to say, he don't know a thing more than we do, but he knew there were people planning something of the sort right enough, and they've sent down an agent to Bolt Hall to look into it."

"They would never have told Papa. Why should they? He was only in charge of ordering the uniforms."

"He was the supplies officer for the whole Peninsular Campaign. Wellington depended on him completely. Then they saddled him with the American war too, and it was too much for him—for *any* one man to handle. Why, they said when he had to leave that it was of the utmost importance for him to be here at Bolt Hall, just in case of such an emergency as this. That's why they've sent the agent down here to us."

"I wonder who the agent is."

"He is under orders not to say, but it stands to reason it must be Benson."

"Of course!" she agreed at once. "He didn't come to look me over at all. I didn't believe it when Biddy said so."

"She don't know a thing about it. Likely that's what Father told her to keep her quiet. He says we're to keep out of the agent's way, and not to go interfering with him."

"We must help him!" she objected at once. She had not yet managed to quite fall in love with Benson, and was ready to accept his alternative reason for being here. Of course his being a spy need not invalidate him as a suitor. Quite the contrary, who more romantic and lover-like than a spy, engaged in daring deeds of national importance?

"There's one thing father didn't know, anyway. I asked him about the ten thousand pounds, and he hadn't a notion what I was talking about. Said I was foxed—imagine, and I only had half a dozen ales, *small* ales. What we must do is get searching tomorrow and find it. The money is to be used to get Boney away safely, you see. Must be it, and if we could find it and take it away, they'd be dished. Jove, but it's going to be an exciting day."

"I'll help," Marie volunteered at once.

"I might be able to use you," he allowed with condescension. "You could strike up a friendship with Madame Monet. She's in on this, or my name ain't David Boltwood. I'll take Benson around to the telescope at the Point and out in the yacht, if that dashed keel is dry. He mentioned wanting to go out, you recall. Funny they'd send down a chap that don't know how to sail for a job like this. Daresay he's a topnotch sailor, but is only pretending he ain't to lull our suspicions."

Miss Boltwood was ready to believe him not only a prime sailor but an admiral, a general, a demi-god. "And the winch and chain. You must teach him how to use that, in case of an emergency."

"I'll show him everything. No need to worry your head, my dear."

"He is very handsome, isn't he, Dave?" she asked a little shyly.

"A regular out-and-outer. I bet he's no kin to Mama at all. I never heard of him before, did you? Mama's whole family were stumpy, platter-faced people, like you."

"You have a more platter-shaped face than *I* have! And Mama's mother was a Benson before she married. Biddy said she has heard Papa mention Mr. Benson before."

"You don't think his name is really Benson!" David asked, amazed at her naiveté. "No such a thing. It's what's known as a cover, for him to have an excuse to be battening himself on us. Whole countryside knows we never have a soul visiting us because of Papa's nerves, and this is to explain it away. He's letting on he's Benson, and come here to give you a gander. If you look lively, you might set up a flirtation with him, but we'll be pretty busy, Benson and I." David's shoulders went back a little straighter as he spoke, somewhat in emulation of the spy who called himself Mr. Benson.

"He would hardly need any special excuse at such a time as this. Everyone has the house full of guests."

"You didn't see any at Bolt Hall, did you? Madame Monet hinting as hard as she could to come to us, and that skint of a Papa . . . Of course, I realize he is not at all well," he added leniently.

"David, do you mean to say you want that vulgar hussy here?"

"There's not a vulgar bone in her body. That's Biddy giving you such antique ideas. She'd pass for a stylish woman in a city, it's just here in this place she ain't appreciated. Why, she's French, and you must know the French are famous for their elegance. I mean to mention it to Benson when I get to know him a little better tomorrow. See what he has to say about it."

"We must try to get Biddy to stop pestering him, too, about the mole on his cheek."

"Has she been at him with her leeches and nostrums already?"

"She talked about leeches for ten minutes. I was ready to sink with embarrassment."

"Lord, what a bunch of flats he'll think us! But I'll drop him the hint she's crazy. Well, I'd better get to bed. Tomorrow is going to be a busy day. Maybe I should just drop in and see if Benson is comfortable."

"It's after one o'clock," Marie pointed out.

"You don't think a spy is in his bed at one o'clock! He'll be working over a secret code or sending a message off to the Prime Minister," he told her, amazed at her lack of percipience.

When David tapped at Mr. Benson's door, there was no reply. A careful peek into the room showed him an empty bed, which was just as it should be. Mr. Benson knew better than to go to bed at one-thirty in the morning. David assumed he was burning the midnight oil in the library, with a decanter of brandy at his elbow to aid concentration, but when he got there, there was no sign of Mr. Benson. If the master was busy, obviously his assistant must not retire either, and for an hour David rummaged noisily through the house looking for ten thousand pounds. He was still at it when Mr. Benson came slipping in at the library door, which he had cunningly left on the latch before leaving. Mr. Benson acted not only mystified at oblique offers of help, but embarrassed to be caught returning to the house of his host after two without having said he was leaving.

"I decided to pop down to the inn to see what was going on," he explained, unaware that Mr. Boltwood had done the same, and knew it was some more hair-raising adventure that had lured the spy out of doors.

"A wise precaution," David said, nodding his head wisely. "Tomorrow I'll take you to the Point and show you the winches and . . ."

"Miss Boltwood has offered to show me the telescope," Mr. Benson answered, rather enlarging on her offer to point out to him the way.

"She'll be tickled pink to tag along."

"I would appreciate your showing me the secret of the mysterious winch and chain, however."

"Be happy to. And don't forget we're going out in the *Fury*."

"Delightful."

"Er, would you care for a glass of brandy, Mr. Benson?"

"Brandy? I cannot think your aunt would approve. She mentioned to me it ought to be avoided at all costs."

"Ha ha, poor old Biddy. You must overlook her odd ways. Crazy as a loon. She'll stick half a dozen of her speckled leeches on you if you give her half a chance."

"I was afraid it was my mole she had designs on," Mr. Benson replied, smiling.

"No, she don't operate. Yet."

"Good. Now, what was that you were saying about brandy? I would like to take a glass to my room."

David was immensely disappointed that they two were not to drink together, but as drinking alone in one's room was a spy's way, he took a glass up with him, and by diluting it with twice as much water managed to get the nasty stuff down before he passed out entirely.

5

Even one guest can seriously upset the routine of a whole household. The next morning, Bolt Hall's schedule was sadly awry. Biddy, scampering through her library for a chapter on moles, human variety, let her niece sleep until an insalubrious eight-thirty, thus missing her morning constitutional. After his late night activities, David did not come to the table till nine, and Sir Henry had succumbed to an attack of gout as a result of all his arduous petitioning, or possibly as a result of the customary glass of wine served at several of his stops. He hobbled to the breakfast table but was in a bad skin. The lines that ran from nose to mouth were etched deep, and the furrows between his eyes pronounced enough that David mentally applied the term "Roman frown." He didn't know exactly what it meant, but it was the phrase used to describe old Romans with similar wrinkles in his textbooks. He had hoped to find his father in better humor, that he might jolly him into a full account of his correspondence regarding the spy. No matter, he'd have to get it out of Benson himself.

Only Mr. Benson sat at the table without being aware he had shattered the day's beginning. "I am looking forward to our ride to the Point to see the telescope, Miss Boltwood," he said pleasantly as soon as he had bid them all good morning.

Having missed her walk, Marie was eligible for a ride. Not even Biddy could deny that, much as she would have liked to. David, of course, immediately volunteered his services in the viewing of the telescope as well, which, removing any hint of fast behavior from it in providing a chaperone, made it acceptable to Biddy.

"We had better wait till Lord Sanford takes his coffee, and see if he would like to go with you," Sir Henry told them.

There wasn't a closed mouth at the table except for Sir Henry's and Mr. Benson's. Who was Lord Sanford, and what was he doing at Bolt Hall?

"Who?" David asked, being the first to recover.

"Lord Sanford. Bathurst's godson. He arrived last night," Sir Henry said with an air of satisfaction.

"Arrived *here?*" Biddy goggled. "I didn't hear anyone arrive."

"He came late. Very late," Sir Henry said, with a hint of disapproval at such irregular behavior.

"What on earth is he come for?" Biddy inquired.

"He was caught in Plymouth with no place to stay, like Mr. Benson, and remembered that I live nearby."

"Are you acquainted with him then, Henry?" Biddy asked, fully expecting more signs of displeasure that a man should be so careless of the proprieties as to come barging in in the middle of the night, unannounced.

"Certainly I know him well. Met him any number of times in London when I was with the Admiralty. Of course we are

35

not close friends. He is a young fellow, a Whig in fact, but Bathurst's godson. I could hardly turn him away in the middle of the night. He is to stay a few days. We must show him some hospitality—an earl, after all."

Any cohort of Sir Henry's from the Admiralty promised to be a dull dog, and the youngsters immediately lost any interest in him. Their only impatience for his arrival at table was due to his holding up their trip to the telescope. For half an hour after they had finished eating, they sat sipping coffee that became increasingly bitter as it aged. Biddy could not abandon her avocation for so long. There were preparations to make for her brother's latest attack of gout, and there were her leeches to be seen to. She went to the reservoir, but the rest of the party was still intact when Lord Sanford sauntered to the table at ten o'clock, yawning into a carefully manicured hand, and bowing almost imperceptibly to everyone.

He was tall and lean, with an aristocratic face, eyes that were half closed due to either fatigue or boredom, a well-sculpted nose, and a lower jaw that would have been described as lantern-jawed had it been a fraction of an inch longer, and might soon be, anyway, if Lord Sanford proved to have a disposition to match his expression. It was clear at a glance that he was every bit as dull as she had expected, Marie decided. As he took up a seat beside Mr. Benson, she had an excellent opportunity to compare them unhindered, for neither of them glanced at her. There was interest, sensitivity, intelligence on the face of their spy, but Lord Sanford looked along the table with very little interest, settling in the end for only coffee. He was stiff, formal, did not give any impression of wishing to make himself loved in any quarter.

"You would know Mr. Benson I expect, Lord Sanford?" Sir Henry asked.

"We have met before I think," he replied, with a bare nod to Benson, who nodded slightly in return.

"We are neighbors," Benson mentioned, causing the table to wonder at such lukewarm greetings between neighbors.

"Are you, indeed?" Sir Henry asked. "I knew you were both from Devon. Well, this is a coincidence."

Nothing whatever was said by either neighbor to this marvelous coincidence. In fact, upon a closer scrutiny, Marie took the idea they were each unhappy to find the other there.

"Are you come to look at Bonaparte, like the rest of the world?" Benson asked, being obviously the more polite of the two, and feeling some further talk between them was required.

"Actually, I am on my way to my residence on the Isle of Wight for a holiday, but as the world is come to Plymouth, I decided to take a detour here and travel back along the coast to Portsmouth, where I keep my yacht for the crossing to the island. I hadn't realized the place had become a circus."

Anyone with the full use of his brain would have realized it of course, but no one said it aloud. "What kind of a yacht do you have?" Sir Henry asked with some little interest.

"An excellent one," was the lord's obtuse reply.

"He means, what type?" David explained.

"Oh, a schooner," Sanford replied, with such a pained face that no further details were sought.

"If you are interested in yachting, you will want to come to the docks after breakfast. We have seven yachts there, ready to run," Sir Henry said.

"Ours ain't ready to run," David mentioned, disgruntled.

Sanford regarded the speakers lazily in turn as they spoke, and sipped his coffee in silence. After a moment he said, "What do the local people think of having Bonaparte so close to them? Do they go in fear of an escape?"

"He will certainly *try* it," Sir Henry answered, "but we are prepared for him."

"I cannot think it at all likely myself he'll make a dash for it," Sanford replied. "His better option would be to negotiate his freedom."

"Liverpool would never hear of it!" Sir Henry objected at once. "You don't think the Duke of Sussex and his set carry sufficient weight to give him any measure of freedom?" He withheld the hated word *Whig* in deference to his guest's politics.

"Sussex's influence is negligible. He likes to play the liberal, but is not influential in the corridors of power. It is more likely Lord Holland who would be of use on that score. He and Brougham are liberal in their views concerning the General. Along with a few of the more enlightened literati, such as Hobhouse, and of course Capell Lofft, the eminent barrister. Byron considers him one of the three greatest men of the century," Sanford said.

"Beau Brummel and himself complete the triumvirate in the poet's estimation, I understand," Benson said with a bland smile.

Sanford regarded him unperturbed. "I think Byron is mistaken to include himself. Coleridge is the more accomplished poet."

Marie could scarcely suppress a smile, and David had even more difficulty holding in a guffaw. Sir Henry was incapable of containing his wrath. "Brummel, that Jack dandy! He has no claim to fame. He is a nobody."

"He invented the starched collar," Sanford pointed out, his eyes widening till they were three-quarters open.

David's titters were not to be ignored at this point. Staring at him and subjecting his high shirt points to a sneering examination, Sanford continued, "Of course he never dreamed some people would carry it to laughable lengths."

With this leveler he turned back to Sir Henry. "You have a neighbor, a Mr. Hazy, who is active in negotiating Napoleon's freedom. I must go to see him."

Sir Henry sat stunned into silence. Mr. Hazy, the local lunatic, who had sworn himself to the legal freeing of that monster, Bonaparte, was a disgrace to the neighborhood. That the godson of Lord Bathurst, a high Tory, should be on terms with him was a crushing revelation. "You cannot mean you are in favor of the scheme!"

"Certainly I am," Sanford replied matter-of-factly.

"He ought to be executed! I have a petition going around to that effect."

"Why is it the common minds always want to execute the giants who come amongst us?" Sanford asked, in the weary tones of one who knew he would get no sensible reply. "Jesus Christ, Socrates, Charles I—the world has only to see a genius to want to put an end to him," he complained, lumping the Deity, philosopher and bad monarch together.

"Giant *devil!*" Sir Henry yelped, pulling from his pocket the petition, already bearing a hundred signatures, some forty of them from his own household. "Here is the paper will see Bonaparte in a grave, where he belongs. Your godfather, Lord Bathurst, supports me," he added, rather prematurely, as the letter to him had received no reply.

"Oh, *Bathurst,*" Sanford said with a dismissive wave of his hand. "Pray don't hold me responsible for his antique views. One has nothing to say in the selection of his godparents. He would not have been my choice, I promise you." He took the petition and scanned it with a derisive smile. "I see *you* have succumbed, Mr. Benson."

"I am in favor of executing Bonaparte," Benson replied,

with a smile of anticipation, enjoying the ruckus. "I take it you don't mean to add your signature, milord?"

"I would as lief sign my best nag over to the pound. This is madness. Bonaparte ought to be returned to Elba, or some more salubrious spot found for him. Actually, one of the reasons I go to Wight is to see whether my residence there might not be used as a refuge. I own rather a fine castle on the island, and Wight has a better climate than the rest of England. Napoleon's health is not good, unfortunately."

"Wight is not ten miles from England!" Sir Henry gasped in disbelief at such madness.

"True, it would permit easy visiting for him, which is one of the advantages of the plan," Sanford agreed reasonably. "If he were agreeable, I would like to set up a military academy there, to give our officers the benefit of his genius."

"We have our own genius! Wellington can teach our lads what they need to know."

"Wellington, another giant, is one of the few who agrees with me," Sanford pointed out. "He says quite openly it is only the bungling of Bonaparte's officers that lost Napoleon Waterloo. Wellington would be happy to see him on Wight. He helped spike the wheel of those bloodthirsty ministers who wanted to send Napoleon back to Louis for beheading. What a conversation that would be—Wellington and Napoleon. I hope I may have the honor to be present when they meet."

"They will not meet, sir!" Sir Henry told him, and, folding up his petition, stuck it into his breast pocket.

"I suppose not, if Boney manages to escape," Sanford admitted. "That would be a dreadful mistake. He can certainly negotiate a good, a very pleasant refuge, if he sits tight and isn't scared into trying to escape by some hare-brained scheme. Surely no one would be foolish enough to try it."

"You may be sure someone will try it," David said, his brown eyes flashing at this impossible stranger. He wondered that his father sat calmly by and heard such treasonous talk. "Everyone says Bonaparte is to be incarcerated on Saint Helena Island, over a thousand miles off the coast of Africa, and he will try to escape to avoid it. This is his last chance. The town of Plymouth is overrun with Frenchies slipped over since Waterloo, come with no other thought than to free him."

"They must certainly be thwarted," Sanford declared.

Sir Henry opened his mouth to object, till he realized he agreed. This was the sole point of agreement between them.

They none of them wanted Napoleon to escape. The Boltwood party was afraid he'd get clean away, and Sanford was afraid he wouldn't. Sir Henry was in no mood to discuss further with this upstart rebel who had somehow got into his house under false pretences, and turned to Mr. Benson.

"You mentioned an interest in seeing my preparations to prevent Napoleon's escape, Mr. Benson. Shall we go down to the wharf now and do it, while Lord Sanford finishes his coffee?"

"I'll go with you," Sanford said, causing chagrin in every heart as he pushed away his cup with a grimace of distaste.

They were soon clambering down the rock cliff from castle to dock, with Sir Henry wincing at every painful step. Benson gave his hand to Marie to aid her, and Sanford walked along behind them with Sir Henry, offering no help at all to the invalid. "Demmed awkward approach to your dock," was his only comment as they went.

"Bolt Hall was put up on the hill on purpose to make attack harder. It is why I have never put in a staircase. The Hall is a fortress, walled all around. The first castle in England that was set up for the garrison having their artillery behind the walls. Show you later when we go back up." But first they had to get down to the dock, to examine the six yachts bobbing up and down in the water, and the seventh, the only one of any size or speed, propped up on the dock on wooden horses, with its keel facing the sun.

"That won't do you much good in an emergency," Sanford said, staring at it with consternation. This was the first statement with which David agreed.

"She can be launched today," Sir Henry replied stiffly, which put David back in his father's camp where he belonged. He went on to point out that the yachts were each equipped with tinned foods, drink, blankets and Brown Besses, procured by means of Sir Henry's former connection with the supplies office.

"A musket with a range of one hundred yards won't do you much good on the high seas," was Sanford's belittling comment.

"If you will look up the garrison wall, you will see there are big guns mounted at the openings," Sir Henry replied curtly. "We'll go back up and you can have a look at them." He was really far from ready to scrabble up the cliff so soon, but had no desire to hear his preparations further denigrated.

"My father finds the climbing hard," Marie mentioned to Mr. Benson, who had remained by her side.

"I'll give him a hand," he volunteered at once. Marie gave him another, so that the three of them went up slowly, while David and Sanford bounded up the cliff at a pace strangely at odds with Lord Sanford's stately bearing.

"Lord Sanford holds some surprising views," Benson remarked.

"The man is a lunatic," Sir Henry declared with vehemence, "and I wish I had not invited him to stay. If he goes calling on Mr. Hazy, I hope the fellow will offer to put him up. They belong together, the pair of upstart Whigs."

"Who is this Mr. Hazy exactly?" Benson asked.

"He is a liberal that lives hereabouts. Was a liberal M.P. some years ago, a friend of Holland. He was always ripe for any foolishness the Whigs came up with. Has given the Prince Regent the devil of a hard time about money, expecting a prince to live in a hovel. His present mania is to set Napoleon free, to do it by an Act of Parliament or some such thing, with the help of other left-wingers like Brougham and this Capell Lofft. And Lord Sanford," he added grimly.

"How would they go about it?"

"No doubt Lord Sanford will inform us," he said through clenched teeth. Speech was difficult in his pained condition, and he said no more. Marie, glancing to her spy, saw his eyes were narrowed suspiciously, as he examined Lord Sanford with the keenest interest.

They had soon reached the plateau that held the garrison wall, entering through a rounded stone archway. There was an area of about fifteen yards depth between the garrison wall and the Hall proper. In this spot were several former fieldhands piling up cannon balls, polishing ramrods, oiling cannons, and generally behaving as they imagined a soldier would behave, which involved a good deal of ribaldry and cursing, till they discerned their employer had come amongst them. Sir Henry strode importantly to the closest gun opening, where a cannon was mounted. He took a grip on the handles and turned the gun from left to right. "Swivels, you see," he pointed out to Sanford, with a vastly superior air. "All my guns do. I can cover the whole seaward mouth of the river that runs in past my place. A ship won't get up the estuary in one piece if I don't like the looks of it."

"Do these antiques actually work? Where did you find such

relics? Are they left over from the Civil War?" Sanford fired off this series of questions without allowing time for replies.

"They are in working order," Sir Henry told him, and didn't see fit to mention that they had not actually done so in the last generation.

"Very effective, if it happens the rescuers decide to bring Boney ashore here. What makes you think they will choose the one guarded dock with hundreds of miles of unguarded coastline? No one would be foolish enough to land him anywhere near here," Sanford pointed out.

"There is very little anchorage anywhere along the coast. Sheer rock cliffs by and large, with a little inlet at Wembury of course, and Sinclair has a neat dock at Sinclair Point, though it doesn't have as deep a clearance as my own. At low tide it is perfectly useless. *I* have had my dock dredged all around."

"Wettering's is dredged, too," David added. Sanford and Benson exchanged a look of consternation. The General had a dozen choices of landing spots no doubt, and here was the entire civilian defense lumped at one spot, with the fact loudly bruited around the town.

"What is the contingency plan if Bonaparte is landed elsewhere?" Benson asked, in a polite voice.

"He won't be landed at all. I have my telescope up on Bolt's Point, keeping a watch on him all day. If he gets off *Bellerophon*, we are after him immediately. This is just in case he is pushed up the estuary while being followed. No saying what turn events will take. But really he isn't likely to get into the harbor at all, as I have the winch and chain oiled up and ready to stop him."

"I have heard a good deal about that winch and chain and am most curious to see them," Mr. Benson said with a pleasing promptness.

Before they could get away, Sir Henry had to point out that the guns were manned all day long.

"And at night?" Sanford asked.

"No point the fellows missing their sleep. They couldn't see a target in the dead of night, but I keep a man posted twenty four hours a day up in the tower, with a trumpet to rouse us if he spots anything. The men could be at their posts in ten minutes."

"That should just about give Napoleon time to slip away on you," Sanford remarked. "Where is this great winch and chain? Let us have a look at them."

"The chain is lying under the water there in the bay," Sir Henry told him, reining in his temper. "Can't see it of course. It is attached to that rock wall at the far side of the bay, imbedded firmly in concrete, stretching across the bay and finishing up inside that square tower there right behind you."

Everyone turned to look at the stone tower, that formed an integral part of the Hall. "May we see it, see how it works, Sir Henry?" Mr. Benson asked. Sanford had already taken a step towards it.

"I was about to show you. Come this way." With a hasty step, Sir Henry got ahead of Sanford as they rounded the corner of the Hall, to enter a narrow doorway, descending first by wooden stairs to the ground level, then by broad rough stone steps into the very bowels of the building, into a large, damp, square chamber that was stone from high ceiling to floor. Set into the stonework was a sturdy double winch with handles for turning, and through a hole in the outer stone wall, a massive chain, each link the thickness of a man's thumb, attached to the winch which was fed out into the bay.

"She's lying slack now," Sir Henry explained. "The chain lies along the bottom of the bay, and is raised by the winches to the surface, stopping all traffic. Makes as dandy a trap as you'd ever care for, and I can't think why it isn't used else-where. An ingenious thing, don't you think, Lord Sanford?"

"Fascinating," he agreed, staring at it, his tone more doubt-ful than enthusiastic.

"Could you show us how it works?" Benson inquired, more keen than the other guest.

"It's not as hard a job as you'd think," Sir Henry said, not averse to displaying the family treasure. "A single man can operate it, a good strong buck. Dave, if you'll just get your shoulder to the winch wheel there." David dashed forward and threw his weight into the task, succeeding after a good deal of effort and several grunts in getting it rolling. While he strained, his father spoke on.

"In the old days, fifteen hundreds, Edward VI used to con-tribute to its upkeep, realizing it was of national importance. Nowadays I bear the expense myself. You saw where the ships were harbored. Twenty yards seaward the chain is at-tached to the opposite wall—cutting out at an angle from the Hall, you see. It runs on a diagonal. If I raise my chain, not a ship enters the estuary. It's priceless, this contraption. In-vented by my ancestor, Sebastian Boltwood, in 1380. It's older than the Hall. There was a fortress here previously, and

43

this square part of the building we stand in is part of the old fortress. It's not patented, my winch and chain. Anyone could have such a rig, but I believe mine is unique. More than once it has kept the enemy from our walls."

"But the yachts there—they lie seaward of the chain, of course?" Sanford asked.

"No, sir, they are protected behind it," he was told.

Sanford blinked in surprise, but Benson spoke out before he could cause further annoyance. He first bestowed some suitable praise on the chain, then asked, "What would happen if the chain broke?"

"It won't," he was told with assurance. "I've had the masonry on the far side inspected, and you can see it is in good repair here. Every link of the chain has been inspected by hand by me. I had it raised the day Bonaparte surrendered, and went out in the *Fury* to inspect it. It will hold. There is a new chain in that chest there," he went on, pointing to a large wooden chest that stood by the winch. He lifted the lid to confirm his boast of a new chain. "Well, Lord Sanford, what have you to say about this?" he asked triumphantly.

"This is a dangerous contraption," Sanford replied in a serious tone.

"Aye, not a ship will get past my chain," Sir Henry agreed, mistaking Sanford's words for approval.

"This must be dismantled at once," was the next remark from the impossible earl.

He might as well have said the Parliament Buildings must be blown up, the Prince Regent assassinated, or Christianity abolished. *"Dismantled!!! Dismantled?"* Sir Henry bellowed, turning an alarming shade of reddish-purple. "Not a link of the Bolt Chain will be dismantled, sir. The defense of England is in its keeping."

"God save England! The chain won't," Sanford said, his own voice rising to an unusual level. "Don't you see, man, it is not Bonaparte's intention to *attack* you? He has no notion of storming your garrison wall. It is his intention, presumably, to escape as quietly as possible. He won't come blasting up the estuary with cannons roaring. Your chain will only prevent those seven yachts from getting out of the harbor to give chase."

"The chain is not to keep us in, but to keep him out," Sir Henry explained, still at top volume.

"Does the chain know that?" Sanford asked with a blighting stare.

"The men operating it do. They know when to raise it and when to lower it I trust. They are not likely to raise it when I give them the signal we wish to leave the dock. They are not morons."

"Thank God the *men* are not. But morons or not, it would take only one turncoat in your organization to sabotage the whole effort. One man at the winch could keep every ship tied up here. You must certainly cut that chain. It is the only safeguard. And get rid of that spare, too, or it might be replaced in time to do mischief."

"Edward VI gave us that chain! Get rid of it? No, sir, I will not. And I won't cut the chain, either."

"Benson, *you* seem to have some influence, *tell* him," Sanford said, turning with an impatient jerk towards Benson.

"I can't agree with you, sir. If Napoleon is removed from the *Bellerophon*, he will in all probability make for land. He can't land at Plymouth for the crowds. There is no good docking between Plymouth and here. It is Bolt's Dock, the closest place, he will make for. The chain is an excellent precaution."

"Good God, man, he won't make for any dock or public place. He'll have men on the clifftop with a rope slung down for him to be hauled up and disappear into the countryside. This chain is a menace. It must go."

"The chain remains, sir," Sir Henry said with an awful gaze, "to protect us when Napoleon tries to land."

There was a most uncomfortable pause while the two uncompromising gentlemen glared at each other. Into the tense silence Mr. Benson said in a perfectly nonchalant tone, "Shall we go to have a look at the ingenious telescope now, Miss Boltwood?"

With a smile of gratitude for his tact, Marie agreed readily, very happy to escape Lord Sanford.

"I'll go with you and see what mischief you've created there," Sanford said in his rudest voice, which was very rude indeed.

6

Sir Henry went back into his Hall, and the others went around to the stables. "I don't have a spare hack," David said in an angry tone to Sanford. "That is, I have offered my spare to Mr. Benson. She is a barb, a sweet goer."

"I brought my own mount," Sanford said, unoffended.

Marie stepped quickly forward to secure Mr. Benson's company, but was soon out-talked by her brother. With a mount to be lent, he had Benson's ear to explain the animal's excellence. Seemingly unaware of his unpopularity, Sanford turned to Marie. "What is Benson doing here?" were his first private words to her.

Unhappy to have been cheated out of a walk with the spy, she answered snippily, "He is a family connection, Lord Sanford. His presence wants less explaining than some other people's."

"Who else is putting up with you?" he asked at once.

"You are the only other guest," she answered.

"And wished at Jericho I assume, from your manner, but you must see that winch and chain are a wretched idea."

"With your love of Napoleon, it must please you that the chain might allow his escape."

"I don't want him to escape. I hope there is no attempt to rescue him at all, but if there *is*, that chain will be damnably in the way. How do the authorities come to allow it?"

"Bolt Hall is private property, sir. My father's private property, and if he wishes to put a chain under the bay, he shall do it."

"The bay isn't his private property. I'll find out who owns the other side, where the chain ends."

"The other side is Crown land, and we have a patent letter dating hundreds of years ago giving permission for the chain."

This exchange of pleasantries saw them at the stable door. When the mounts were led out, there was surprise on David's face to see Lord Sanford's mount, an Arab stallion, a thoroughbred with flaring nostrils, a wide, deep chest and neat legs.

"Nice bit of blood," he was startled into saying, looking jealously at the animal.

"Thank you, I am a little particular about what I ride." A passing glance to David's own mount said without words that he saw the attitude was not mutual.

They set off together, the four of them. David was not about to admit there was a horse in the kingdom could outdistance his own, and by urging his gelding on relentlessly he managed to keep pace with Sanford, which pleased Marie very well as it gave her a chance to talk to Benson.

"What is Sanford doing here at this time?" he asked repeating the other man's question regarding himself.

"Father is a close friend of Lord Bathurst. It is his being godson to Bathurst that accounts for it. How unfortunate he should have come."

"He won't find the company to his liking, Miss Boltwood. I don't think you will be long saddled with him."

"Who is he, anyway?"

"A member of the *ton* in London. A fashionable fribble. It is pretty clear he has come here to make mischief. He has no real interest in anything but parties and his jackets, and his various estates, of course."

"I wish he would go on to Wight as he mentioned doing."

"I hadn't realized he owned a place there. His major seat is Paisley Park, in Devon, not far from Oakhurst, my own place. You must have read of it in the guide books. A huge heap, full of art-works. A bit of an art collector in his spare time, which is all of his time."

"He is very unfriendly for a neighbor. He hardly spoke to you."

"Oh, I am beneath his lordship's touch. You will have noticed he holds himself very high. Thinks he owns the world."

"That will not influence my father. He will not destroy the winch and chain."

"We must see he does not. Such an excellent safeguard. You had no idea Sanford was coming to you? It was not arranged in advance?"

"No, I heard nothing of it."

"I was afraid he meant to give me some competition," Mr. Benson said with a rallying little smile that set Marie's heart racing.

She looked at him with large, surprised eyes, holding a

question. Biddy had said he had come to court her, implied it, and she blushed as it dawned on her that their spy might have two reasons in coming. "He is very disagreeable, is he not?" she asked.

"I find him so, as he is so much more eligible than myself. But then Sir Henry Boltwood's daughter is not the vulgar sort to be dangling after a title, I trust."

"Oh, no!" she assured him at once, with a ravishing smile.

Unfortunately, Lord Sanford chose that moment to draw his mount to a halt and await the others. David came up to Benson to point out to him the excellent view they were approaching. They continued four abreast towards the telescope.

"This is too far from the Hall to be of any use," Sanford said, looking behind him down the hill to the Hall. "How do you communicate if your man happens to spot anything suspicious?"

"The lookout runs down the hill," David told him.

"Where is his horse?"

"He doesn't have a horse. He runs down on foot," David answered, hardly able to keep a civil tongue in his head. Then he dismounted, as did they all, and with a pointed look at Sanford, he offered Benson first look out of the telescope.

Benson put his eye to it and looked out to sea, where the *Bellerophon* was visible, surrounded by many smaller craft. Behind him, Sanford looked around the point. "Those bushes there offer excellent concealment for anyone wishing to knock out your guard," he said to David. "You ought to have set it up in a clear spot."

"Pity you hadn't been here to tell us how to go about it," David answered.

"It certainly is. It will have to be moved."

"It isn't being moved. It took us three hours to get it up, and it's staying right here," David said, in much the voice of his father.

"Cut down the bushes then," Sanford advised him.

With roughly an acre of brambles and thorn bushes to be done away with, this speech was taken for pure ill humor. David turned away before he could utter some unforgivable rudeness. Benson, turning from the telescope remarked, "I make it over a hundred boats there, out on the water. Plenty of chance for mischief."

"The very number ensures safety," Sanford contradicted.

"No one would be foolish enough to attempt a rescue with a hundred witnesses standing by."

"They most of them leave at night, and *naturally* the rescue will be attempted at night. Anyone should know that much," David said curtly.

"Very likely," Sanford agreed, to everyone's surprise, till he added, "when your father has called off his watchmen." Then he walked forward and looked into the glass. "They're kept at a good distance, I see."

"A hundred yards," David informed him—really Mr. Benson, though Sanford, of course, heard it as well.

"Too close," the latter said.

"Admiral Keith doesn't seem to think so," David said at once, not to let the meddler get away with anything.

"I don't see how any of those little boats could hope to effect a rescue," Sanford said next. "We'll have to run into Plymouth and get a better look. Your father said the *Fury* was ready to launch, Mr. Boltwood. We could hack into Plymouth and back before lunch. Shall we go now, and take *Fury* out this afternoon?"

"That's up to Mr. Benson," David answered, liking the suggestion nearly as much as he disliked the speaker.

"Excellent," Mr. Benson agreed, and the men turned away, but Marie had not had a look yet, and went to the telescope. There was little enough to be seen. Even with the powerful telescope, one could not hope to actually recognize a face aboard *Bellerophon*. There were men there, but if one of them was Napoleon there was no way of telling it. Still the very idea of his being so close to them sent a shiver down her spine. During the whole of her remembered life, the name Bonaparte had been an evil charm, a bogey to strike fear into a child's heart. He had been a favorite threat of an old nanny. "I'll turn you over to Boney," the woman used to say at the first sign of recalcitrance. And now he was here, a prisoner. How she'd love to see him.

"Hard to believe he's really out there, isn't it?" a voice asked at her shoulder. She recognized it to be Lord Sanford's voice, and was annoyed. "I wish we could get a better look at him," he added.

"I can't think why anyone would want to see him," she replied, lifting her chin and immediately turning away, to lend credence to her lie.

"No doubt that is why you were using the telescope, to avoid seeing him."

She racked her brain for a setdown, and found none. "Shall we go?" she asked instead, directing her words to Mr. Benson.

They returned to Bolt Hall to inform Sir Henry of their destination, but he had gone off to round up more signers for the petition, and it was Biddy they had to deal with. "You won't be back in time for lunch. We eat at twelve-thirty," she said.

"So early? We've just had breakfast," Sanford exclaimed, being an urban bird.

"My aunt had her breakfast at eight o'clock," David told him.

"Go ahead without us. We'll eat later in town," Sanford decided for them all.

"Marie, you'll not go with them. You won't want to eat at the inn at such a time as this," Biddy said at once. Marie was dismayed. She loved to eat at the inn any time, most especially at such an exciting time as this.

"Three gentlemen must be sufficient protection for Miss Boltwood, even at this time," Sanford said with an authoritative air. "Come along, Miss Boltwood. I shall hold myself responsible for her," he said to Biddy, and the matter was closed. Marie had never been closer to feeling in charity with him, and if only he had then fallen back with David for the trip, she would have forgiven him all. But he kept by her side the whole way, pestering her with a dozen pointless questions, and keeping her away from Benson.

"Are there many Frenchmen about the quay?" he asked.

He had been there himself—he knew, but an answer was required. "Yes, swarms of them. I never saw most of them before. They are trouble-makers, rough looking types, every-one of them."

"Are there any amongst them who strike you as gentlemen?"

"No, I just said they are all rough, common people."

"Gentlemen in disguise is what I meant. A rescue would take money and brain power."

"There are no gentlemen. There is one *lady*," she added, her mind flitting to Madame Monet. "But of course a woman would not be actively involved in it."

"What is her name?"

"Madame Monet."

"Pretty?"

50

"That depends on your taste. Some people seem to find her so. She is of a certain age—blond, full-figured. Rather attractive, in a vulgar way."

Sanford nodded with a little smile, apparently liking this type very well, Miss Boltwood thought. "Madame Monet, eh?" he asked. There was an odd tone to his voice, but as Marie was more interested in the other half of the party, she took little note of it.

As they approached the city, David began outlining the obvious to Mr. Benson. Bolt Hall lay to the east of Plymouth, and as they approached the city, it was seen sloping down the hill to the Plym. Boats of all sizes and degrees lay in the harbor, some arriving, others leaving, and still others with activities going forth aboard—men seeing to sails, ropes and supplies. Already the quay was stiff with people come to see the *Bellerophon* riding anchor within view, flying the white ensign of the Royal Navy, and signal flags of various colors. Sanford studied the signal flags with interest, but said nothing.

"This is the estuary of the Plym River," David explained. "Plymouth is situated between two rivers, the Tamar on the other side. This inlet is called Catwater, and on the other side it is called Ham-Oze. This is the more picturesque in my opinion. We'll ride into town and walk along the Hoo, if you don't mind being crowded. You will get the best view of Billy Ruffian from there."

"Billy Ruffian, that is another name for the *Bellerophon* I take it?" Benson asked, nodding at all the odd scraps of information thrown to him.

"Yes, it is what the crewmen have named her, and of course the whole crowd of landlubbers have become sailors since the ship anchored within view. Anyone in town could tell you she carries seventy-four guns, and is under the command of Captain Frederick Maitland."

They dismounted and walked along, enjoying the sun, which was dissipated to a glow by the hazy air, but still warm enough that the salt air from the ocean was welcome. They jostled elbows with fishmongers, sailors, children, soldiers, ladies and housemaids till they had reached a good position on the Hoo, an elevated esplanade that ran along the edge of the sea, and was the favorite spot for regarding the ship. David, who always brought a small hand telescope with him when he came into the city, handed it to Benson to train on *Bellerophon,* but its ineffectual lens showed no more than the same view seen from the point, a large ship riding the waves, with indistinguishable shadows moving about on board.

Unaware of the machine's weakness, Sanford reached for it. "I think we could get a look at him if he came out on deck now," he said, training the glass on the ship.

"He is nothing to see I promise you," Benson remarked casually.

"What—have you *seen* him?" David asked.

"Yes, I was in France when he escaped from Elba, and met him once. He is a short, obese, unkempt gentleman with thinning hair and bad teeth. Awkward in his movements, and slovenly in his dress. He wears his uniform open at the neck, and can be rude to people when he wishes."

"Petty complaints about the greatest genius of our age," Sanford said.

"Ah, do you put him a rung above Beau Brummel?" Benson asked.

"Several rungs below in toilette, from what you tell us. I begin to perceive I must invite Beau to Wight to smarten the Emperor up."

"I made sure his toilette would be of interest to yourself, Sanford, so interested as you are in your jackets. And with what other detail can you cavil? He is short, certainly. Five feet six inches, to be precise."

"But somehow, you know, it seems inappropriate to measure Napoleon Bonaparte in *inches*," Sanford objected.

"How would you measure him, milord, in pounds?"

"No, it is not my practice to assess people in pounds and pence. I assume that was your meaning, Mr. Benson? You are interested in the fortunes of your friends, one hears." He just glanced to Marie as he said this, a meaningful look, though it meant no more to her than that Sanford was extremely rude indeed.

"It was pounds and ounces Mr. Benson referred to," she said angrily.

"Ah, was that it?" Sanford asked with a light laugh. "It was giving us the figure in feet and inches, but not in pounds and ounces that led me astray."

Benson ignored the whole pass, like a gentleman. "He is aging besides," he added. "Forty-six years old."

"And how many months and weeks?" Sanford inquired courteously. He was again ignored by Mr. Benson, and the rest of the party as well.

They fell silent, looking across the gray-green water, shimmering with a silvery-gold light, and flecked with white caps where the wind ruffled it. "The wind's rising. We'd better be getting on if we want to take *Fury* out," David said.

"In a moment," Sanford said, again trying to adjust the telescope to give a clearer picture, but with no success. "What is that island there, just off the coast?" he asked Marie.

"St. Nicholas Island," she told him. "One of Cromwell's officers was imprisoned in the castle there. General Lambert. And the other large stone building on land facing it is the citadel of Plymouth, very old. The lighthouse there in the sound is to warn sailors off from the Eddystone Rocks. Very treacherous, for they are concealed at high tide. There have been some dreadful tragedies caused by them, but they help protect the harbor and can be navigated well enough with the help of the light and a little familiarity."

Sanford could not feel any attempt would be made to land Bonaparte here at such a crowded spot, nor was it likely a rescue operation would depart from here. "Let's go over and have a look at Ham-Oze," he said, again walking with Marie.

"It is not so picturesque here at the Tamar," she pointed out. "The repairs and refitting are done here. Those ramshackle buildings are warehouses and storehouses and so on." There was a good deal of busy activity going on, but again of a very public nature. Not a likely spot for conspirators.

"Maybe you'd like to have a look at the Royal Naval station while we're here, Mr. Benson?" David asked.

He was not averse, but it was the thorn in their side, Lord Sanford, who suggested they go in and say hello to the officers. David suggested going along to the inn to await him, but Benson, too, was curious to go to the station, so they all went along. It was no less a personage than Admiral Lord Keith, commander of the navy in the area, that Sanford asked for when he stepped in. He was told the admiral was at sea, aboard the *Tonnant*, and the officer, Captain Wingert, asked if he could be of assistance. Wingert was a young officer, brown-haired, apple-cheeked, and very keen. It was his youth perhaps, or his relatively junior rank more likely, that set Sanford's back up.

"Are you the second in command at the station?" his lordship inquired in a haughty accent.

"No, sir, Rear Admiral Rawlins is second in command, but he's very busy. Can I be of assistance to you?"

"No, I will see Rawlins."

"I'll see when he'll be free, sir," Wingert said, and sent off a message, remaining with the callers himself till Rawlins' arrival.

"I see supplies are to be put aboard tonight," Sanford commented idly.

Wingert stared at him. "May I ask how you know that, sir? No one has been told outside the station."

"I read the flags," Sanford told him.

"Oh, you read semaphore," Wingert said, satisfied with the explanation, but unhappy with the fact.

"In a shipping community, I cannot be the only to do so. Keith should have set up a secret communications system. Are there not tight precautions taken for the loading?" Sanford asked.

"Certainly there are."

"Night seems a bad time to do it. Daylight would be better."

"Are you sent down by the Admiralty, sir?" Wingert asked cautiously, feeling no other reason could account for his didactic manner, and that in this case Rawlins would wish to be told.

"No, I am here as a concerned citizen," he was told, in a lofty manner. There was a plethora of concerned titled citizens making themselves obnoxious to Rawlins, and Wingert realized his duty was to be rid of this one as soon as possible.

"We are working under Admiral Keith's orders, sir," Wingert told him in a polite tone. "A pair of ships go out, both armed. Every precaution is taken."

"How about the stuff put aboard, the food, the drink? Where are they procured?"

"From our own naval stores. It was the first move Admiral Keith made when we took Bonaparte, to set a guard on the storehouse twenty-four hours a day, to see nothing was tampered with. It would be easy enough to dope the wine or something of the sort, and set the stage for a takeover of the ship. But nothing is left to chance. The supplies will be taken aboard after dark when the sightseers are gone, and it will be done under close supervision. Only naval vessels are allowed within one hundred yards of *Bellerophon*. Fears of an escape are exaggerated. If any vessel other than a ship of the British navy were to get too close, they would be shot out of the sea in a minute, and it isn't likely one of our own vessels would free him."

The visitors listened closely to this, nodding their heads in approval of this strict surveillance. It struck Marie that any

54

effort to free the General must die unborn, and her hopes of being engaged in some romantical adventure were very slim indeed.

"I expect the men who are used for any communication of this sort are hand-picked, too?" Sanford asked.

"There wasn't time for that, unfortunately. It is the regular crews that are used. It all happened rather quickly, of course," Wingert replied. "But I think the British navy is to be trusted."

"What makes you think anything of the sort?" Sanford asked, his face a mask of astonishment. "The crews of these ships you speak of, if they are like every other ship afloat, are made up of sailors who were pressed into service against their will. One can hardly imagine patriotism forms any small part of their makeup. They might easily be bribed to help Napoleon escape."

"Still, they are Englishmen. . . ."

"Yes, if they aren't Yanks, pulled off American vessels during the blockade of America."

"I assure you, there are no such persons aboard any of our ships here," Wingert told him.

"Well in any case, they're only human beings like the rest of us. Everything has its price."

"What do you consider the price for Napoleon Bonaparte, milord?" Benson asked him, in no serious way at all.

"It would be very high indeed," Sanford replied, unsmiling.

"Thank you. You know I always like to assess everyone's worth, but could you suggest a figure in pounds and pence?" Benson asked, with a little smile towards the Boltwoods.

"No, no, Benson. I merely hinted it was your *friends'* fortunes you were interested in. With your deep-seated disgust of Napoleon's open jackets, I acquit you of having made a bosom bow of him. But about the navy, the men are press-ganged and the officers largely culled from younger sons with their pockets to let."

"In that case though, sir," Wingert pointed out with deference that hid his anger, "it would be a whole ship that would have to be bribed, and while we make no claims to being other than human, I doubt you would find a whole shipful of venal seamen."

Sanford listened, then answered, "It wouldn't take a whole shipful, would it? Only a captain. The men would do as they're told."

Marie's hopes soared at this speech, seeing that she might

yet get in on an adventure. She considered the discussion, then said, "But if he—this hypothetical corrupt captain—managed to get Napoleon transferred to his vessel, where would he take him? If he made for France or America, the whole navy would be after him and give chase."

"Yes, and I wish you could convince your father that he wouldn't make for Bolt Hall, either," Sanford added. "What he would do is make for an unguarded spot of coast and scramble upon a rope, to hide out somewhere till the heat died down."

"I expect that is why Admiral Keith takes such careful precautions," Wingert said, wishing to be finished with these visitors.

"He should do the shipping in daylight," Sanford said, returning to this finished point.

"An interesting idea you spoke of, Sanford, but our hypothetical captain wouldn't have Napoleon turned over to him without signed orders from Admiral Keith," Benson mentioned.

"Or Rawlins," Wingert added. "He is in charge during Keith's absence. It is he who gave the order for transferring supplies."

"I suppose you're well acquainted with this Rawlins?" Sanford asked.

"I know him fairly well. He doesn't strike me as a man who would sell his honor. Of course, I've only been here a month myself."

"You are a swift judge of integrity, Captain," Sanford told him in a supercilious way.

"It is all nonsense," Marie said impatiently. "If any attempt were made to free him it would not involve the British navy. He would slip over the side of Billy Ruffian some dark night and swim to shore, or be picked up by a small waiting boat." Then with a laughing eye towards Sanford she added, "which would take him to Bolt's Dock, where the winch and chain would stop him."

She was surprised to see a little flash of amusement in Sanford's lazy eyes, but Wingert spoke up, distracting her. "No, it could never be done that way. His cabin door is not locked, but it is guarded twenty-four hours a day, and if he goes above he is watched. There are men posted all around the decks of the ship. Poor Boney couldn't throw a crumb to a gull without having a gun at his back."

"A guard would be easier to bribe than a captain," she pointed out.

"No one can get to him to bribe him. The ship is incommunicado, except for official dealings with the British navy."

"Anyone who is already on board can get to him," Sanford objected. "Better check the supplies being put aboard tonight for secret letters, too."

"What a suspicious bunch we are. I see the captain narrowing his eyes at us. Who shall blame him?" Benson asked, laughing. "One would think *we* were trying to spring him to hear us. I assure you, Captain, *I* came along only to bear Lord Sanford company. When Napoleon is spirited off, I trust you will arrest Sanford, and not me."

"*When* he is spirited off, Benson?" Sanford asked with a challenging smile. "I see it is already considered a *fait accompli* in your mind. I spoke of unlikely possibilities only."

"Upon my word, you have the mind of a spy, milord. You leap on an innocent word. *If* he is set free. Is that better?"

"Much better. But then it is the unconsidered word that reveals our true thoughts, is it not?"

"You see, already I am guilty," Benson joked, "and it is yourself, Sanford, who raised the subject of corruption in the King's navy. I shall hold *you* guilty *if* any plan is discovered to turn that monster, Bonaparte, loose on us again. Who but you could afford it? Certainly *I* am not wealthy enough to bribe even a lowly guard. My comparative poverty must be my proof of innocence."

"Your poverty as compared to what, Benson?" Sanford asked with a meaningful look.

"Compared to, let us say, yourself."

"Ah, but it is poverty that is the motive, Benson, so you have thrown yourself into suspicion again," Sanford riposted, the whole discussion being made in a light, bantering way. "I am too wealthy to be bothered picking up a million pounds or so only for delivering Napoleon."

"Delivering him to *whom?*" Marie asked. "Who is it that wants him so badly he would pay a million for him?"

"Who indeed?" Benson seconded her. "I could find more amusing uses for a million pounds than a slightly used Emperor. By the by, is it actually a million pounds bruited as the going price? By Jove, I am tempted. But then I am such a wretched sailor, I'd probably lose him between Billy Ruffian and shore."

"You have an unaccountable reputation for *losing* things,"

Sanford said, still smiling, but in a rather unpleasant way that made Marie wonder what he was talking about. Benson, she noticed, looked uneasy, uncomfortable.

"You haven't told us who is willing to pay so much money for him," she reminded Sanford.

"He still has many influential friends in France, and other places. But about the round figure of a million, it was chosen at random. You might find the price to be considerably lower when you actually try to sell him. Between the bad teeth and the thinning hair, he might be devalued to a hundred thousand or so." He turned to Benson. "I'm afraid I can't give you a closer estimate than that. As to the odd shillings and pence, you can make your own guess."

At the mention of the familiar figure of one hundred thousand, David gave a start of recognition. He looked to Benson, and saw the flash of understanding in his eyes, but soon Benson was laughing nonchalantly. "I don't deal with generals in pokes. If you hear of a firm offer for a million, let me know. Otherwise I'll leave him for someone more purse-pinched."

"But who is more purse-pinched than you, my dear Benson?" Sanford asked in a silken, hateful voice. "Shall we be off, folks?"

"Will you not wait to see Rawlins, milord?" Wingert asked.

"I can't dawdle about all day. I'll be back soon. Tell him I was here. And tell him I disapprove of loading the supplies at night."

Holding in all his spleen at the various slurs lavished on the navy, Wingert bowed and said he would inform Rawlins of the pleasure awaiting him, and of the suggested change in hours of loading.

The party repaired to the inn.

7

Having arrived at the inn at the common hour for the noon meal, they found the place was filled to the doors. Not a private parlor nor even a table in a corner was available. "We might as well go on home," David said, looking around, and seeing a long wait would be necessary.

Sanford and Benson were also scanning the room. Benson turned to leave, but Sanford beckoned to a harried waiter and had some words with him, passing a folded bill into his hand. He soon turned back to the others. "There is a private parlor about to be vacated," he said. "We will just have time to wash up."

This trick would better have come from the spy, but still it was a relief that they were to stay, and Sanford was forgiven his finesse. They were soon ensconced in a cozy parlor that offered a view of the main street of Plymouth, busy with pedestrians and clumps of people standing talking about the wonderful doings in town. Sanford suddenly jerked to attention, and Marie, noticing him out of the corner of her eye, followed the line of his gaze to see Madame Monet sauntering down the street, again wearing her garish peacock-blue ensemble. She looked closely at Sanford, and wondered that he should smile in pleasure at such a common looking woman, though really she was rather striking in a way, and more particularly from this distance. There were several masculine heads turning to admire her. Sanford looked back to the table, intercepting Miss Boltwood's scrutiny of him.

"Madame Monet, by any chance?" he asked, indicating her with a nod to the window.

"Yes, she stays here at the inn." As Marie spoke, Madame turned in at the door.

"Excellent," Lord Sanford said, and arose at once to go to the door of the parlor and on out into the hallway. Before a minute was up, he entered the private room with Madame on his arm. David was secretly delighted, but as Benson wore a disapproving scowl at the woman's appearance, he schooled himself to wear a similar face. Marie noticed Benson's instinctive withdrawal and approved his taste.

"Madame tells me she has the pleasure of your acquaintance," Sanford said to the Boltwoods. "I have convinced her to join us for luncheon, as she will have to wait eons for a table. You know Mr. Benson, Madame?" he asked, looking to the new guest.

"*Je crois que non,*" she answered, examining Benson with avid interest and those strategic eyes, her best feature.

"I thought it might be possible, as Mr. Benson was on the Continent after Napoleon was sent to Elba," Sanford remarked.

Mr. Benson, already on his feet to acknowledge a new lady amongst them, bowed and said he believed he had not previously had the pleasure.

"I am happy to be able to give you the pleasure now," Sanford said, and introduced them.

"What brings you to Plymouth, ma'am?" Sanford asked next, when he had seated her beside himself and offered a glass of wine.

She explained her motive, the Château de Ferville requisitioned, her wish to see Bonaparte gotten rid of. "Sir Henry, there is a man who knows what he is about," she finished up.

"You refer to the petition?" Sanford asked.

"Bien entendu. I have signed it, me. I approve."

"I don't," Sanford said bluntly. "I am surprised that a gentle-born lady like you should be so bloodthirsty, Madame," he went on in an arch tone. Marie was surprised to see this arrogant creature sinking to flirtation.

"As to bloodthirsty, the General has shed more than his share. Time for him to pay now the debt to society."

"He has more than repaid it," Sanford said. "He has advanced military strategy by a century, and civil law by a millenium in France. The Code Napoléon is the best thing ever happened to France. Now you, as a French lady, Madame, must appreciate that."

"Quant à ça, he did little enough for us women. *We* are chattels still in France, as elsewhere," she countered.

"Oh but women are incapable of looking after themselves, and must be protected," Sanford pointed out, with a face so serious and noble that Marie took the idea he was roasting Madame. A wicked flash leapt out at him from those two azure pools that were Madame's eyes.

"Protection! I received no protection, nothing, not a sou, for my husband's home. Were it not for *les saphirs Monet,* my necklace of which I have spoken to the Boltwoods many times, I would be destitute. Had I been a man, I think some recompense would have been made to me. But they think nothing of robbing a helpless woman. It has left me uncomfortably short of money, and it is very expensive living at an inn, so very inconvenient. I appreciate your kindness in having me at your table, Lord Sanford. The meal times are the worst of all, standing in a line like a pauper waiting for a loaf."

"I am surprised you choose to stay at an inn," he said.

"Surely some of your friends would be charmed to have you visit them."

"Ah, but I have no friends in England. This is my first visit here." The eyes flitted between David, Benson and Sanford. It was not a demanding or angry look, but helpless, pathetic. Even Marie felt an involuntary spurt of pity, which she soon controlled.

"You are friends with Sir Henry, I think you mentioned?" Sanford asked, creating an extremely unpleasant situation for Sir Henry's offspring, who knew they dare not offer Madame the hospitality of Bolt Hall. Nor did he leave it at that, but pushed on to embarrass them even further. "You must explain Madame's plight to your father," he said to Marie.

"Sir Henry is not at all well," Benson explained, upon intercepting a desperate glance from Marie. "It upsets him to have company in the house."

"Nonsense! He already has us," Sanford went on. "I cannot think such a *charming* lady as Madame Monet would discommode him in the least. She would be company for Miss Boltwood—the *elder* Miss Boltwood, I mean," he explained to Marie, whose heart fell at the inappropriateness of this remark. There was a thundering silence while Sanford and Madame looked hopefully from David to Marie, all in vain. "I wish I had a home here myself that I might offer you shelter, Madame," he said after the long pause.

The Boltwoods were as one in wishing the same thing. "You are too kind," Madame told him, eying the inhospitable pair with diminishing hope. She soon settled on David as the more susceptible, but he was forced to sit with his tongue between his teeth, feeling an utter fool, and knave into the bargain.

"If Sir Henry's hard heart is not touched by your position, Madame, you must do me the honor to come to me," Sanford continued. "I would be happy to welcome you at Paisley Park, in Devon, or on the Isle of Wight, where I shall shortly be going myself. Or in London, if you prefer the city. You would like London, and London would be *aux anges* with you," he added with a glowing smile. Strange the way his face softened with a smile, Marie noticed. Nor was Madame untouched by all his gallantry.

Her eyes spoke volumes of gratitude, and her lips said a few words. "You are too kind, Lord Sanford. Please not to think I am unappreciative, but I must stay here till

Bonaparte's fate is decided. It is of the utmost importance to me. Perhaps later . . ."

"Your presence can make no difference one way or the other," Sanford pressed on, seeming to be determined to get her to one of his establishments. "You would be happier waiting out the interval in the comfort of a decent home. Don't say no, or I shall fall into the sulks and ruin our little party." But his smiling face made clear he was far removed from the sulks.

Madame beamed and flapped her lashes at him. "I cannot leave Plymouth, the area."

"I don't understand just why it is you came," Sanford said, "putting yourself to so much inconvenience. Would you not have done better to stay with friends in France?"

She looked a trifle disconcerted, but rattled on gaily. "I like to be where there is action. Vienna for the Congress, Plymouth for Napoleon's capture—I am the sort who follows the excitement."

Listening to this and admiring her with three-quarters of his faculties, David noticed that Benson was observing her dispassionately, and soon it occurred to him that this was no real reason. Certainly, she was here to spy and engage in the plot.

Madame, her eyes flitting around the table, was eager to change the subject. "After the excitement dies down here, I shall be happy to go to a private house and await the next event. Are you very sociable and merry at Paisley Park, Lord Sanford?"

"If *you* will come to me, I guarantee every interesting person in the country, both of them, will come to me as well."

"Is that Byron or Napoleon you are excluding?" Benson asked. "I take it Beau's presence is assured."

"You should know, Benson, as Madame Monet has already expressed her dislike for Napoleon, that it is the General who is excluded," Sanford answered.

"After the bourgeois types I have been exposed to at the inn, the noise and disturbance till all hours of the morning, the poor service, I would hardly object even to the General."

"You cannot remain here! This is absurd," Sanford said, completely taken in by this tale of woe, Marie assumed. Yet Madame had not given a single good reason for having subjected herself to all this squalor.

"Oh, I shall survive," Madame assured him bravely, with

just a little trembling of her lower lip. The lips were not so killing as the eyes.

"If Sir Henry can't be talked into it, I shall speak to a friend of mine, Mr. Hazy, who will certainly . . ."

"Mr. Hazy! But he is for Napoleon Bonaparte! Sooner I would put up with torture than stay with him. You must know I was joking to say I would not mind Napoleon himself, Sanford, and Mr. Hazy, he, too, is abominable."

By this reckoning Lord Sanford would be equally abominable, but it was observed by Miss Boltwood that he let up on his praise of Bonaparte. He preferred the charms of an aging French widow even to those of an aging Corsican General, it seemed. The food arrived, causing a welcome diversion. The Boltwoods were bestowing smoldering glances on Sanford, who sat impassive, refusing to comprehend. They were all hungry, and every mention of Madame's going to Bolt Hall was out-talked by praise of the raised pigeon pie and mutton.

Mr. Benson was firmly with the Boltwoods in not wishing to have Madame under the same roof as himself. Marie, watching him, noticed him covertly examining the woman, a look of disgust on his sensitive face at her vulgar outfit, her lack of breeding at encouraging every mention of placing her where she was so obviously not wanted. Seldom had she suffered through such an unpleasant repast, which no doubt was responsible for the haste with which she declined dessert, coffee or any of the other treats pressed on her by Lord Sanford, who had become by some means the host of the meal. The Boltwoods and Benson hastened to the door while he settled the account, but noticed over their shoulders that he went back to speak to Madame, bowing low over her hand, joking, flirting outrageously, and taking several minutes to do it.

"Another example of poor taste on Sanford's part," Benson said, in a condemning way.

"Aunt Biddy would be furious to know what he is up to," Marie said, to David, but with no effort to conceal her speech from Mr. Benson.

"The outside of enough to be offering hospitality on the part of another and when it was pretty clear you were both against it. I would say *we* were *all* against it, but it is no affair of mine."

He had made clear all the same that he considered their discomfort his own affair, and won a smile from both his companions. At length Sanford joined them, and began immediately exhorting the family to charity on Madame's behalf.

"You had better speak to my father about it," David said with a stiff face. He was doubly chagrined by the affair. In his secret heart, he would have liked very well to ask her.

"I shall certainly do so the moment we reach the Hall," Sanford answered, then offered his arm, so lately clutched at by Madame, to Marie. She looked at it as though it were a dead rat before turning pointedly to accept Mr. Benson's escort. There was only one other thing to be done before leaving the town. David wished to obtain a copy of the booklet that explained the flag language used by the navy. As it was no secret document, he got ahold of it at the ships' chandler shop, and stuck it into his pocket for the ride home.

The wind continued rising as they rode along to Bolt Hall, a good stiff breeze off the ocean, that sent David's curled beaver flying off his head, and caused Marie's skirts to billow in a bothersome way. These were only minor irritations; the real disappointment in it was that the trip out to see Boney must be postponed to a better day.

Biddy told them with ill-suppressed glee that they had waited too long to go, and it couldn't be done today.

"It's only a gentle breeze. The *Fury* could take it," Sanford objected, looking to the men for agreement, and finding none.

"I doubt very much my stomach could take it," Benson admitted. "I am no sailor, I fear."

"*You* must be, Mr. Boltwood, as you live on the coast," Sanford continued, undaunted as usual by one negative.

Much as he disliked to admit to Sanford any inferiority in anything, David knew his father would skin him alive to be taking *Fury* out into the teeth of a gale. Furthermore, his major reason for going was to help Benson along, so he replied, "The keel is not dry yet."

"Your father said she could be launched today," Sanford reminded him.

"We'll wait for tomorrow, so that Mr. Benson can go with us," David replied firmly.

Sanford expressed his displeasure by lowering his brows and staring at them. In the saloon, he sat drumming his fingers on his knee in a way to set everyone's teeth on edge. He soon arose, saying, "I'm for a jog about the countryside. Is anyone coming with me?"

David looked to Benson, who had taken up a magazine to thumb idly through it, with no apparent intention of doing anything else, so of course David too had to remain at home. He was eager to get searching for the chest of gold, eager to study the flag language, even more eager to reach a first-name basis with the spy, and start sharing secrets.

Marie wished to join in the search too, and looked away so that she might be excepted from Sanford's canvas of companions. "Will you be kind enough to come with me, Miss Boltwood?" he asked her averted cheek. She turned on him a face full of reproach, approaching hatred. He looked startled to have engendered so much hostility. She waited a moment before answering, hoping Biddy would rescue her and forbid her going out, but Biddy, influenced possibly by the title, said only, "You won't want to go too far. We'll have rain before nightfall. Wear your serge riding habit, Marie."

This advice was not followed. Many of Biddy's wise counsels were ignored, especially when Sir Henry was absent. Marie arose, cast a withering eye on Sanford, and went for her bonnet and gloves. She did not take him for a sensitive man, nor a feeling one, and was a little surprised when he uttered some words strangely resembling an apology as they walked towards the stable.

"I hope I haven't forced you out against your will," he said.

"No, certainly not," she answered in a controlled voice.

"I can perfectly well go alone if you could point out to me some few facts about the neighborhood."

"I am going with you," she replied curtly. She spurned all offers of assistance in mounting her mare, and as they rode across the meadow, she said not a single word.

"It is certainly kind of you to accompany me. Nice to have someone to *talk* to," he said after five minutes' silence.

"I will be happy to tell you anything you wish to know."

"I would like to know why you are in the boughs."

"I was referring to your interest in the neighborhood. What is it exactly you wish to see?"

"What I would like to do is get the general lay of the land," Sanford began, giving up on any effort at conciliation. "Discover where it is possible to dock a ship, and if there are any empty houses or buildings of any sort in the area. Anything that might be used in rescuing Napoleon is what I mean," he concluded.

"You are undertaking single-handedly to thwart the rescue attempt, are you?"

"It begins to seem I may have to act alone. In any case, I

65

take a strong personal interest, and will certainly do what I can to see he is not stampeded into any foolish attempt at escape that will more likely see him killed."

"You are determined to save him for your Isle of Wight residence, are you?"

"Just so. One dislikes to envisage the Emperor running from pillar to post, like a chased hare. He is too great a man for that indignity. His retirement must be carried out in a manner befitting his station."

"His station is that of a prisoner of war! He's lucky he isn't to be thrown into Dartmoor Prison with the rest of them."

"Is that your real feeling, or are you influenced by your father? I had the impression you shared my admiration, this morning at the telescope. You looked enchanted, enthralled, when you were looking out to Billy Ruffian?"

"I was enchanted with the idea that he is captured."

"You would actually like to see him executed? You would enjoy to see that great man's head on a spike, or to see him hanging by the roadside?"

"No, Lord Sanford, *I* think he should be beheaded in the Tower of London, to lend all due dignity to his position as the greatest menace that ever bestrode the world."

She expected some argument, but he just shrugged indifferently, saying, "It takes all kinds. We'll go this way." He pointed eastwards, as they had traveled west in the morning, and his conversation throughout the ride was of a business nature. Sinclair's Dock was pointed out, a few promontories were given a superficial examination. Every lane and byway had to have its termination explained in detail, and if it featured a building at all, a little jog was made to inspect it. Just the dull, stupid sort of a ride to fray the nerves. Not a good gallop the whole time. There were no homes standing empty within two miles of Bolt Hall. The closest place of any interest in that respect was a barn, all that remained of a once thriving farm that had burned down three years previously. He displayed some interest in the barn, the more so as there were plentiful signs of traffic leading through the field to it, a regular path beat, and a shiny new lock on the door. Marie knew very well this was the local cockfighting barn, but was so miffed with Lord Sanford that she wouldn't satisfy him by telling him. He tethered his stallion to a fencepost and walked quickly all around the building, trying doors with an eager air, but failing to gain entrance.

"I must see what is going on in there," he exclaimed in excitement.

"There is a window, but it is very high up," she pointed out. It was a good eight feet from the ground, and impossible for Sanford to see through.

"If I lifted you up on my shoulders you could get a peek in," he suggested, looking at her hopefully.

The image this suggestion conjured up was so bizarre she could hardly hold her lips steady—herself clambering up on this haughty man's impeccable shoulders. "I would prefer not to," she answered primly, and remained where she was, on her mare's back.

He exhaled a breath of air angrily, giving her a corresponding look.

"There is an old door lying on the ground. I believe they have put on a new door. My, there must be something *very* interesting going on in there, for someone to have taken such a precaution. I wonder if you could lean the door against the barn and climb up," she suggested.

He immediately went to the door and hauled it up, examining the decaying wood uncertainly. "If you held it secure at the bottom I could use it as a ramp," he said.

As this promised some amusement, she agreed. "I would be happy to," she told him, hopping down from her mount.

It made an extremely wobbly unsafe ramp. Sanford's foot went right through the wood on the third step up, taking a gouge out of his beautiful Hessians and also jarring his knee. "My valet will have my hide," he said, but was not hurt, and continued balancing his way up with a good deal of agility.

Marie was uncertain in her mind afterwards whether she might have prevented the accident. Just as Lord Sanford approached the point some good five feet from the ground and was leaning precariously forward to get his fingers on the windowsill, the door gave a lurch. She tried to grab it, but with his weight, it was difficult. Or maybe she didn't try so very hard—that was what caused her to wonder later, for really she was overcome with a strong desire to see him tumble ignominiously in the dust. In any case, door and lord both went crashing to the ground, where a very ungentlemanly oath left his lordship's lips. He cast a look of utter loathing on Miss Boltwood, who said in a show of dismay, "How clumsy!" as he struggled out from under the door, where his leg was pinned. His first step caused a wince of pain and another oath.

"I've sprained my godda—my ankle," he said. "What a time for it! If you had let me lift you up as I wanted to, this wouldn't have happened."

"It wouldn't have happened to *you!* It would be *me* you dropped, instead of the door."

"Not a decent sawbones for miles around, I suppose. What the hell am I to do?"

She expressed not a single word of commiseration, but suggested blandly that she would bring his horse to him, and if he could control his temper till they got back to the Hall, her aunt was very good with a splint or fomentation, whatever was required.

His long jaw looked two inches longer at this suggestion. "Where is the closest doctor? I don't want an amateur quacking me."

"Plymouth," she answered. "You have to ride past the Hall, in any case. I expect you will want to stop and change over into a carriage."

She led his stallion to him, and said in an innocent voice, "And you *still* didn't get to see what is in that barn. But you must not worry that it is a gang planning to hide Bonaparte out there. I have just remembered—David said the other night that it is used for cockfighting nowadays. That would account for the new door and lock, and the traffic. It has several chairs and tables and so on, that must be kept safe. I wish I had thought of it sooner."

"I'm sure you do," he said, glaring at her, and suppressing all show of pain, as it seemed to give the young lady so much pleasure.

8

When Miss Boltwood and Lord Sanford reached Bolt Hall, the latter felt unable to go farther without some restorative. Glancing to the dock, Marie saw David and Benson were there, seeing to having *Fury* removed from the wooden horses and returned to the water. Her strong impulse was to abandon Sanford and run down to join them, but training won out in the end, and she assisted him into the house, where the servants without any urging ran for Miss Biddy.

She came dashing in, delighted to have a patient. He was not the Prince Regent and he was of no use as a leech victim, but a sprained ankle was not to be despised, and a sprained noble ankle was a rarity. She took him to the morning parlor, called for splints and cotton, for boiled water, and before Lord Sanford knew what she was about, she had his beautiful Hessian, the artwork of the famous Hoby of St. James's Street, being cut from his foot with a large pair of scissors, for the ankle had become swollen and the boot would not draw off. Off came the sock, to reveal a nasty purple swelling half as big as a turnip.

"I'll just reduce this swelling first," she informed him. "Ice. I'll need chopped ice, Marie. Run to the kitchen and have Cook chop some ice in a tea towel and bring it. How did you manage to do this, Lord Sanford?"

"I slipped off a ladder."

"Ladder? What ladder? I thought you were going for a ride." In her mind reared up a ladder into a hayloft, and for what reason he should have been taking Marie into a hayloft was as clear as noonday.

Marie, aware of her aunt's every idea, for she seldom kept them to herself, informed her of the truth. "Lord Sanford wanted to see the cockfighting barn, into it, I mean, and put a ladder to the window."

"Actually it was a door I was using," he augmented.

"You went as far as Steele's? No wonder this is such an angry swelling. It's had time to expand, and the heat of that sock and boot is the worst thing for it." Her professional concern easily won sway over suspicion of amorous goings-on once she had an explanation.

That Biddy, an elderly lady and a stay-at-home, knew at once Steele's was a cockfighting barn removed any last vestige of doubt that Marie had been making a May-game of him the whole time.

"Lord Sanford was very eager to see it," Marie said. "Just an old empty barn with a table and a bunch of chairs. I cannot think why he bothered. It seems so very foolish."

"Would you be kind enough to get the ice, ma'am, before my ankle explodes?" Sanford asked in a quelling tone.

By the time she returned, there was no mention being made of calling in a real doctor or of continuing on to Plymouth. The subject of leeching, however, had arisen. "I'll just wash off your arm and put three or four leeches on it," Biddy was saying.

"That won't be necessary," Sanford said firmly.

She persisted a few times, outlining the peculiar excellence of her own leeches, but upon discovering there was a fine graze on Sanford's wrist where he had tried to break his fall, she relented and settled for the splint and the wrist bandage.

Marie was required to hold splints straight while the cotton was wound around them, later to run for basilicum powder and a plaster for the wrist, and at length for a glass of sherry. When she brought the sherry in, Biddy reached out to take it for herself.

"I'll make you up a posset, Lord Sanford," she promised gaily. Doctoring was about the only thing that put Biddy in a good mood.

"No, thank you. Possets disagree with me, but a glass of that sherry . . ."

"You never want to take straight spirits on top of an accident! It thins the blood, and makes you giddy. You want a few drops of wine in a nice posset, curdled."

The grimace that lengthened Sanford's jaw showed pretty clearly that he wanted nothing of the sort, but Marie, tired as she was of running, volunteered at once to fetch the ingredients, and did so, then sat smiling while Biddy heated the milk at the little portable spirit lamp that was an integral part of her doctoring equipment. So handy for warming the linseed oil and melting pinguid.

"Really I feel fine! I wish you will not put yourself to the bother of a posset," Sanford pleaded, trying once again to rescue himself.

"No bother," Biddy insisted merrily, smacking her lips over the sherry. "I always make Henry take one after I leech him. It will be ready in a minute."

"The doctor knows best," Marie added mischievously.

"Does the doctor not think Miss Boltwood requires a posset after her trying ordeal?" Sanford asked with a threatening glance at Marie.

"I had no ordeal! I feel fine."

Biddy spared her a quick glance. "You *do* look a little flushed."

"No, no, I feel fine."

"You're bound to be upset, watching Sanford take such an awful tumble as he did."

"It didn't upset me in the least."

"Well it should have, if you had any proper feelings. Here, there's plenty of milk. You have some of this posset, too," Biddy persisted.

"Doctor knows best," Sanford repeated with a satisfied smile, lifting his glass to salute her. "*À votre très bonne santé, Mam'selle*," he continued, and drank without quite gagging.

She scowled at him and took a tiny sip, wrinkling her nose in distaste, then set it aside. "I'll get Lord Sanford a walking stick," she announced in a moment, thinking to get away without taking her medicine.

"You drink up your posset," Biddy commanded. "I'll get it. Henry has an old blackthorn walking stick in the hallway." She bustled from the room, her thoughts winging ahead to consider further therapies for her noble patient. He was within ames-ace of a purge, though he didn't know it.

"Drink up your posset," Sanford said in a stern voice.

She went to a potted palm and poured the drink on it, washing it in with some of the hot water to hide the traces of milk. "Hot water is very bad for plants," he said, wishing he had waited and done the same.

"Hot posset is very bad for me."

"Serves you right. Why didn't you tell me it was a cockfighting barn, and save me all this bother?"

"It is a conspiracy," she told him laughing. "I always take my beaux to Steele's barn, to provide patients for my aunt. It is the only pleasure she has in life."

"Then it is Mr. Benson you ought to have taken, is it not? I assume he is your beau, and certainly *I* am not. I observe languishing looks passing between the pair of you. You are choosing poorly, if I may be forgiven saying a word on a matter that does not concern me."

"I don't expect *that* would prevent you, as it did not seem to stop your all but inviting Madame Monet to come to Bolt Hall. But I'm afraid I cannot agree with you that Mr. Benson is undesirable."

"Is that what has you incensed, my friendship with Monique?" he asked with a speculative look.

"Monique! Upon my word, you work fast, Lord Sanford. Already on a first-name basis after an hour's acquaintance."

"I get on more quickly with some ladies than others, Miss Boltwood. Are you not curious at all to hear why I consider Benson a poor match for you?"

"Not particularly."

"I shall tell you, all the same. He is all to pieces. Was required to sell his property at Devon, not too far from Paisley Park, which is how I came to hear of it. He has managed to keep it pretty close, for what purpose you may imagine."

"No, I can't imagine."

"You are dangerously unimaginative. He wishes to nab an heiress while he is still *considered* eligible. Once the word gets out, he will not be welcome in such homes as this."

"That's not true! He is as rich as may be."

"He is virtually penniless. It must be gambling, though he has not the reputation for it. A strange thing, he was required to sell out. It is usually a gentleman's last resort, to sell his patrimony. I assume he had already disposed of all other assets. Well, a word to the wise."

Marie was aware of a strong feeling of disappointment. She didn't think Sanford was lying, making the story up out of whole cloth. Why should he do so? He was not personally competing with Benson for her, had no reason to invent such a story. She considered this, worried. Those few remarks Sanford had made that morning about Benson being interested in the fortune of his friends—this was what he had meant. And Benson had disliked it very much, had not questioned the remarks, or contradicted them. There had been tentative hints from Benson that he was interested in herself—the word "competitor" had arisen with regard to Sanford. She fell to wondering if Benson were indeed trying to attach her before his position became known. It was such a low, underhanded thing to do. But she soon dismissed the idea. He was not here because of her at all. He was here as a spy, and his dangling after her was only an excuse. He had not really made up to her at all strenuously. He was only being friendly enough to give the illusion of caring for her, to fool the likes of Sanford, for example, and the illusion must be maintained, to prevent people from guessing his real reason for being here at Bolt Hall.

"Mr. Benson is connected to us, a relative of my mother. My father may accept an offer from him on my behalf despite his poor luck in losing Oakhurst."

"Estates are not lost by poor luck, Miss Boltwood, but by poor management. Your father will not accept any offer from him once he hears of Benson's position, and I trust you will tell him, that you not put me in the undesirable position of having to do so."

She looked, but made no reply. For a moment she wondered if Benson were even Benson. David had said he was not, but then Sanford, a neighbor, recognized him, so of course he was really Mr. Benson.

Soon Sanford was continuing with ideas of his own, dangerously accurate ideas. "Or am I mistaken in thinking he is here because of you? Is there another reason for his presence?"

"There is no other reason, except that he wants to see Bonaparte, of course," she answered promptly, to change the subject before he should tumble to the truth.

"He has already seen Bonaparte, and not taken much pleasure from the sight, either, to hear him speak."

"To see all the crowds and commotion, I mean—like yourself."

"You'll soon be rid of him then."

"Do you dislike him so much?"

"I dislike anyone who wishes to see Napoleon killed," he replied, quite clearly including the present company.

She smiled in derision. "Pity, but you will be in poor shape to thwart any attempt to rescue him all the same."

"As it is one hundred percent your fault that I am incapacitated, it is only just that you help me. We really want the same thing, for our different reasons. We both want to prevent his being taken off Billy Ruffian. I, because I think he deserves better than a life of hide-and-seek, and you, because you want him beheaded."

"I don't! I mean—I would be satisfied to know he is where he can do no harm. I don't really care whether he is *killed*. I am not so bloodthirsty."

"You have an odd way of showing it. No, I don't refer to your signing Sir Henry's infamous petition, but to my poor battered self. You set me up for that fall, and if you have any right to the name of lady, you will help me. Well?"

"What do you want me to do?" she asked, though it was ninety percent curiosity speaking. She had very little intention of helping him to do anything.

"To talk your father into . . ." He was interrupted by the reappearance of Biddy with the walking stick.

"Not very elegant, but that little ornamental malacca stick you usually carry isn't up to your weight, Lord Sanford. This is a sturdy one."

He looked with grief at a very ugly, knobby stick that was two inches thick at the narrow end, four at the top, more closely resembling a tree trunk than a cane. "Thank you. That looks very serviceable," he said, standing up to test it, hobbling around the room, and looking with sorrow at his favorite Hessians. He was cautioned not to overdo it, then soon handed over to his valet to be aided upstairs, as it was time to change for the early dinner.

Marie went to do the same, thinking as she went of poor Mr. Benson's misfortune in losing his home, and of her own hefty dowry, really quite sufficient for two to live comfortably. As she pinned a velvet bow amidst her curls, she realized she was in the paradoxical position of being not at all disinclined to accept any offer from him if he did make one or make up to her in any serious way, but if he was clearly dangling after her in his impecunious position, he was not at all the thing.

His behavior over dinner told her exactly nothing. He was a shade more than polite, and a shade less than lover-like. Behaved, in fact, like the family connection he was, come to see Napoleon and not to court the daughter of the house, on whom he bestowed just the right amount of attention to do credit to her youth and sex without singling her out in particular. And she was disappointed with him. But then, there was really no course open to Benson that could please her. Such a course was certainly open to Lord Sanford. He had only to leave her alone and she would have been well pleased, but he came to sit beside her as soon as the gentlemen had taken their port, taking up the other half of the sofa she had mentally assigned to Mr. Benson. David was trotting at Benson's heels like a puppy, leading him from the rear to a private corner to draw out his book on the flag signals, to discuss with his fellow spy how useful a tool this would be to them. He assumed Mr. Benson's ignorance on the subject was a further part of his cover, and determined to keep a secret his own mastery of the code if he ever got on to it—dashed hard.

Sanford meanwhile took up the other half of Marie's settee, hoping to avoid Biddy. He thought he had failed when she came running to him with a pillow and footstool, but she only arranged them under his slippered foot, then went to sit beside Henry, to try to pester him into using vast political influence to get her a dozen Hungarian green leeches from Turkey. The best Hungarian leeches, oddly enough, were immigrants to Turkey.

Sanford looked at Marie with a smile of relief at Biddy's departure. Miss Boltwood looked back with a scowl as black as pitch. "*Now* what have I done?" he asked. He was not accustomed to such ill usage at the hands of nubile young ladies.

"Nothing," she answered abruptly, looking across to the other side of the grate, where David was heard to call Mr. Benson Everett. Her brother was making long strides with the spy, while she always got stuck entertaining this lantern-jawed nuisance.

"Ought I to have done something?" he inquired, in an effort to discover the reason for her latest fit of pique. "You will notice I refrained from broaching the subject of Madame Monet at dinner, taking your not so subtle hint that it was none of my business to try to get her here."

"I suppose you *will* ask Papa as soon as you can get him alone."

"No, actually I was about to ask *you* to do it for me when Biddy interrupted us in the morning parlor earlier. You will recall we were discussing your owing me some help due to having crippled me."

"That is *your* interpretation of the matter. I cannot feel I owe you anything because you so clumsily fell off the door."

"No dice on Madame, eh? *N'importe*, I have alternative plans for her. I'll introduce my other request. About the winch and chain . . ."

"If you bring that subject up again, Papa will invite you to leave!"

"My godfather would take that sorely amiss," he told her, having a sharp idea what made him tolerable to Sir Henry. "He'll take back his inkwell. That chain really is a menace. You must see it."

He explained again briefly his reason for thinking so, and much as she disliked having to agree with him, she was obliged to admit to herself (certainly not to him), that there was some inherent danger in it.

"I'll discuss it with Mr.—my father," she said. But of course it was the London agent who must make this important decision. Again she looked across the grate to David and Benson, hearing fragments of a conversation in which she was longing to participate. The word Bonaparte was heard—plan—rescue—Madame Monet—all syllables to excite her greatly. And there Lord Sanford sat with his long jaw, waiting to be entertained.

She turned to him with her best smile and asked with an interest wholly feigned, "Your property on the Isle of Wight, do you usually summer there?"

"It was my uncle's place of retirement. I have often visited it in the past. He died last year and left it to me."

This brief answer was soon expanded by ingenious questions. Miss Boltwood sat nodding and smiling while a house of stone in the gothic manner was being described to her. "How nice," she said, then led him on to a description of Paisley Park. He seemed not at all loth to give her a rundown on some pictures recently purchased from his Italian agent, which left her free to try to hear the other conversation in the room while she was told of bargains discovered in unlikely spots, brushwork that suggested Rembrandt, and chiaroscuro that might quite likely denote the work of Caravaggio.

"Isn't that nice," she said, when he came to a stop and looked at her as if he expected a comment.

"We should have preferred to find the work was authentic," he answered, regarding her with astonishment.

"Oh! Oh, yes, indeed, so vexing to find one has been taken in," she said with a guilty start. "But then there is no telling with Rembrandt, is there? I heard somewhere that he had painted about three hundred paintings, and there are seven hundred passing for Rembrandts in England alone, so obviously many collectors must be in the same position as yourself, having works that are not authentic."

"Very true, but it was the Caravaggio I spoke of," he told her. He then sat back with his lips closed and regarded her steadfastly, as if he had run across an interesting portrait of doubtful authenticity. His eyes were of a very dark blue—bright, penetrating beneath those half-closed lids. They held a question. She felt too foolish to demand any further details, and after an uncomfortably long silence which he showed no interest in breaking, she forced out a statement.

"I don't believe I'm acquainted with the work of Caravaggio," she said.

"We have already discussed Caravaggio, ma'am. Or rather *I* have discoursed on him. What would you like me to talk about next? My stables? I can run on for hours uninterrupted about my horses. If I pitch my voice low enough, I think my speaking will not interfere with your listening to the more interesting conversation."

She blushed up to her eyes. "I'm sorry," she said in a rather small voice. "I was preoccupied with something else, you see." Her eyes darted across the grate to Benson.

"I shouldn't lose too much sleep over missing out on Benson, if that is what has been distracting you. It can hardly be called a lasting attachment as I am given to understand this is his first visit. Your father will not allow a match, but there can be no harm in your amusing yourself with a flirtation, so long as you know he is ineligible. Like most young ladies, I expect you have your head full of nothing but beaux and balls."

"I am not a flirt, Lord Sanford, if that is what you mean to imply."

"I noticed. You can well use a little practice. Shall I try my charms on David and give you equal time with Mr. Benson?"

This conversation, had it been carried on in a joking way, would have surprised Marie, for her companion had no air of frivolity about him. Its being said in a perfectly serious manner threw her for a loss. She hardly knew what answer to make, but wished it to be in the nature of a setdown. "That is not at all necessary," she replied, and knew she had not succeeded in her wish.

"You are thinking I would have only a poor chance of success, but really it is yourself who is at fault for the dull nature of my conversation till now. Conversation, like a love affair, requires the participation of two parties. I don't usually rattle off the excellencies of my possessions unless asked specifically about them, preferably by a knowledgeable speaker. Even then I can be diverted by a strong enough show of indifference. It would have been easier on us both had you told me your wish. I'm curious myself to hear what Benson is up to. He don't seem to have romance on his mind. Not reading your signals at all."

He proceeded to turn his shoulder on her and sit listening quite shamelessly to the other two, even cupping his hand behind his ear to aid hearing. Bereft of a partner, Marie, too, looked to her brother, and was soon straining her ears to overhear what he said. The talk had taken a turn towards cockfighting. It was redwings and duckwings and Welsh mains that were being discussed.

Some few moments later Sanford turned back to her. "I've heard enough lies about their gamecocks. How about you?"

"Yes," she answered, looking with fascination to hear what outrage he would come up with next.

"Good. I've been thinking, with this game leg I could use my yacht. I think I'll have it sent down from Portsmouth."

"Would that not take a long time? How long do you plan to stay?"

"Till I'm kicked out. How long do you figure that will be?" he asked with a quizzing look. "Providing, of course, that I am silent on the subjects of French widows and winches and chains, and restrict myself to a litany of my art-works."

"How long do you find people can usually stand you?" she asked. Even the oddest manner of conducting a conversation is eventually got on to, and she was coming to see that no formality was necessary with Sanford.

"Depends on their level of tolerance. I spent the years between my twenty-first and twenty-third birthdays with the Devonshires at Chatworth. They were very tolerant, and so must their guests be. Then, till I was twenty-five I battened myself on the Somersets at Petworth. For the last five years I've shortened my visits to eighteen months. When my hostess is so sullen as the present one, however, she may expect with luck to be rid of me within the twelvemonth."

A reluctant smile was forced from her. "You must admit you have not put yourself out an inch to be agreeable."

"I have a feeling I might have dislocated myself a mile without much better results. Being agreeable to malicious females is no part of my plan, unless it should be necessary to bring you round my thumb to get your help."

"I don't wind easily. Would you not do better to seek the help of the gentlemen, Mr. Benson and David?"

"Probably, if they weren't a jackdaw and a puppy—respectively, you understand. The whelp will grow into a too solid citizen, like his father. But I always find women more amenable, so shall concentrate on you, instead. We shall be taking a little trip tomorrow, you and I."

"You can't go anywhere with that sprained ankle!"

"I didn't mean to infer we would *walk*, ma'am. And we shall take care to hide it from your aunt. I would prefer to get away without either posset or tree stump. My malacca will carry me. It is no prolonged voyage I plan to make in any case. I must get over to see Hazy."

"My father will never allow me to go there!" she said at once, happy for such an unexceptionable excuse to refuse him.

"Your aunt tells me you are on terms with Mrs. Hazy. Yes, I have been busy buttering her up behind your back. She winds very nicely. There is a period in there between forty and fifty where a persistent gentleman can do anything with a spinster. Around the mid-fifties they become quite impossible."

"Gentlemen become impossible some twenty-five years younger."

"You are too sparing of the butter boat, ma'am. A little butter softens up the toughest old bird. Speaking of which reminds me of another point of interest. Tell me, as a resident hereabouts, what do you know of this Rawlins who seems to be the bigwig at the naval station during Keith's absence? He is important, as it seems Keith means to stay aboard the *Tonnant*. Liaison between the *Bellerophon* and shore must be in his hands. Are they capable hands?"

"They have been known to tremble."

"What does that mean?" he asked very sharply. The change from his former playful attitude was very marked.

"Oh—I have never heard his integrity questioned. I don't mean to blacken his character. He is an older man, fifty or so, but not from the local area. He came here a few years ago and has kept pretty much to the station. The thing is—it was a demotion, you see. They say he drinks a little more than he should. Not a drunkard—he would not be long in his position in that case, but I have overheard the officers share a joke about him from time to time. I know several of them, meet them at the balls and so on."

"I see," he said, considering this with a look of concentration.

"Surely you don't think the navy would be instrumental in helping Bonaparte escape!"

"I can give you a better answer after David takes us out in his yacht, to see at close range how things are handled aboard. If things are as Wingert told us, I don't see how else it could be done. We'll do that in the morning, and go to Hazy in the afternoon. I don't plan to quite keep you from Mr. Benson all day long, you see. He will be with us on board, and in the evening I insist on entertaining David, to give you a full hour to bat your lashes at Benson."

"I don't bat my lashes at men," she said, anger arising again at this contemptuous way of putting things.

"Have I been singled out for special marks of attention? I am honored, Miss Boltwood," he said with a bow of his head.

"You certainly have not!"

"The draft from your fanning has nearly blown me from my chair. Such *long* lashes. And still she glares! That was a *compliment*, Miss Boltwood."

She was on the verge of some extremely ill-natured remark when Biddy interrupted them to remind Lord Sanford he wanted to retire early with all those wounds, and she had a nice paregoric draught simmering for him, a little camphorated tincture of laudanum, with a drop of clove oil for taste.

"You see how she spoils me," he said to Marie. "I have just been telling your niece, Miss Boltwood, how well you and I go on. Really, you are too kind to me, and I a virtual intruder, uninvited. With this sort of care I may lengthen my visit indefinitely."

Biddy smiled fondly, at either the butter or the simmering draught. She was back within a minute carrying her brew. It was absurd to think of a grown man going to bed at eight-thirty, but Sanford submitted to the laudanum with a suspicious meekness, and drank it down. "That clove oil gives it a delightful taste. Could I have a little more?"

"Oh, laudanum is *strong*, Lord Sanford. You only want a touch of it, just a soother, not a real sleeping potion."

"You shouldn't make it taste so delicious," he chided gently, while Marie fumed at his duplicity.

He said good night to everyone, complimented Biddy again on the excellent walking stick, and was trundled upstairs with the help of a stout footman. At last Marie could join David and Benson, just in time to hear her brother say, "Everett and I are going to rattle into town and see what's afoot."

He nipped upstairs to freshen his toilette before leaving, and Marie was at his heels. "Have you discovered if Mr. Benson is the spy?" she asked.

"Of course he is. He can't say so because of the Admiralty wanting it kept secret, but it's all we ever talk of, Everett and I. The *real* reason we are going into town is to supervise the putting aboard of those supplies. A chance for trouble there, though Ev says likely Rawlins will have such a tight security no harm can come. We don't want to set Rawlins' back up, and will just watch it from the shadows. We must be there, just in case."

"I wish I could go with you!"

"No place for a lady, my dear."

"What else have you been doing?"

"I told him about the chest of gold, and we have been looking around for it. You might scour the house tonight while we're busy at the quay. Ev says it is an excellent thing for me to learn the flag signals of the navy. He suggests I spend what time my other work allows at the telescope at Bolt's Point, reading the flags."

"That sounds very boring," Marie pointed out.

"Aye, half of our work is of that routine nature, but it must be done. It's not all shooting and fighting as an outsider might think. Ev has spent hours standing out in the rain on a dark night, just waiting to see if a certain person goes into a certain building, or what have you. But then there is no knowing when the case will break, so there's an excitement even in the waiting."

She told him about her trick on Lord Sanford at the cockfighting barn, and he had a crumb of praise for her. "It would help Ev and me if you could keep that mawworm occupied. Ev is not at all happy he is with us, and Papa will want me to taggle after him, as he is a lord. Ev didn't say so, but I don't think he trusts Sanford above half."

"Sanford feels the winch and chain are dangerous, David, and I must confess he has half convinced me."

"That's just what I mean! Wanting to cut our chain, and it the best safeguard the coast has to keep Boney out."

"Yes, but it could keep all the yachts in the harbor if it were raised at the wrong time."

"It won't be! Who would raise it? There's no one here but us and the family servants—faithful as dogs, everyone of them. And of course Sinclair and some of the other yacht owners might be here, but to be thinking *they* would be for Bonaparte is nonsense. Ev feels it is our dock would be used for landing, right enough, and I agree. Nothing but sheer rock cliff between Plymouth and here. Sinclair's dock another mile away. We'll be his target right enough, and that chain must be on guard at all costs."

"Well, I don't believe Sanford wants it cut for any mischievous reason. He is just not too bright."

"He's a fool, and a danger to our whole proceeding. Trying to get that Frenchie, Monet, battened on us."

"Everett dislikes the idea?"

"He can't stand her, and feels she's suspicious, too."

"Sanford didn't actually speak to Papa about inviting her."

"Much good it would do him. With that bad leg of his, he won't be able to do much harm, anyway."

"He is going to see Hazy tomorrow."

"Is he, by Jove! I wish I could tag along and hear what they have to say."

"He asked me to go with him."

"Good! Excellent—keep your ears cocked, and let me and Ev know what is said between them."

"He mentioned I might visit with Mrs. Hazy. I don't suppose I'll be able to overhear him."

"You must make a point of it. He seems a little sweet on you, Sis, and it would be a great help if you would jolly him along and see what you can worm out of him."

"I don't expect Father will let me go to see Hazy."

"I'll speak to him," he told her, and could waste no more time on his sister when the master spy was awaiting him below. He was off, and Marie passed the next hour futilely searching the spare rooms for a chest of gold. At last fate had sent two gentlemen to them, and what did they do? One went scampering off with David, and the other to bed at eight-thirty at night. She was very little better off than when the family had been alone, and felt ill used, indeed.

9

The morning dawned fair and clear, with a stiff but not dangerously strong breeze to give the party clear sailing. It was evident to Marie how Sanford had spent his evening when he came below with a handful of letters for posting. She offered to place them with her father's outgoing mail. As she went to his office, David nipped smartly out after her. "Let's see who he's writing to," he said, thinking there might be some fuel for Benson here. He was eager to identify the enemy, and had found no one more likely than Sanford. He flipped through the envelopes—Portsmouth—that would be to have his yacht sent down. He mentioned that. Bathurst—his godfather, nothing in that. Paisley Park—his country seat, that would be estate business. "Look at this, Marie! Three letters to ladies." Missives to such harmless dames and damsels as his great-aunt Theodora, Lady Gower, Lady Carmain and Miss Elizabeth Arnprior were each considered scrupulously for signs of intrigue. It was David's opinion that one or the other of them was a code name for some treacherous French agent, but short of opening them up, he could not determine which ought to be confiscated, and when he mentioned it to Benson, he was told to let the letters go.

They went down to the dock, the descent difficult for Sanford, but he was helped by the other gentlemen. The *Fury* was in the water, her crew at their posts. She was a sleek, trim yacht with a crew of four, and spacious seating for guests. David instantly became a captain, using every nautical term at his command. With Sanford incapacitated and Benson apparently as inexpert a sailor as he had claimed, he had the show to himself. They drifted out past the harbor and tacked westward towards Plymouth. With a good breeze bellying the sails, they were not long in reaching the area that was densely cluttered with boats come to view Billy Ruffian.

They realized as they got close that the ship was more carefully guarded than they had thought. At the closer distance, it was observed that four naval barges stood guard, one on each side and another fore and aft. Guns were manned, and several glasses were trained on the hovering craft. A voice boomed out from a megaphone when David inadvertently invaded the forbidden one-hundred-yard limit, but they stayed as close as they were allowed. With the help of David's hand telescope, they would be able to see even Boney's bad teeth if he should decide to come on deck.

They remained for half an hour, bobbing up and down, while Benson, turning pale then green, suggested at five-minute intervals that they leave. "But he might come up on deck," David reminded him.

"I would love to get a look at him," Sanford added.

At last there was a stirring commotion on board *Bellerophon*. One could almost sense the tensing of the various men at their posts, see their heads turn as one to stare at something. It could only be the General. Marie held the glass, but with the naked eye Sanford saw a dark form, somewhat shorter than the two men who accompained him, advance along the deck. He was visible only from the waist up. His gait was solemn, his head at a proud angle, and on it sat the familiar tri-corne hat, its sole ornament a red, white and blue cockade.

"It's *him!*" Marie breathed ecstatically. Wordlessly, Sanford removed the glass from her fingers, his own trembling with excitement, she noticed.

He raised the glass and adjusted it. Held in sharp focus was a face, familiar from pictures, yet totally unfamiliar. It was human, and it was sad. Also it was pale; the man was not well. Thin, dark straggly hair was brushed forward, and the eyes were two dark holes. There were deep lines from nose to mouth, a square jaw and a sagging chin. Sanford lowered the glass to see his uniform. It was dark green, rather plainer than one would expect, adorned with thin red piping, gold epaulettes and buttons. There was a ribbon across his chest, the Legion of Honor, and three small medals of some sort. As he looked, Napoleon turned aside, giving a view of his profile—double chins, nose slightly hooked. His hand went up—he seemed to be taking snuff. He sniffed in, but did not sneeze. At Tor Bay the crowd had doffed their hats; here there was total silence. It was a respectful silence, as though the throng knew they were in the presence of someone whose equal they were unlikely to see again.

Sanford felt a hand on his sleeve, and saw David's hand reaching for the telescope. Regretfully, he gave it over. All around on the water there was a dead, staring silence. Unconsciously, Sanford removed his hat. A few onlookers did the same. Marie felt a warm tear start in her eye and pulled out her handkerchief, but on an impulse she waved it instead. The General noticed the flutter of white, lifted his hat and bowed in her direction. She felt as if she had been singled out for a special honor. David was smiling fatuously, and she preferred not to glance at Mr. Benson. "Let's go. We've seen him," she said, blinking away the telltale tear.

"He looks very pale," Sanford remarked, and retrieved the telescope for a last look.

"He'd be better off dead than locked up like an animal, with everyone staring at him," Marie said, angrily.

"I doubt if he thinks so," Sanford replied.

As they spoke, the General turned his eyes from the crowd all around to look across the water to France. There was defeat in the line of his shoulders.

"Damme, he can't be let go free," David said, yet in his own heart he was saddened to see the eagle chained. Felt an inexplicable urge to change sides. "If it was death he wanted, he could have gone back to Paris. Louis would have been happy enough to oblige him."

"Please take us away, David," Marie urged. David shouted to the crew, and they left.

"I'll show you the other possible landing spots I mentioned, Ev," David said. He pointed out Wetherington's, Sinclair's and a few others, but for the most part the coast was cliff. Then it was back towards Bolt Hall.

"I don't see any chance of Bonaparte getting off that ship," Sanford remarked. "As guarded as a virgin queen. It would take a man of war and a pitched sea battle."

"A sudden leap overboard is his only bet," Benson agreed. "In his poor health, I don't think that likely either. He'd never make it to shore. They'd lower boats and go after him. I begin to think it is all a tempest in a teapot, people discussing a rescue attempt. He is safe as a bird in a cage."

Rapidly recovering from his momentary switch of allegiance, David found this line of talk highly unappetizing. "A masquerade at night might work," he decided, wishing he could communicate this intelligence to the General. "One of the seamen rigged up in his uniform and wearing his hat—in the dark of night, who'd know the difference? While the masquerader struts around the deck, luring all the watchmen to one side, the real Boney slips quietly over the other. His best bet, easily."

Sanford frowned, realizing that there was a possibility of success in such a scheme. "Don't mention that to anyone!" he exclaimed. "Lord—what a dangerous idea! It wouldn't be impossible at all. You're a *menace*, David Boltwood."

David flushed with pleasure at this high compliment, and looked to Benson for further praise. Benson was already edging to the side of the yacht, preparing for the onslaught of nausea that he felt inevitable. It was a blow for David to see his master spy was actually as unseaworthy as he claimed.

"It sounds entirely feasible," Marie added, smiling that it had once again become possible for Bonaparte to escape, and therefore have to be caught. She too was recovering from her bout of pity.

"A masquerade is his best bet, certainly," Sanford repeated. "It's either him masquerading as a British seaman, or a whole shipful of rescuers masquerading as a crew come to transport him elsewhere, and that would take some arranging."

Benson shivered and reached his head over the side. Marie turned away, to give the illusion she was unaware of his disgrace, while Sanford advised him not to try to hold back. Let it all out was the quickest relief.

There was no mention of going for any pleasure cruise with one of the party in such wretched straits, and they went immediately to Bolt Hall, where a nice warm posset was awaiting Lord Sanford. He had no luck in passing it along to the real invalid. Benson was given a paregoric draught.

After lunch, Sanford's curricle was wheeled around to the front door, and Marie went with him, not too sullen, as she felt now she might be of a little use to Benson in this expedition to Mr. Hazy, if she could arrange to get within earshot of the conversation. Her father, strangely enough, had not said a word against her going. It was a matter that puzzled her greatly, but then David had said he would talk him into it. She felt a little twinge of regret that she would be missing out on more exciting adventures at home, till she discovered Mr. Benson had taken to his bed to recover, and David was to spend his afternoon at the telescope, reading the flags.

Mr. Hazy, a gentleman of considerable means, lived in a good style in a half-timbered home in the Elizabethan style, some few miles east of Plymouth. His politics were felt locally to be from the same era as his home, Marie told Sanford with a smile.

"Our ideas have deteriorated badly since then, all right," he agreed.

Mr. Hazy was an elderly gentleman of a country cut, with his hair grabbed behind in a tail, and he was wearing an outmoded jacket, but his ideas were in fact liberal and advanced. After a little preamble regarding the general situation, Sanford asked if Mrs. Hazy were home, glancing to Marie as he did so. Hazy followed his look, not too happy to see Sir Henry's daughter listening to his every word. "No, she is out visiting. She will be sorry she was away." And so was he.

He had a low opinion of women's minds, however. He considered them about one step up from a monkey's, and was eager enough to speak to Sanford that he thought he might take a chance. "What do you hear in London regarding the liberal branch of the Whig Party's plans for Bonaparte?"

"Only their *wishes*, I'm afraid, as it is the Tories who will decide. It is difficult to arrange congenial terms for him when he is a prisoner of war."

"Prisoner of war! No such a thing," Hazy replied promptly. "He is not a prisoner of war in the least. We won't let them away with that trick. Of course whatever is done must be done with the concurrence of all the Allies. It is not only England that *was* at war with him."

"You don't consider him officially a prisoner of war then?"

"The war is over. Once peace has been declared, one ought *by law* to free prisoners of war, so unless they mean to turn him free completely they cannot call him that."

"It is an irregular situation. He put himself under the protection of English law, or tried to, with his Themistocles-letter to the Prince Regent. If he is granted privileges of a citizen, it would mean a trial. That will never be tolerated by the Tories. He is not a citizen of England."

"A foreigner on English soil or in English territory, which certainly includes Plymouth Harbor, is given the privileges of a citizen," Hazy pointed out. "He would have access to habeas corpus, for instance. Since the time of Magna Charta, you know, it is the law that 'No free man shall be arrested or imprisoned, etc.—nor will the Crown proceed against him save by the judgment of his peers.' Article thirty-nine, I believe. And where will you find a jury of peers for Napoleon Bonaparte, eh? There's the rub."

Sanford listened closely, then replied. "The normal rules are suspended in times of war or rebellion. To quote Cicero, 'Inter arma silent leges'. The laws are silent in times of war."

Marie's ears nearly flew from her head at this introduction of the name Cicero.

"But we are no longer at war. That would apply during a period of martial law perhaps, certainly not at the present. Bonaparte might be considered a rebel, I expect. Or as a last resort, the House of Commons could always pass an act of indemnity to cover whatever action they decide to take. Liverpool and the cabinet will do exactly as they see fit, and I'm sure the Allies won't stand in their way. For that matter, though France is not at war, Napoleon as an individual might still be."

"He surrendered voluntarily."

"Bah, voluntarily! What choice had he? He has walked into a trap. He will be dealt with very severely. Under no circumstances is he to be landed on English soil. And that is where the Whigs come in," Hazy finished up.

"You have some plan to get him on terra firma for a trial you mean?" Sanford asked.

Marie, realizing Hazy was casting worried glances at her as a possible pipeline to her father and the Tories, asked innocently, "Would you mind terribly if I had a look at your wife's new *Belle Assemblée*, Mr. Hazy, as I see you gentlemen mean to discuss politics?"

"You must forgive our bad manners, Miss Boltwood," he replied with satisfaction. "We sha'n't be more than ten minutes on the subject, then I shall take you out and show you my rose garden." He handed her not one but a stack of recent fashion magazines collected by his wife, who was sartorially more modern than her spouse.

"I can amuse myself with these," she answered, smiling inanely at the stack. Then she opened one and sat, scanning its pages with every appearance of interest, while her ears stretched to overhear every word.

"So, what is the plan?" Sanford asked in a lowered voice, by no means inaudible, but pitched low enough to indicate he was attempting secrecy. Marie turned a page and ran her finger under a line of print, as though her whole concentration were diverted from them. Holding no suspicion of cunning on the part of a mere female, Hazy proceeded to outline the scheme.

"Capell Lofft—there is the genius has found our way out. The situation is this: old Admiral Cochrane, commanding the squadron in the West Indies, was accused by a fellow named MacKenroth, a lesser British official there who wished to get some attention for himself, of incompetence and cowardice in not attacking a French squadron that was coasting nearby. Cochrane was furious, as you may imagine, and promptly brought an action against MacKenroth for defamation—did it in London at the King's Bench Division. Well, Jerome Bonaparte was part of the French squadron that I spoke of and MacKenroth, wishing to make as big a stir of it as he could to get notoriety, called not only Jerome Bonaparte but Napoleon as well, as witnesses in the trial to follow. Nonsense, of course, but the issue of writ is granted as a matter of course on payment of the fee. So there is a writ out for Napoleon to appear as a witness for the defense in the case of Cochrane vs. MacKenroth. Issued in June, too, before all this business blew up. It is now a priceless document. Of course the catch is that it must be delivered in person to Napoleon Bonaparte by either MacKenroth or a process server. MacKenroth is coming to Plymouth in person to do it. It can be served on either Napoleon or Admiral Keith, his guardian. Keith will try every trick to avoid it, of course, but if we could get it done, English judicial law decrees that he must then appear in court. Would have to land, you see, and remain here till the case was over. It would give us months to work out a suitable fate for Napoleon. I think the people might well relent during the space of several months, might come to feel pity for him in his weakened condition, and show some decent humanity. They treat him with respect when he comes up on deck of Billy Ruffian. They're sick and tired of our own wastrel monarch—what a contrast they see in Bonaparte."

Hazy's eyes were aglow, his cheeks pink. Risking a close look at him, Marie was struck with the notion that she never *did* believe before that the man was perhaps a lunatic. His ardor seemed to imply that the next step would be to replace their Prince Regent and mad king with Napoleon Bonaparte.

"You plan to keep this a close secret, I fancy, that Keith not catch on there is a writ to be served on him?" Sanford asked.

"Unfortunately he knows all about it. MacKenroth's aim was never *secrecy*. He has been hollering it all over town. Our only alternative is to give the thing every publicity, and then get that writ to Napoleon. It will be the aim of the entire Tory Party and the navy to prevent it, but it must be done."

Not only Marie but Lord Sanford as well sat stunned at this disclosure. "No one is allowed near the *Bellerophon* but official navy vessels. How on earth could the writ be delivered?" Sanford asked.

"That is why we must publicize the matter, try if we can turn public opinion in favor of it. Only fair and just, after all, and we have the reputation for liking justice in this country. Lofft has written up a passionate letter and it is to be published in the *Morning Chronicle* on July 31, next week. I expect there will be an avalanche of letters in support of it. Indeed, we mean to see there is. I have had my clerks scribbling them up by the score, and hope you will do the same, my lord. Be sure to use different names for each, of course, and get them posted by friends throughout the country. There must be no hint of manipulation in it. Real names, and the wording changed, not identical in each. We are not without friends in the cause."

"If only we could inform Bonaparte of this, he would resist any risky scheme of rescue. There is always a danger of his being accidentally shot in such an affair," Sanford said.

"You may be sure he knows all about it," Hazy laughed. "We have not been quite sitting on our thumbs, Sanford."

"How is this possible? The precautions surrounding Bonaparte seem very tight to me."

"Let us say it is done by mind reading," Hazy informed him with an arch look. "There are ways."

Marie sat, tense, waiting to hear Sanford press on for an explanation of this mysterious business. She could hardly credit her senses when he asked blandly, "You think the scheme has any chance of success?"

"Till we see how Lofft's letter is received in the country, we are not quite despondent. We have other irons in the fire. Savary is trying to swing a deal with Sir Samuel Romilly, is in touch with him by letter. British law by tradition takes precedence over ministerial decisions, and we don't plan to let those dashed Tory ministers in London have it all their own way. We would prefer to do it legally, you must know. We none of us wish to end up on the gibbet, and till we see if the habeas corpus works, we sha'n't do anything desperate. I hope you won't either, Sanford."

The warning note in Mr. Hazy's voice caused Marie to look with a keener interest at Lord Sanford. They knew little of the man. Was it possible he had the reputation of being even more of a lunatic than Hazy? That the latter should warn him to prudence sounded like it. Was it *possible* that the man behind the plot, Cicero, was Lord Sanford? He soon spoke out in a very sane voice.

"No, certainly not. It would be reassuring to know his other supporters are aware of how matters stand, though."

"They will know soon enough. July 31, there is the date to look for. Keith has such a tight rain on Boney there is little chance of his ever escaping. The only element desperate enough to try it is that which is in it solely for the money. There is a rumor running around, you know, that the friends of Napoleon have put up a reward of a hundred thousand pounds for any party that effects a safe rescue, but it seems to me it would cost more than that to carry off such a rescue, and the riffraff that are in it for the money could never raise such a sum."

"I doubt it would cost that much."

"Something very much like it, to bribe the King's navy. Well now, I think it is time we stopped boring Miss Boltwood, and go out to have a look at the rose garden."

Miss Boltwood appeared so immersed in the magazines that she had to be appealed to twice before she heard the invitation. When she looked up, she mentioned that she would adore to have an Empress gown, if only Papa did not think them decadent.

Lord Sanford sat in the saloon with his ankle resting on a footstool while Hazy cut a bouquet for his female guest. They all had a glass of wine together, then the company left.

"Well, that was a bit of a nasty surprise!" Sanford said as they drove down the road.

"Nasty? I thought you would be all in favor of it," she said, surprised at his spontaneous reaction.

"I don't think any scheme that depends on the humanity of the common people for its success is likely to get anywhere," was his damping answer.

"What would you rather see done then?"

"I would prefer to see the ministers take a positive and benign view. I wrote to Bathurst this morning, urging such a plan on him." Just as Marie was thinking what a pompous and stupid man he was to think his opinion would weigh with the cabinet, he added, "And I told him what a good home his inkwell had found, too. The pride of Plymouth."

"I'm afraid you'll have tough work convincing the cabinet to change their mind."

"Some few of them are not entirely averse. Wellington secretly admires him, and he is quite a tower after beating Boney at Waterloo. It is Liverpool himself who is adamantly for this wretched rock of a Saint Helena. We'll sit tight and hold ourselves ready to balk any scheme of the money-grubbers to get him off that ship. At least on that one point we are in agreement."

"Why didn't you ask Hazy how he communicates with Napoleon?"

"Unnecessary."

"It would be helpful to know!"

"I *do* know, ma'am."

"How does he do it then?"

"I'll be happy to deliver any messages you care to send him. But nothing in the nature of hate mail or 'It serves you right,' mind. He has enough troubles without that."

"You don't know at all. You're just saying that because you're ashamed you were too slow to ask him."

He directed a lazy smile at her. "I have plunged to idiocy rather quickly. Not ten minutes ago you were worried I meant to dash out and pull him off Billy Ruffian all by my slow self. You really are having very poor luck in putting me in a pigeonhole, aren't you?"

"A pigeonhole is too small to hold a fox," she answered, every bit as confused as he mentioned.

"Oh I think it a great misnomer to call me a fox. I am not at all *sly*, only clever."

They were soon home, to find Benson had recovered his

health and gone to the winch and chain room for another investigation of this oddity. David had just returned from a very long and dull session at the telescope to say there was nothing more interesting going on than a request for some books for Napoleon, or maybe it was hooks, he wasn't quite familiar with his flags yet. Sir Henry was in a dudgeon that Mr. Sinclair had called and refused to sign the petition. "He, calling himself a Tory all the while! A closet Whig is what the fellow is. I've a good mind to send his yacht home, but he'd only use it to go after Bonaparte and free him. What had Hazy to say?"

Marie was astonished to hear Lord Sanford give a pretty accurate and complete account of the visit. But then the letter was to be published in the paper, and upon consideration she decided there was no secret in it. Sanford then excused himself to hobble upstairs to pen more letters—postdated and addressed to the *Morning Chronicle,* she assumed. She relayed a few details he had omitted to David, who immediately grabbed her by the hand to go after Benson.

They found him just closing the lid of the enormous chest that held the extra winch chain. "What an ingenious device this is," he complimented again, but was perfectly willing to exchange this topic for Marie's news. She dredged up every detail she could remember.

"An excellent job!" he complimented her, while she flushed with pleasure. "The habeas corpus will never work, of course. The crux of the matter is delivering the writ, and that will never be done. I begin to see Sanford wants close watching, though. His yacht coming down, and this secret means of communication—he might mean to undertake delivering the writ himself. It will be well for you to remain on terms with him, Miss Boltwood. Such an unpleasant chore we saddle you with!"

When he smiled at her so warmly, he could have asked her to remain on terms with a wild buffalo. She expressed every willingness to do what she could to help.

"What should we do next?" David asked. "I am worried about the ten thousand pounds, Everett. On our doorstep, the man said. Where the deuce can it be? I've searched high and low. It ain't in the house."

"Such a sum would not be so very large—more heavy than huge. You've tried the cellars and attics?"

"Every hogshead and trunk in the place."

"If it is being used in preparations to free Bonaparte, then it must be being used every day," Marie said. "I mean, if someone is to be bribed, as David mentioned—the masquerade scheme, you recall—and to hire a ship or carriage or rent a house to hide out in—well, it must be close to the person who owns it. It seems to me we should be trying to figure the person at the bottom of it all—Cicero. Oh, Mr. Benson! *How* could I forget? Sanford—he used the very word Cicero today at Hazy's."

"What did he say exactly?" Benson asked, his eyes starting with excitement.

"Something about the laws not being used during times of war. A quotation from Cicero, he said. Is it not a great coincidence?"

"That's *all* he said? Nothing about Cicero actually being here?"

"Oh, no, nothing like that. I don't remember the Latin, but it was only with reference to some quotation. I nearly fell off the chair when he said it."

"That pretty well clinches it then," David decided. "Had my suspicions about Sanford all along. Sending out all those letters and so on. He's Cicero."

"Sanford would never involve himself in such a risky business," Benson disagreed.

"In it up to his neck, Ev," David pointed out. He was fast coming to consider himself an equal partner. "Making up to Monet, trying to cut our chain, bringing down his yacht. Plain as the nose on your face."

"It does come to seem a possibility," Benson allowed uncertainly.

"Well then, *he* must have the ten thousand pounds," Marie pointed out.

"He'd never miss it. Very wealthy," Benson said, falling into line with his pupils.

"We've got to get into his room and find out," David said, his blood warming to the delightful task. So much more worthy of him than sitting at the telescope.

"He's there now, writing letters to the newspaper," Marie reminded them. "It will have to be tonight."

"You distract him for us, Sis," David directed. "Make up to him a bit and see what else you can find out."

"It is unfair Sanford should be so generously rewarded for his dealings," Benson said, with a little jealous flicker of the eyes towards Marie.

She read volumes into it. "I'll direct some gentle hints about Cicero," she decided.

"Don't make it too clear we're onto him," David warned.

"Oh no, I'll be as subtle as anything."

A course of action decided upon, the gentlemen then forgot all about Cicero, and spoke of a ride before dinner. Marie went to the study to bone up on Cicero, that she be not totally unprepared to discuss him with the present-day Cicero. A dusty volume, all in Latin, was her only finding, but she brushed it off and took it with her to ponder over unintelligible words.

10

There were guests to dinner that day, the Hopkinses, owners of one of the yachts harbored at Bolt Hall, and signers of the petition. No mention was made publicly of the depths to which Miss Boltwood had sunk in accompanying their guest to Mr. Hazy's house, but the name arose and was heaped with contumely. After the taking of port, David and Benson did not return to the saloon. The others were told by Sir Henry that they had gone into Plymouth, which filled Marie with regret. But she had her job to do, and walked straightway to Lord Sanford, under the pretext of seeing if he wanted a footstool.

"My ankle is recovering, thank you. We can dispense with the stool, but do please sit beside me and fan me with your great long lashes."

She ignored this piece of impertinence. "So boring for you, having to miss the trip into Plymouth with David and Mr. Benson."

"You can't imagine how much it vexes me to miss out on the treat," he replied, telling her he was in one of his foolish moods. "I'm thinking of asking your aunt for a cup of laudanum to put me out of my misery."

"Hush, or she'll hear you."

"Oh but I didn't mean *permanently* to extinguish this flame that flickers in my carcass. I meant only a soothing draught.

You see, the pleasure of the Plymouth circus will soon be mine again. I plan to go tomorrow, incapacitated or not."

"Still there is this long evening to be got in. Would you like me to get you something to read? Cicero, perhaps?" she suggested with an innocent stare.

"He was never one of my favorites, to tell the truth."

"What was his philosophy? What did he write, exactly? I have just been glancing at this book by him, but it is all in Latin, and I can't make a thing of it."

"How odd that you should *try*, if you are unfamiliar with the language. You aren't missing a thing. He wrote a great many tedious epistles to himself and his friends, along with some minor treatises, one on friendship and another on old age being particularly admired—by the critics only, you understand. Real people don't read them."

"That sounds very dull," she said, frowning at the knowledge that anyone should take such an uninteresting code name. "Why is he remembered then?"

"I don't hear him every day discussed. Why did you recommend him?"

"You mentioned him today at Hazy's place, quoted him, and I was just curious."

"You have no other interest in Cicero?" he asked, regarding her closely, so that she began to fear her subtlety was lacking.

"No indeed! How should I? Is he famous for something else?"

"The only other fact generally mentioned about him is that he was named Cicero due to a wart shaped like a pea on the nose of an ancestor. *Cicer* being Latin for pea. Plutarch is responsible for the story. Plutarch is a more interesting gentleman altogether than Cicero. I would highly recommend Plutarch's *Lives,* if you are looking for something to read."

Plutarch was of no more interest to her than a sermon on trans-substantiation. She regarded Sanford's nose, innocent of warts, and asked, "Did any of *your* ancestors have a wart?"

"Very likely, but if so, it was not on the nose. I have never noticed one on either the living or the portraits of the deceased. Is *your* family prone to warts, Miss Boltwood? A new career for your aunt."

"No, we haven't any. That is, Uncle Heffernon has one on his hand, but that could have nothing to do with it."

"With what?" Sanford asked, slightly at sea, or pretending to be. She wasn't sure.

"With Cicero," she answered.

"No, I shouldn't think it at all likely you will trace a family connection with a Roman who died B.C. But if you are looking into the matter, his name actually was Marcus Tullius."

She became aware that Lord Sanford was roasting her, and quickly abandoned the subject.

"You are going to Plymouth tomorrow, you say?"

"Yes, but I sha'n't pester you to accompany me, as I have failed to live up to my promise. I said I would entertain David tonight and let you have an hour with Benson, but they've both run off on you. And his little bout of *mal de mer* this morning made the sail quite useless to you. A very unsatisfactory lover, your Mr. Benson."

"He is not my lover," she disclaimed, but she wished he would behave more like one.

There was a canvasing for participants to play cards. Lord Sanford was drawn into the game. Biddy took up her needlework and went to sit beside Marie on the sofa. "How did you make out with Sanford at Hazy's?" she asked.

"Fine."

"He is extremely eligible, Henry tells me. And such a nice young man. Very proper notions. He asked me if I would have any objection to your accompanying him to see Hazy before he asked you to go. That indicates a nice regard for the civilities."

It indicated rather to Marie this Sanford had made good his boast of bringing Biddy round his thumb. Benson, on the other hand, had sunk very low. "He is much better off than Benson," Biddy continued. "There is something about Benson I cannot quite like. He was hinting, ever so carefully, to discover of me what your dowry is. He knows from Henry of course that it is ten thousand pounds, but he was trying to find out if you come into more from me, or some other female relatives. I dislike such a conniving rascal as that. Trying to hide his aim by mentioning some cousin or other who is interested in making a match, but it is himself wants to know."

"He is not here to court me, Biddy."

"Of course he is. Why else in the world do you think he is here? And we have heard a very unsettling fact about him. I don't know just where Henry heard it, but someone told him Benson has lost his home—Oakhurst you know, a very decent property."

"I know where he heard it! Sanford told him," Marie said, her heart beating angrily.

"Very likely. It was well done of him to tell, if it is true. They are both from Devon—certainly Sanford would know. And another thing, Benson drinks *brandy*. A great deal of it. The decanter on the sideboard is nearly empty, and no one here drinks it, you know. Sanford never touches brandy. He has an excellent constitution, Sanford. He would be a good breeder. He is nearly recovered from that sprain already, and without leeching. He will have it it is my help that cured him, but I did nothing out of the ordinary. Perhaps the splints and bandages were put on with more care than a mere doctor would have used . . . However, what I mean to say is, he would make an excellent husband for you."

"That dull old stick, with a chin six inches long!"

"Nonsense, he is a *little* long-jawed, of course, but it doesn't show when he smiles. I like him very well. I shall speak to Henry. I daresay he came here to look you over. All a faradiddle, his coming to see Boney. You don't see him jauntering off to Plymouth three times a day like Benson and David. He would stay with his friend Hazy, if that were the case. One cannot quite like that little Whiggish streak of course, but he is young. He'll outgrow it and turn into a sensible Tory in the end."

The mention of Hazy and Whiggish streaks made Marie realize that this was an excellent opportunity to search Sanford's room for gold. She'd surprise Mr. Benson and do it for him. She made an excuse to go upstairs. As she slipped along the hall to his room, she took care not to make any noise lest his valet should be listening in the next room. The door was unlocked, and she went in, carrying a lighted taper as she assumed the room was unlit during Sanford's absence. She found no trunks or cases, though he had certainly brought some with him. He was always well turned out, and had already worn three different jackets, including his formal wear. She looked through the drawers, under the bed, in the clothes press, all without success. Then she noticed in the corner a large cardboard box—not a part of the room's furnishings, but his own. She removed the lid, her heart quickening, to discover one good boot and one cut down the side—the result of Biddy's ministrations. She took out the good one, then heard a sound at the door. Her heart pounding, she blew out her taper. But it was no good. Sanford entered carrying a lamp in his hand. He softly closed the door behind him and set the lamp on the dresser, looking at her with a sardonic smile on his face the whole time. For a long minute he said nothing, just looked while the smile turned to a gloating expression. "Well, well, to what do I owe the honor of this call, ma'am?"

She was speechless with embarrassment. What was there to say? "I—I was just seeing if you required anything," she answered. "Fresh towels or—or anything," she finished lamely.

"You ought to have given yourself a light. You must have had some trouble discovering the state of my towels in the dark. Ah, but your candle has—gone out. Allow me to assure you, my towels are quite unexceptionable. I have not been using them to clean my boots, as you apparently thought," he added, glancing at the boot that she still held in her hand. She dropped it and looked at him in confusion.

"Now, what are you *really* looking for?"

"Nothing."

He turned and slid the bolt on the door locked. "I hope it isn't going to be necessary for me to search you? Dear me, what a precarious position you put me in. I will be expected to do the right thing by you if Miss Boltwood should happen along to check up on my towels and find me unbuttoning your gown."

"You wouldn't *dare!*" she gasped.

"Don't put too much faith in your aunt's high opinion of me. Benson put you up to this, did he?"

"Certainly not! It was my own idea."

"Hogwash! What is it you're trying to discover?" He advanced towards her, a menacing expression on his face. She backed up till she ran against the wall, and still he kept coming.

In a panic, she said, "I was just curious to see if you had written letters to the *Morning Chronicle*." She knew it sounded absurd, but the truth must be concealed at all cost, whatever he thought of her.

"And posted them in my boots? I see." He strolled slowly to the desk and lifted a sealed envelope, whose existence she had not even been aware of, with her eyes looking for a much larger piece of guilt. He examined the seal, and set it down, satisfied that it was untampered with. He regarded her fixedly, tapping the envelope against his other hand. "And *had* I written to the *Chronicle?*" he asked.

She hesitated, reckoning the odds that his one letter was to the newspaper. "No," she said.

"Who did I write to?"

"I forget," she said.

"No, Miss Boltwood. You're lying in your teeth. We'll have the *truth* now, if you please."

"I didn't *steal* anything, if that's what you think!"

"No, I didn't think it was money you were after, and I am wearing my diamond stud. So, what was it brought you here? I would like to conclude it was a social visit merely, but alas you *knew* I was below-stairs."

Her tongue touched her lips as she tried to calculate what actual danger she was in. Under her father's roof, he couldn't do anything to her. "This is the last place I'd come to for agreeable company!" she said sassily.

He looked over his shoulder to the locked door, and advanced from the desk to where she stood, placing himself squarely between her and the door. "You're not home free yet, my girl."

"You will not quite dare to *murder* me in my own home, and if you have any other alternative in mind, you had *better* murder me, or you will find yourself facing a judge and jury."

"It is not the custom for a peer to be sent to trial for turning an upstart over his knee and giving her a well-deserved spanking. What, did you think it was seduction I had in mind? You have a very odd notion of my preference in females. Go, before I lose my temper and box your ears," he said, not even angry, but with a dismissing gesture, as though she were a naughty child. He unlocked the door and closed it quietly after her, then went into the next room to give his valet a tongue-lashing for not having the communicating door open, and not guarding his room.

Marie ran to her chamber and flung herself into a chair, mortified to the bone. Where would she find the courage to tell Benson and David what a botch she had made of it? She did not have the courage to return belowstairs that evening, but stayed in her room and prepared for bed, inventing a headache in case Biddy came to get her. As she sat before her mirror, dressed in an elegant rose night robe, brushing her hair, she was struck with the idea that she was looking a little better than usual. The eyes shone and the cheeks were flushed after her ordeal. She *felt* horrid, but she *looked* well. More than one gentleman had seen fit in the past to compliment her on her appearance. Indeed she enjoyed a good deal of popularity with the naval officers. Why did Sanford imply she was unattractive? What did he prefer in females, if not young, pretty ladies of good fortune?

She recalled his gallant smiles and compliments to Madame Monet, that fat old French blonde. It was not her *notion* of his preference, but the preference itself that was odd if *that* was what he preferred. Yet she realized that somewhere in David, too, there lurked a streak of admiration for Madame. Even Papa was polite to her, and men in general showed her a great deal of attention. What was it that attracted them? The woman was vulgar, pushing, not so pretty really except for the eyes, and getting along in years. The more she compared Madame with herself, the more vexed she became with Lord Sanford, till she remembered how differently Mr. Benson had reacted to the French woman. *He*, a gentleman of sensitivity and taste, had been disgusted with her. This thought cheered her, till it was followed by the realization of how dreadfully ineligible Mr. Benson was. She began to wonder if spies were paid well for their work—if they would be allowed to keep ten thousand pounds they came across during a case, as sailors kept prizes of war. She would make a very determined effort to find that money tomorrow.

11

Morning found Benson, David and Marie at table together, coming after the other Boltwoods and before Lord Sanford, that late riser. "Did anything exciting happen last night?" Marie asked them.

"I should say so!" David told her, his eyes dancing. "There was a dandy hassle at the inn. A couple of bucks down from London set up a row with the local fellows that ended up with half the town in on it."

"Your sister refers to Napoleon," Benson said, with an understanding glance to Marie. They exchanged a look that was almost better than words. They understood each other. "No, last night was quiet. And the night before, the loading of supplies was carried out without incident as well. The time is not quite ripe yet."

"The seamen say they didn't get a glimpse of Boney at all that night. He is kept belowdecks when there is anything of that sort going on, just in case. He's guarded as close as may be. If he don't tumble to my idea of a masquerade, he's there for good. Till they take him to Saint Helena, I mean."

"Did you have any luck discovering whether Sanford knows about Cicero?" Benson asked her.

"No, I didn't," she confessed, and hesitated to admit the rest of her disgrace. She settled for saying only that she had searched his room, and found nothing.

"Doubt he'd keep it in his room," David said, picturing in his mind's eye a pile as high as a mountain of gold sovereigns.

"More likely stowed in the bottom of his trunks," Benson allowed. "Where would they be, David?"

"Depends on how long he's going to billet himself on us. Either toted to the attics, or in his valet's room. They ain't in the attic, come to think of it. I looked there, so they must be in the valet's room. Take a look there when you get a minute, Marie. Ev and I are going into town."

"Perhaps Miss Boltwood would care to come with us?" Benson asked.

She smiled her eagerness, but David wouldn't hear of it. "Too dangerous. We'll be listening in on suspect conversations and that sort of thing. Take up a stand beside dangerous looking batches of men, Frenchies or what not, and hear what they're plotting. We might bump into Monet. Don't frown, Ev. I know you don't like her, but she's French, you know."

"And Sanford gets Miss Boltwood to himself again," Benson said, with just a little edge of jealousy in the voice to cheer her.

"I sha'n't enjoy it!" she assured them both.

"Enjoyment has nothing to do with it," David rounded on her. "Told you half our work is of this unpleasant sort. Haven't I sat at the telescope till I have callouses on my behind? It won't hurt you to talk to Sanford. Someone must keep an eye on him, and we have to go into town."

"We are going to stop at the naval station, as well, and give Rawlins the hint regarding David's dangerous idea of Napoleon masquerading as a British seaman," Benson informed her. "Rawlins must be informed of that possibility."

She was sorry to hear that this possibility of escape was to be snatched away from the General, but her spy had to do his job, and she lauded his foresight. David dashed into the hall to check the mail before leaving, and Benson turned to Marie. "I wish you might come with us," was all he said, but the eyes, the tone, offered musings for a whole morning. He wore a serious expression as he left—perhaps with a little something of sadness in it. She could not say he was making up to her, but she liked that he regretted his ineligibility.

She sat on alone, disturbed as to what line Sanford would take after the evening's work, but prepared to meet him. "Good morning," he said, rather coolly. He was hardly limping at all, using only the malacca stick to assist his halting steps.

"You plan to go into Plymouth?" she asked brightly, relieved that he chose to ignore the whole incident between them.

"Yes, but if you plan to give me fresh towels, I wish you will present them to my valet," he said.

This silenced her. He sipped his coffee in silence for a moment, then turned to her with his lazy smile. "Don't pout, Miss Boltwood. It don't become you. You will have the whole morning to chase Benson."

"He's already left."

"Left for where?" he asked with quick interest.

"Plymouth, to see Rawlins."

"I am on my way there myself."

He spoke of no dangerous activities that need exclude a lady. A trip to the naval station was always welcome, and as he had smiled at her, she hoped he might request her company. Her other activity of watching him could hardly be carried on with him away, and she had really no idea of sneaking into his valet's room. "I don't know what I'll do with myself," she said, with an entreating eye.

"All at loose ends, are you? A good opportunity to look into Plutarch."

"I don't read Latin."

"How lucky for you it has been translated into English, quite excellently, by Sir Thomas North. You can tell me all about it this evening."

He ate a very light breakfast then went away without saying an interesting word to her. When David and Benson returned, she discovered Sanford's real reason for not inviting her along with him.

"You'll never guess what he's up to!" David said. "He was strolling along the Hoo with Madame Monet. Had her right on his arm, and what did the pair of them do but go to a real estate agent's office."

"Oh—he's buying a house for her!" Marie exclaimed. She felt such a jolt of anger she hardly understood its cause. The fat blonde was preferred so much to herself that he was buying her a house, and he scarcely knew her.

"Hardly *buying*," Benson objected. "Hiring one is more like it, as your father has had the good sense not to ask her here."

"And he letting on he was going to see Rawlins!" Marie said, still irate.

"He did see Rawlins," David told her. "What a cake he made of himself. He came in just as we were leaving, before he picked up Madame, and said in that toplofty way he has that he trusted Rawlins would warn Maitland of the idea of the masquerade, when he had already assured us he would. He was jolly glad we slipped him the clue. He hadn't thought of it at all. Rawlins is an excellent chap. Sanford insisted he do it right while he was there, just to make sure it got done right. Gad, but he's hard to take. Rawlins was ready to wring his neck. I wish he'd go on to Wight, or move in with Madame."

It was really Madame that Marie wished to discuss, and this gave her the opportunity. "What excuse can he give for hiring a house for her? Surely it is very strange he would do so, on such short acquaintance. It looks so very odd. What will everyone think?"

"They'll know very well what to think," David answered. "Setting her up as his mistress. Plain as a pikestaff."

Benson coughed uncomfortably at discussing such a matter before an innocent girl, and said, "I hardly think that is his reason, David. He is sorry for her in her position."

"Pooh! She brought the position down on her own head. Said right out she goes running around after trouble. Where did she *think* she'd stay when she came here without knowing anyone?"

Marie knew it was mere politeness made Mr. Benson express his lenient view, and while she appreciated his sensitivity, she was not fooled into believing him.

David contradicted him baldly. "He's having an affair with her, the trollop, and paying through the nose for the privilege."

Subsequent events left no doubt whatsoever in the matter. He was seen with her several days in a row. When at last a

103

neighbor threw a rout and invited the Boltwood household and guests, he declined the invitation on the grounds that he was unable to dance, but he was dancing at Madame's skirts nimbly enough. He fell out of consideration as a menace to the safeguarding of Napoleon altogether. He was doing absolutely nothing to either rescue Napoleon himself, which had once been thought possible, or prevent anyone else's doing it. He was just plain running after a vulgar French widow. He spent the better part of his days in Plymouth with her, and as he was away from Bolt Hall half the nights, it was naturally assumed they were spent in the vine-covered cottage he had rented for her. If he returned to see Mr. Hazy he went alone and told no one, and if he wrote any letters to the *Morning Chronicle* in support of Capell Lofft's appeal, he did not leave them at Bolt Hall with the rest of his mail. David contrived to lure his valet into the kitchen to allow Benson to search the trunks which Marie had failed to do, but they contained no gold.

"That seven-day beau wouldn't have the wits to get a dog out of a cellar, let alone free Napoleon Bonaparte," David declared. He was disappointed that Sanford was so innocent. He had found no other party to take his place as Cicero. They were making very poor headway in unearthing the plotters. And the moon was waning, too. In another week they would be at the darkest phase. "Some moonless night," the plotter had said, and David took it quite literally.

Lord Sanford was not Cicero and he was not very often at Bolt Hall, but he was not entirely absent from it. His preference in males proved every bit as peculiar as in females. With two young, lively gentlemen in the house, he struck up a relationship—one could not actually call it a friendship—with Sir Henry. They would sit together in the study of an afternoon or evening for an hour, sometimes chatting amiably, at other times with their voices risen to a pitch that indicated a total lack of amiability. They also took an occasional ride about the environs. This last sociability was easily understood by the youngsters. Sir Henry would like it to be known to his neighbors that he had a lord, a godson of Bathurst, putting up with him. Just why Bathurst's godson should put himself out to the extent of chatting with farmers and squires was less easily understood, but then he always enjoyed to tell people what they had been doing wrong, and perhaps that accounted for it.

His yacht, the *Seadog*, arrived five days after sending for it, and he went to Plymouth to sail it to the Hall himself. Sir Henry went down to the dock to admire it grudgingly, and was close to being pleased with his noble guest. "She will be an excellent addition to our fleet," he said, looking with just a little regret at a yacht that was larger, finer and faster than his own. There was a distinct possibility it would be Lord Sanford, and not Sir Henry, who led the flotilla in the capture of Bonaparte. Still, it was a flattering addition to his preparations, to be able to say that Lord Sanford had had his *Seadog* shipped in from Portsmouth.

"I don't plan to dock her here," Sanford told him.

There was a stunned silence while this information was digested. "Where will you keep her then?" Sir Henry asked, wondering if the navy had requisitioned it.

"I'll leave her here for the time being, till I speak to Sinclair. I want to dock her at Sinclair's—it's the closest place, and I don't want her hemmed in with that damned winch and chain if she's needed in a hurry."

The battle of the winch and chain continued unabated. Sanford urged its removal oftener than was conducive to peace in the household, but Sir Henry held fast. He had another blow to send him reeling, as well as *Seadog* going to Sinclair's. Lord Bathurst had replied to his letter regarding the petition in the strongest terms, saying he must by no means consider circulating such a pernicious document—fuel to the Whig fires hinting at a vengeful attitude that would further arouse the pro-Napoleon faction, and disgust the neutral element that would agree to safe incarceration, but not accept violent death. The petition, now three hundred signatures strong, was regretfully consigned to the filing cabinet. Bathurst himself was in poor aroma, and his godson clearly wished at Jericho. Only the inkwell retained its luster.

An unlikely ally for this troublesome lord was found in Biddy Boltwood. She cared nothing for either the petition or the schooner, but she did approve of a gentleman who required her professional services, and Sanford proved a virtual hypochondriac. He was plagued with a mulitude of ailments from oncoming colds to headaches. It was the sprained ankle and scratched wrist that first endeared him to her. His quick recovery spoke well for her talents and his constitution, then with his little aches and pains they reached an easy footing. She was in the process of persuading him an occasional leeching would free him of that bit of bad blood that manifested itself in these free-floating maladies. He was not yet agreeable, but had relented to the extent of watching Sir Henry being leeched, and accepting that it didn't hurt in the least.

His arranging a tidy private cottage for Madame Monet was of course known to Biddy. She approved. It had nothing to do with his carrying on with her—it was pure humanitarianism. The fellow was so big-hearted he even cared for Napoleon Bonaparte. Like his Whiggishness, this rampant philanthropy would be cured with maturing. Meanwhile it removed the possibility of Madame billeting herself at Bolt Hall, which was no small benefit. Biddy set out on a campaign of urging Sanford on Marie, who took every opportunity to insult him.

He returned early from Plymouth one afternoon, complaining of a little pain in the liver, an organ that had hitherto given him no trouble. "I can't think what caused it," he said, frowning, "for I *never* touch brandy, and haven't been over-indulging in wine, either. What do you think, Miss Biddy? I had some shellfish at Madame Monet's that tasted well enough, but was done in a peculiar sauce. Spicy."

Biddy knew French sauces for culprits. "It's the cream," she informed him knowingly. "Full of hot spices and cream and unnatural herbs, those French gravies—why, if there wasn't brandy in it you're lucky. French sauces have inflamed more pancreases than you can count. I'll relieve it for you at once."

He foresaw a posset, and began recovering. "I really don't think curdled milk . . ."

"Curdled milk? No such a thing. It would destroy a pancreas already saturated with cream. You want vacuum relief. I'll get out my hood."

He listened, transfixed. "A nice high hood I have got ahold of from a medical friend," she told him. "They are using it in Scotland with excellent results. The Scottish doctors know what they are about, say what you will."

A tin affair, shaped like a very deep bowl with a vaulted bottom was soon being brought in, along with the movable spirit lamp. She heated up the cavity of the hood and the metal while she ordered Sanford out of his jacket and shirt. She likewise commanded Marie from the room, for of course an innocent young female was not to be exposed to masculine flesh on such a wicked part of the anatomy as the torso. She rather wondered if she should have let her see his bruised ankle—it had been a particularly attractive bruise. She explained that the hot air in the hood would create a vacuum when it cooled down. She got it as hot as his skin could bear, and clamped the hood on him, forming, in theory at least, an hermetical seal. "The vacuum draws up the flesh and relieves the pressure on the pancreas," she told him. She held it on tightly with both hands while it cooled, giving him a discourse all the while on her leeches. Sanford had owned up that his mother was fond of a leeching.

"How's that?" she asked after the tin hood had achieved room temperature.

"That feels remarkably better," he told her. "Wouldn't the vacuum be even stronger if you put very cold cloths over the hood? The lower temperature would contract the trapped air even more."

"Well now, I never thought of that! It was not mentioned in the instructions that accompanied the hood, but it sounds very likely. I think you've hit on an excellent idea, Sanford."

"Yes, and if we could mask the lip of the hood with some material such as cloth, you could make it hotter, too. The tin is a conductor of heat—you can't get it any hotter than skin can stand."

"I wonder it wasn't thought of sooner. I'll glue a band of cotton around the lip of it before I use it again, and use cold cloths on it, too. It would double the hood's efficiency."

She had already liked him better with every affliction; this entering into improvements in machinery was pure delight. Together they could pioneer new techniques, advance the frontiers of medicine. She determined that this patient should not slip irretrievably through her fingers. Marie must be made to have him. "We'll do as you suggested, and give you another treatment tomorrow if it recurs," she said happily, hoping that a recrudescence, a very slight one, might occur.

"You ought to set up your shingle," he told her, buttoning his shirt. "All doctors should be women. They have such a soft touch, not poking at you with ice-cold fingers like the male doctors. It is a great pity a woman like yourself must remain a talented amateur, Biddy."

This was the first time he had addressed her without the Miss, and while she abhorred forward manners in the young, she was pleased. Their relationship was exceptional enough to warrant the familiarity. "I enjoy dabbling in it," she admitted.

"Dabbling! You use the wrong word. You are an expert. I wish I could take you along to the Isle of Wight with me. How Mama would adore to meet you."

"I have never been to Wight," she answered, not disliking the idea at all, and also seeing the possibility of pushing Marie forward. "I should like to go some time. Marie has never been there, either."

"Perhaps you will both do me the honor of going there with me a little later on, when Boney is dispatched."

"I doubt we would want to go if *he* is there," she said.

"Bonaparte? What the devil would *he* . . ."

"That is your hope, is it not? To get him to Wight."

He laughed deprecatingly. "Say dream rather than hope. It would never be allowed. But how useful you would be if he should come to me."

Her dreams of glory soared to new heights. To be physician to the Emperor! "Oh, my!" was all she could say at the moment, her heart fluttering and her face pale. From that moment onwards, her declared aim was to get Marie and herself to Wight, and to make Sanford her nephew-in-law. To this end, she began besieging Henry to hold a party, an out-and-out ball. There was nothing so romantic as a ball in her view. Her own sole offer of marriage had come at a ball, and while she had felt not the least inclination to accept the offer, still a ball featured in her daydreams of romance.

"A ball, at a time like this?" David asked when he heard of it, and looked to Ev to see what the master thought of this frivolity.

"When?" Benson asked.

"Pretty soon—before Boney is taken away and all the crowds have left," David answered.

"It must be later," Biddy pointed out. "There'll be no moon to speak of then. It is a nuisance to have to go out in a carriage at night when there is no moon to light the way. Here in the country the roads are pitch-black on a moonless night."

"Yes, but if we wait, everyone will have left, and we don't want to throw a ball after the crowd is gone," David pointed out.

It was Biddy's ball, and she pointed out the number of other activities that cluttered up the next week's calendar. Still she realized that if Lord Sanford, too, had gone, there would be little point in throwing a ball.

"August the fifth we have free," she said, thumbing through a book of engagements. The other busy nights were occupied with such revels as meetings of the parish board and her own church board monthly assembly.

"Let us make it August the fifth then," Benson suggested.

His was the last wish to be considered, but David took the idea up strongly, and August the fifth was set on as the date. Plans for the ball had to be rushed forward with an unaccustomed haste, tearing Marie away from Benson and David with the writing of invitations and preparations, but there was little enough going on in any case. David continued spending some hours a day at the telescope on the point, while Benson tried his hand at becoming seaworthy, or at least conversable with a knot and the working of the winch and chain. He spent a good deal of time at the dock and in the winch room, where he was making a scale drawing of the mechanism to show some friends. This pleased Sir Henry, who foresaw future glory in it. Benson spoke of a scientific journal he subscribed to that might be interested in publishing an article on it. Biddy advised Marie it was all an act on Benson's part to continue his stay at Bolt Hall, for he had no real reason to do so now that they knew he was penniless.

This continued to plague Marie, but at least her would-be lover confessed his predicament to her. It was on a particularly warm night in early August, when he went out into the garden just before dinner. With David usually dogging his steps, she had very poor access to him, but David had not yet come down to dinner, so she went out after him. The letter in the *Morning Chronicle* had been published and reached them that day. It was much discussed.

"Do you think there is any chance of the habeas corpus succeeding?" she asked him, as a prelude to more personal conversation.

"Certainly not. It is foolishness on someone's part to try to stop anyone from taking a more desperate action to free Napoleon. The government itself might well be behind it, with no intention of carrying it through. I wonder if it will work."

"I suppose you hope it will," she ventured.

"Certainly I do," he said, then smiled, looking much younger. "No, I don't, though. It would be fun to go after him, wouldn't it?"

She was happy to see he was not only a clever agent, but also a human being, with sentiments similar to her own secret ones. "I expect you have had many exciting adventures in your work." David had given tantalizing hints of exotic scrapes in Europe, but she had heard nothing firsthand.

"I have been involved in a few escapades," he admitted

109

modestly. "There were some intrigues at the Congress of Vienna, as you may imagine. That old devil Metternich gave us a rough time."

"How interesting."

"Still it has caused me some personal hardships. My being caught up in this work leaves me little time to manage my own affairs at home. The fact is, Miss Boltwood, that while I was in Vienna, my man of business was so foolish as to set an enormous mortgage on Oakhurst, my place in Devon, where I am a neighbor of Lord Sanford. My man did it to pay some outstanding debts. I had given him my power of attorney as I was not able to keep in close touch with him. By the time I got back, the affair had gone too far for me to do a thing about it. The mortagee had foreclosed, taken over my place, that had been in the family for three hundred years. It was an infamous thing, but my own fault entirely. I could easily have raised a loan, for I am not quite without prospects and friends, but on the day the mortgage was due, Lord S—the mortgagee—foreclosed on me, without giving me a chance to make other arrangements."

"Could you not buy it back?"

"No, he would not sell, or not at a reasonable price in any case. So I have lost my home, and . . ." He came to a stop, while she listened eagerly, her heart going out to him.

"Well, in that circumstance, you know, I cannot say to you what I should like to say. Oh, not that I am completely in the basket—far from it. Considerable cash came to me after the sale, after the mortgage was paid off, and I stand to inherit something from relatives, but a man without a home to take a bride to has no business taking a wife."

Her heart was hammering. It had bothered her, that one fact of his having lost his home, and not told them, but now he had done it, and the facts were not so desperate as she had feared. He had something—one could always buy another home. "That would make little difference to *some* ladies," she told him, hoping her tone let him know she was amongst those uncaring of a roof over her head.

"It would always make a difference to me," he said, looking away across the rolling lawns, while he heaved a deep sigh.

"The case is not desperate. If you married a lady who had some money in her own right . . ."

"Never! I don't wish to stand accused of fortune-hunting, have no desire to live off my wife. Till I bring myself around,

110

I have no right to be courting anyone. Indeed, I have no right to be here at all," he said.

That he *was* here despite not having any right occurred to her, of course, but she had the answer to that. He had come as a spy, and ended up a reluctant lover. She wanted to assure him she understood, appreciated his scruples in telling her how he stood, and proceeded to do so.

"I can't think how anyone would be so low as to take advantage of your absence to cheat you out of Oakhurst," she finished up. "Who was the man? What was his name?"

"The name is no matter. He was a neighbor who coveted my place. A noble gentleman, one even with whom I am well acquainted. It was all legal, however, and I cannot blame him for snapping up Oakhurst, despite his having twenty-five thousand acres of his own, and that is only at Pais—only one of his estates. He has others."

The whole dreadful truth slowly descended on Miss Boltwood. The unsaid name, Lord S, the unnamed property, Pais—Sanford being a noble neighbor, in possession of other estates. "Well I think that very underhanded of Lord Sanford!" she exclaimed, her nostrils flaring with anger.

"I didn't say Lord Sanford! Where did you get the idea it was he?" Benson asked in open chagrin.

"You were too much the gentleman to say it, but I see it all now. No wonder he was so intimately acquainted with your position. He put you in it himself, then went prating to me of poor management on your part!"

"Did he say so?" Benson asked, offended. "Now that is doing it a bit brown, when he had a pretty good idea why I was at Vienna. But pray, say nothing to him. He is your father's guest, and I wouldn't have any unpleasantness under your roof for the world. I have pretended not to understand his little slurs."

"I shall certainly tell him what I think of him. Not that he doesn't *know!*"

"No, please, you must not. I wouldn't have it happen for any consideration. The matter was legal, there was no wrongdoing in his foreclosing the mortgage. He was well within his rights. I wouldn't satisfy him to think I held a grudge. You must promise me you will say nothing. Please, Marie," he asked, grabbing her hands. "Do it for me."

How could she resist such an appeal, with her given name used in his emotional state? How could she resist such a gentleman, who forebore telling her he loved her because

Sanford had stolen his property, who forebore even being nasty to his victimizer, or allowing her to be? Such magnanimity went beyond anything she had ever encountered or even imagined. Somehow while she looked at him, with her two hands held firmly in his, they moved a step closer. They were in the privacy of a bower, with no chance of being discovered unless someone should enter the library at the unlikely moment of ten minutes before dinner. Their eyes were locked, Marie's heart beating wildly against her rib cage. Soon their lips were approaching the touching point. She closed her eyes, anticipating the inevitable embrace, when suddenly she felt Mr. Benson stiffen and drop her hands. She opened her eyes in surprise to see Lord Sanford smiling at her mockingly from the edge of the bower. How had he got there without being heard? He had sneaked up on them silently as a cat.

He continued looking at them both a moment, then glanced up to the sky. "Looks as if we might get rain," he said, and walking forward, he sat on a hard wooden bench, threw one leg over the other and leaned his arms along the back of the seat as though to say, I mean to stay. "Or perhaps you two weren't noticing the sky? Love, they would have us believe, is blind."

Marie could contain her temper no longer. She had promised Everett she would say nothing about Sanford's stealing Oakhurst, but she had scores of her own to settle with him. "It must be, if you can think Madame Monet is pretty!" she flashed out.

"That is a blindness I share with the rest of the gents hereabouts. She is much admired."

"She is not admired by any gentleman of any taste or discernment or common decency!" she shot back.

"*Common decency?*" he asked, raising his brows. "How did that moral judgment get into a discussion of beauty? Bad taste, which is to say a taste at variance with your own, may be termed ill-advised, but surely not a challenge to common decency. *Chacun à son gout. I* find her utterly charming."

"You would!" Marie said in a scathing way. She turned immediately to leave, then turned back and took Mr. Benson's hand. "You will not want to be alone with your *ex*-neighbor, Mr. Benson. Come with me. I want to speak to Father."

"I wouldn't want to pester Sir Henry with this business," Everett told her as they hastened away.

"I don't intend to. I only wanted to get away from that horrid Lord Sanford."

She glared at him over dinner with all the venom a pretty, young face with long-fringed eyes could produce. She failed to hear his request for ham, or any other remark he directed to her, but was solicitous to hear Benson's slightest whisper, and to see he was never without a full plate. Biddy took her to task for it when they retired to the saloon, raising again the point of Benson's poor judgment in staying on. How she longed to tell her the whole! That Benson was here on delicate official business, that he was without an estate only because Lord Sanford had stayed out of the hospital long enough to steal it, but she was reduced again by her promise to venting her wrath on Madame Monet.

"I wish you will stop harping on that point, Marie. Naturally you are jealous, but . . ."

"Jealous! Jealous of that fat Frenchie! I don't care a hoot if he marries her. They're a good pair."

"You should care if you hadn't more hair than wit. Such an eligible *parti*, Lord Sanford. I wonder how his pancreas goes on. I'll relieve it again before he goes to bed this night. I'll show you later how it is done, in case he requires the treatment when I am not there to perform it."

Marie turned aside in vexation, only to see Lord Sanford entering the saloon in advance of the others, limping directly towards herself. She hopped up and went to the magazine table, in hopes that he would sit with Biddy and discuss his pancreas, but he stood waiting to see where she would sit, and as soon as she took a sofa by the grate, he came forward and sat beside her, ruining any chance for a cose with Mr. Benson.

"I have spoken to Biddy about you two coming to me for a visit. Has she said anything to you?" he asked.

. . "*Biddy?*" she asked with a proud stare. "*Miss Boltwood* has said nothing to me." Her ears were ringing with the constant plans in this regard, but she wouldn't give him the satisfaction of knowing what an uproar the invitation had caused.

"I have achieved a first-name basis with Biddy—like Monique, you know. She has professed a strong interest in seeing Wight, and thought you would enjoy it, too."

"Our tastes are quite different. I dislike all islands very much."

"What a pity you were born and reared on one."

"England is different—a whole country."

113

"How about coming to Paisley then? Right in the heart of the island, with thirty thousand acres."

"I have heard twenty-five thousand, but then you have *added* some acres recently, have you not?"

"A few, not quite five thousand, however. How did you hear that?"

"There isn't much I don't hear," she replied, stiff as a ramrod.

"Funny you didn't hear Biddy mention my invitation."

"I suppose Madame Monet will be there?"

"No, she is desolate to have to refuse me, and so am I desolate."

"Well, I must refuse you as well," she said, and flung open a magazine.

Benson and David went to a farther corner and were soon deep into talk. Sir Henry, with no petition and no parish business to busy him, suggested a hand of cards. Biddy and the boys were lured into it with him. Miss Boltwood, finding herself alone with Sanford on the sofa, set aside her magazine for a hard-covered book three inches thick. She opened it at the first page, hoping her companion would take the hint she did not wish to talk.

"Plan on some heavy reading, do you?" he asked.

"Yes, I enjoy to read."

"I'm impressed to see how quickly you've picked up Latin," he said after a moment. As her angry eyes focused on the letters, she saw them to be composed of a multitude of words ending in 'ibus.' At a loss for any explanation in her defense, she turned to attack instead. "What keeps you from Madame Monet tonight?"

"My pancreas. And the weather, of course. You were too well occupied with Benson before dinner to notice the dark clouds forming up. His conversation must be extremely diverting."

"It is," she answered with a smug smile.

"How very strange, and the rest of the world finds him a dead bore."

"Is that why you were so eager to be rid of him as a neighbor?"

"No, that isn't why. It is not necessary to be bosom bows with one's neighbors. It was his being an absentee landlord allowing his estate to become badly run down that occasioned the general rejoicing when he left. A falling-apart old rabbit warren of a place detracts from the whole neighborhood. The

114

people who bought it have fixed it up very nicely. Cut down the pasture in the front lawn, replaced the windows, and are speaking of putting in floors and ceilings."

"The *person* who bought it can well afford to, I expect."

"*They* seem to be well to grass."

"I expect the walls, if they bother to install any, will be decorated with bogus Rembrandts."

"You think *I* mean to palm off my forged Caravaggio on them, I expect. No, I don't go out of my way to make enemies. In a few cases, however, it seems to happen in spite of my best efforts."

"I wonder why that would be."

"That matter of taste we were discussing before dinner, in the garden, must account for it."

He tried a few times to rally her into conversing but failed, and before long he went to say good night to everyone. Biddy mentioned repeating the vacuum treatment, but he pronounced her too good a physician to require a second treatment. The card game did not last long. A neighbor from the parish board came to talk to Sir Henry about a possible addition to "the situation," which required the privacy of the beloved office to keep it from Marie's ears. She'd have to wait and hear from Biddy who the girl was. Marie offered to take his place at the card table, but looks were being exchanged between David and Benson. It soon came out that Mr. Benson had to go out somewhere. The night was wretched, with rain threatening at any moment, and to stop Biddy's protests, Benson let on he was only going down to the winch room for another look at it, but his cohorts knew it was more important business taking him into a howling storm.

Before long, Marie discovered the exact nature of his business. "He has a line on the money," David said. "Thinks he might know who has it, and where it is hidden. I offered to go with him but he says it is too dangerous for us both to risk it. If anything happens to him this night, all this affair will rest with me. One of us must survive to carry on," he said gravely, unconsciously straightening his shoulders and lifting his chin to meet the challenge.

"You should have insisted on going with him!" Marie adjured at once, but already Benson was off on his dangerous mission. All they could do was sit and wait, and pray for his safe return, preferably with the money.

He hadn't been gone ten minutes till Biddy picked up her needlework and retired to her room. Before much longer,

Sanford sauntered down the stairs looking for her. He had changed from his black jacket, was wearing a sort of lounging coat, a new fashion that David had not come across before. It was longish, made up in maroon velvet, very elegant. When Sanford saw the Boltwoods sitting alone, he asked, "Where's Benson?" in a sharp voice.

"Out," David answered. "He didn't say where."

"It must be an important matter to take him out on such a night as this. Didn't he say where he was going?"

"No, he didn't."

"We do not feel it our right to question our guests," Marie added.

He turned without another word and went to his room. "That fellow gets under my skin," David remarked idly.

This opened the doors to the whole of his heinous conduct. She didn't feel Benson would object to David's knowing it. Upon hearing how he had diddled Ev out of Oakhurst, David's ire knew no bounds. His quoting Cicero, his insistence on cutting the chain and all his other misdeeds were recalled and discussed, with the fairly recent crimes of planning to take *Seadog* to Sinclair's dock thrown in. Suddenly he jumped to his feet with a totally new and extremely damning piece of evidence. "Did you notice that jacket he wore?"

"Yes, I thought it looked very strange. Too long for a jacket and too short for a dressing gown. What was it?"

"I didn't mean the cut! I meant the buttons."

"I didn't notice the buttons."

"How could you miss them? They were *brass*."

David was partial to a brass button himself, the bigger the better, so she wondered why this fact had him excited. He continued, "Don't you remember—the night I heard the two spies talking I thought one of 'em was a military man—he had brass buttons. It wasn't an officer at all. It was Sanford, wearing that jacket. It had two little rows of smallish brass buttons, just like an officer's jacket. A bit of a military cut to it, too. Of course it was him! What would an officer be doing here at two o'clock in the morning? He had just arrived—you mind Papa told us the next morning he got here very late. The first move he made when he got here was to keep a rendezvous with his partner, whoever *he* is. I've got to tell Ev this."

"You can't tell him till he gets back. We don't know where he's gone."

"We know now where he's gone, right enough."

"Where?" Marie asked in puzzlement.

"To Madame Monet's. I've had a pretty good notion all along she's in on it, and this pretty well proves it. If Sanford is Cicero, and hiring her a private house and all, you know what it's for. It's the headquarters where all the arrangements are being made to rescue Boney, and it's where the gold is hidden."

"It's not right on our doorstep."

"He hadn't taken it there yet when I heard him say that. Use your head, woman. Can't you figure out anything? Ev's tumbled to it and gone there to get the gold. I'll have to nip along and warn him Sanford knows he's gone. No saying he won't follow him, for you saw how excited he was when he noticed Ev was gone. Made quite a point of trying to find out where he was."

"Benson should have asked you to keep an eye on Sanford."

"He'd gone to bed, letting on his liver was cutting up. All a hum so Ev would think he had clear sailing. I've got to go at once."

"Why don't you check and see if Sanford is going out first?"

"Can't wait. Ev warned me you have to be ready to move on a moment's notice. I've got to get there *before* Sanford and warn Ev. You keep your eyes open here at home and see if anything new turns up. Now that we *know* Sanford is Cicero, you may notice something. Now that we know where to look for trouble, I mean."

David was gone, and Marie sat on mulling over their talk. She couldn't think of a single new vista of investigation opened up to her as a result of Sanford's established guilt. Even, she wondered, if a set of brass buttons were not flimsy evidence on which to accuse him so positively. But of course the brass buttons were only one link in a long chain. His every move since coming to them was suspect. Even his *being* here was suspect. Why was he? Not a connection nor a suitor, only a meddler who happened to have a title and the gall to push himself in where he was clearly not wanted. Not even the decency to behave with propriety towards his hosts. That "odd notion of my preference in females" rankled still.

12

For some time Marie sat wondering what she ought to do, but no inspiration came to her. At length she decided she would at least check the stable and see if Cicero had in fact gone out at all. She was quite surprised to see the Arab stallion standing in his stall. Had Sanford taken his curricle then? No, the grays too were munching hay, and a rapid review of the other stalls told her there were no nags out but David's and Benson's. She was just turning to go back into the house when she heard a step at the doorway. Quick as a wink, she slid into her own mare's loose box to conceal herself. By patting the animal's nose she kept it quiet, and by peering between the slats she saw the newcomer was of course Sanford, with a dark cape thrown over his clothes so she couldn't see if he wore the incriminating set of brass buttons. He went immediately to the stand to lift his saddle down, so he was going out, all right.

Before he had got the saddle buckled, a groom padded forward, Sanford's groom.

"Qu'est-ce qu'il y a?" the man asked. A Frenchman! He had a French groom.

"Je crois que la nuit est venue," he answered.

I think the night has come? How absurd! Of course it was night time. Or did he mean *the* night—the night on which Napoleon was to be rescued?

"Il n'y a pas de lune," the groom mentioned. No moon! *"Vous aurez besoin de moi?"*

"Non, j'irai seul," Sanford answered off-handedly, spurning any help. *"Tu restes ici, et n'aies pas les yeux en poche."*

Don't keep your eyes in your pocket? She pondered this. He meant of course that he would go alone, and the groom was to keep his eyes open here.

"Compris," the man replied jauntily. *"Vous avez le pistolet?"*

"Bien entendu!" Sanford answered, patting a bulge in his pocket.

Of course he had a pistol. Naturally a traitor would not run about unarmed. The saddle was buckled on, Sanford hopped up and went out of the stable, while Marie waited on tenterhooks for the groom to leave, that she might dash out after Sanford and see which way he had gone. The stubborn Frenchman took his time about leaving. It seemed an hour he stood looking all around with a suspicious eye, but at last he turned and walked off towards the grooms' room, and she could make a hasty dart to the yard to watch Sanford.

He was off to Madame Monet's, she assmued, but was no longer sure. If this were the night Napoleon was to be rescued, he might be going elsewhere. And David and Benson wasting their time spying on Madame Monet! She soon realized it was no such a thing. Only David was gone there. Benson had somehow discovered this was the night, and was already out in advance of Sanford to thwart his plans. She felt a swelling of triumph, also considerable relief to know the whole onus was not on her own slim shoulders. How noble of Everett to have gone alone, to keep David out of danger. It was just like him.

Looking around in the darkness, for with the heavily-clouded sky there was a very poor illumination, she saw Sanford headed not into town but off up the hill to Bolt's Point. He was going up to the telescope. To await a signal before going into action? She had to discover of course, and in a flash she was back in the stable, very silently and carefully leading her own mare out the door. The Frenchie might come back and discover it gone, but she must take the chance and hope he had his eyes in his pocket. Her own had some trouble keeping Sanford in sight. For minutes at a stretch she lost him, but from time to time he was visible, proceeding directly to the telescope. When she came to a point about a quarter of a way from the summit, she realized she could not go barging in on horseback, and tethered her mare to a tree, only to see that Sanford had done the same thing not ten yards away. She wasted precious moments backtracking and going off to the left to keep her own mount invisible from any chance comers. She couldn't believe Sanford was to do the whole by himself.

Creeping forward as silently as a bat, straining her eyes into the distance, she saw only one form on the summit by the telescope. The thorn bushes might conceal others, but she thought Sanford was all alone, using the telescope now, or trying to. She could not believe he could see a thing in the

119

darkness. Then suddenly a light flashed, right in his hand. Once, twice, three times, and it was covered again. He had a covered lantern he was signalling with. How had he got it? It must have been up here waiting for him. He hadn't taken it out of the stable.

Then he waited. No further signals were given, but he walked to the very edge of the precipice and leaned over. He was carrying something in his hands. Not a large object, and apparently not heavy, as he moved swiftly, lightly. A rope, she decided at last, catching some little glimpse of a longish object bobbing from his fingers. He then lay down on his stomach and threw the rope over the cliff. There wasn't a single doubt in her mind that she would soon see Napoleon Bonaparte being hauled up that rope. Often she had heard Sanford mention this exact means of escape for him. But how stupid Sanford was! He should tie the rope around a tree. His own weight was not great enough to safely tether the rope at this end. He would go sliding down the cliff himself, and Bonaparte on the other end of the rope. And wasn't that a just fate for the pair of them? She realized it was not the fate she wanted for either one. She was seized with a trembling that shook her whole body to consider such a calamity.

Just as she was on the verge of dashing forward, the man began to rise. He stood up, reeling in the rope, empty, to judge by the speed of his movements. Then she saw it was not quite empty. There was some small object attached to its end. Sanford fumbled with the knot, removing the object. It was small, cylindrical in shape, and had a little sheen to it. A metallic tube of some sort. It was not Bonaparte himself that was the object of tonight's operation, but a message only. So it was no idle boast that he knew how the secret messages were relayed. He had managed to bribe a good swimmer to carry messages in a sealed metal tube. That must be it. He had probably passed on David's idea of a masquerade to Napoleon, and was getting the General's response. Instructions as to how he must proceed ashore to complete the escape.

All worry for Sanford's safety vanished. She had to get the message, had to find out his plans. What to do? But again there was movement at the point before she could do anything. A silent black shadow darted out of the bushes, and Sanford crumpled to the earth. The metal tube was snatched up, and the attacker disappeared back into the concealing darkness. A secret smile of pride and triumph glowed on her face, unseen. Benson, on the alert, knowing every move in advance, had come here and got the message away from Sanford. His whole plan would soon be revealed to the London agent. Her instinct was to rush forth and congratulate him, but the crumpled heap on the ground began to stir, and she remained hidden. It sat up, rubbing its head, and suddenly the air was rent with a truly wicked curse. Then the man got to his feet, looked all around, and soon flew right past her. She shook her head in bewilderment. It was not Lord Sanford. It was Benson!

Everett had come to receive the message, and Sanford had somehow discovered it, and gone after him. It took her a moment to recover from the shock, but as soon as she did so she darted out from behind the bushes to offer her services to Benson. She was too late. He was already pelting down the hill on his horse. Where had he had it hidden? She hadn't seen a sign of it, nor heard a single whinny. The excitement over, she returned at a slower gait to untie her own mare and go home. She lingered a while, purposely going slowly to allow the men to get out of the stable before she should enter. When finally she went in, all mounts were accounted for except David's. For once *she* had been on the scene, and *he* had missed all the fun. She mentally corrected the frivolous word—activity.

She was extremely curious to hear all about it from Benson, and went to him to console him on his loss, and of course devise plans for the message's recovery. The night's excitement was not over yet. She flung her pelisse off in the kitchen and dashed up to the saloon, to find him looking through a book with a somewhat bored expression on his face, as if he had been there an hour. He was not disheveled nor perturbed in the least.

"Mr. Benson!" she cried in surprise. "I thought you would be going after Lord Sanford to get back the message."

He blinked his eyes and frowned. "I beg your pardon?" he asked.

"You don't have to dissemble with me. I saw the whole. I went to the stable after David left . . ."

"Where did David go?" he asked.

"After you, to Madame Monet's. He thought you had gone there, but when I went to check to see if Sanford's horse was gone, Sanford came into the stable, and I followed him to the Point."

"You shouldn't take such risks, Marie. I'd never forgive

myself if anything happened to you. And do you mean to tell me Sanford went up to the telescope tonight?"

"But you were there! Surely it was *you* he hit on the head and stole the message from."

"My dear girl, I haven't an idea what you're talking about." He demanded an explanation from her, and at its termination, he said, "But it wasn't *me*. *I* have been back from town this half hour, and was wondering where everyone was. I waited up only in the hope that you would come downstairs again, as it is not at all late."

"I made sure it was you! Of course in the darkness I really couldn't see very well. I thought it was you, and saw what I was looking for, I suppose."

"I am flattered you were looking for me."

"Who could it have been, I wonder."

"Someone else who is mixed up in this. There is more than one plan to rescue Bonaparte—half a dozen of them, I daresay. But Sanford claims he, too, wishes to stop any attempt, you know, and he has heard somehow of this plan and caught the fellow up. It was well done of him."

She tried to explain to him the error of his thinking. The brass buttons on the coat, unseen by him, were mentioned, along with all the other suspicious behavior. She thought she had convinced him, and her next speech was, "You must get that message from him. I am convinced it was a message from Napoleon."

"He has already read it. Not much point in going after it, except that it would be well for us to know, too, of course."

"We must know. It is *crucial.*"

"Yes, I'll take care of it. I don't wan't *you* involving yourself, my dear." His glowing eyes regarded her tenderly, sadly.

"Let me help you," she offered.

"That is not necessary. I have ways."

A pretty good way soon presented itself as Lord Sanford strolled down the stairs, wearing again his brass-buttoned jacket. Marie looked at the buttons, then with great significance to Benson! "I'll detain him—you go and search his room now," she said in an undertone. He sat a moment chatting so his departure would not be too obvious.

"Back are you, Mr. Benson?" Sanford asked in a normal conversational tone.

"Yes, I had some business in Plymouth."

"What sort of business does one conduct at night? Sounds like romantic business to me."

122

"You mistake, Lord Sanford. It is not *I* who conducts his amorous business in Plymouth."

"One hears it is France you prefer."

"It isn't Mr. Benson who favors Frenchies for his amours, either," Marie said angrily.

"I thought otherwise," Sanford remarked with an air of indifference, and took up a seat. "Where is David?" he asked.

"Was his mount missing when you came back, my lord?" Marie asked, looking a challenge at him.

"Back? I haven't been out," he answered.

"Dear me, what a state your room must be in, that you have muddied your boots while lounging in it," Marie said, glancing to his boots, where slight evidences of mud were visible along their edges.

"I didn't like to mention it, but it is in need of a sweeping out," he replied, his lips held steady with just a little difficulty. "Mind you, I am not complaining! The *towels*, for instance, are changed morning and night."

Mr. Benson yawned, stretched, and said he thought he'd call it a night.

"Not a bad idea. I'm for bed, too," Sanford said at once, looking at him with a sapient eye.

"Ah, before you go, Sanford, might I have a word with you?" Marie asked, smiling winningly.

"If Mr. Benson will promise not to be jealous. But really he doesn't seem to be bothered by the green-eyed monster at all," he answered.

Benson's face assumed an angry hue, but he said nothing. He arose and strode out the door.

"Now what, I wonder, can suddenly account for your deigning to smile at me, and wishing to speak to me?" Sanford asked.

"I hope it is not so unusual as to occasion remark when I smile at a guest under my father's roof," she began, searching wildly for a topic to detain him.

"That must depend on the guest. Mr. Benson would not find it unusual. *I* have reason to."

"I have been thinking about your very kind invitation for my aunt and myself to visit you at Wight," she said, hitting hastily on a subject that might be stretched out to a quarter of an hour.

"Dare I hope you are overcoming your aversion to islands?" he asked with polite interest, and a twinkle in his eye she could not quite trust.

"As you pointed out, I was born and bred on an island, and I daresay once one got to Wight she would forget she was surrounded by water."

"My home is right on the coast. It would be difficult to forget."

"But I live on the coast here, too, and never think of the ocean at all."

"Not even when you go to the dock, or out on the *Fury*, or to Bolt's Point to use the telescope?" he asked.

She swallowed at the mention of the telescope and said, "Never think of being on an island, I mean."

"In that case you might contrive to be comfortable at Wight."

"I should like to hear something about it."

"Certainly, I shall be happy to talk to you for half an hour, and you must doze off or listen, just as you see fit. How long does Mr. Benson require abovestairs?"

She gave a guilty start, her eyes darting towards the staircase in the hall.

"No, no, I have no notion of interrupting him. He sha'n't find a thing there, and would not be nearly so interesting as yourself to lock in with me in my room. One clout on the head a night is enough for him, don't you think?"

"It wasn't he at Bolt's Point," she said, seeing no point in pretending to misunderstand him.

"Certainly looked like him."

"I thought so, too, but it is only because we *expected* to see him."

"I wasn't at all sure it would be him. I hoped, for your sake, it would not be."

"What do you mean?"

"It is a trifle incriminating, don't you think, that he was in secret communication with the *Bellerophon?*"

"Incriminating! Oh, no, it's . . ." She pulled to a stop, unsure how much she dared to tell, but knowing at least she ought not to reveal Benson's secret job.

Sanford regarded her closely. "Don't get yourself mixed up in this, Miss Boltwood. And don't put too much faith in Mr. Benson's lovemaking. He is not eligible."

"He told me about losing Oakhurst! *All* about it," she added in a tone of significance. "He does not pretend to be wealthy."

"Does he pretend to be unattached?"

"*Pretend* to be! He *is* unattached."

124

"Did he actually say so?"

"No, not in so many words, but he is, of course."

"If you say so," Sanford replied, with a look that told her she was a fool. They were ex-neighbors, these two. Was it possible Mr. Benson had a girl friend, even a fiancée back home? She soon solved this mystery. He *had* been courting someone, some mercenary girl who turned him off when he lost Oakhurst. Still, she was curious to hear it confirmed and asked, "Did he have a friend, a lady friend, in Devon?"

"Not to my knowledge. He was seldom there," was his unhelpful reply.

"What did you mean then?"

"Ask him. I've driven enough spokes into the poor devil's wheel for one night. Do you figure he's had time to finish his search yet? I'm getting mighty tired."

It hardly seemed to matter if Benson should be discovered, since Sanford knew exactly what he was doing, anyway.

"We'll have a glass of wine and give him five minutes more," Sanford decided, and poured two glasses from the decanter on the table, handing one to Marie.

"To success!" he proposed, and they both drank to this ambiguous toast, with a little pointless conversation. Then Sanford said good night and went upstairs, to find his door innocently closed. There was no sign of Benson. With a wicked gleam in his lazy eyes, he stepped along the hall to Benson's room and tapped on the door. "She's waiting for you in the saloon," he said.

Benson returned below, to hear that Sanford knew exactly what they were up to, which accounted for the lack of success in finding the tube or message. She was eager to drop a hint as to Benson's being attached, but his mind was not on the subject, and she had no chance to introduce it. They decided together, really Benson convinced her, that Sanford had only been working on his own to intercept the message devised by some other party trying to mastermind the escape. But when David returned, his hair wet and his boots soaked, for the rain had at last come down, he threw them into doubt. He had to hear how he had missed out on all the excitement, of course, then had a discovery of his own to alarm them.

"My night wasn't completely wasted anyway, for you'll never guess who was visiting Monet! Rear Admiral Rawlins, in a plain dark jacket, not his uniform."

"What on earth would he be doing there?" Marie asked,

125

feeling an angry thrust that yet another gentleman had fallen under the trollop's spell.

"Making right up to Sanford's girl," David explained. "Sitting on the sofa together, close as inkle-weavers, with their heads together laughing and talking."

"You don't mean he was making love to her!" Benson asked.

"Couldn't hear what he was *saying*, but Rawlins didn't have to run up any flags for anyone to read the gist of it. Billing and cooing—Lord, what a sight! That old man and Madame."

"This is outrageous!" Benson said, jumping to his feet.

"Known all along what *she* is," David pointed out. "Wouldn't I love to drop Sanford the hint, though."

"No!" Benson said, the word a sharp command.

"Just razz him a little is all I mean," David countered.

"No, David, in our business personal feelings have no place. You have misunderstood the matter, no doubt. Rawlins has become suspicious of Madame, and is following his own investigations. The likeliest way of discovering anything from a woman of her kidney is by lovemaking. He was only trying to find out what she's up to. Naturally the navy is suspicious of French persons who came to the town just at the time Napoleon was brought here. I wouldn't want Sanford to know what Rawlins is up to."

"But you said Sanford is doing nothing but trying to stop anyone from rescuing Napoleon," Marie reminded him.

"Lord, where did you get such an idea! Sanford is Cicero!" David shouted. He had been absent during the period when Sanford had been whitewashed.

"He is a dark horse," Benson decided. "He may be fairly innocent, or he may be playing some deep game. We'll just keep an eye on him. There is a reward of one hundred thousand pounds for whomever frees Bonaparte, you recall, and it may be that he is trying to stop anyone else from doing it in order to claim the reward himself."

"But he's rich as Croesus," Marie pointed out. "He wouldn't take such risks for money."

"He admires Napoleon. He may be doing it to secure the reward money for Napoleon. And one hundred thousand pounds is a considerable prize. Even to Sanford it would be something. What a lot of art-works he could buy for that sum," Benson said.

"What a lot of mortgages he could snap up," Marie added

with a speaking look at Benson, who smiled warmly to show her he understood.

"Oh, by the way," David said suddenly, "I expect something ought to be done about Sanford's groom."

"How did you know about his being French?" Marie asked, for during their multi-faceted discussion this point had been neglected entirely.

"French? Is he, by God! I never knew that," David exclaimed. "He spoke English as well as anyone when he showed me the Arab stallion's points."

"What did you mean then?" Marie asked.

"He's been knocked out cold. Was lying on the stable floor when I came in. I roused up John Groom to see to him, but I ought to tell Sanford, maybe."

"I wonder what could have happened to him!" Benson asked innocently. Marie looked at him with an approving smile. He had checked not only Sanford's room, but upon finding it empty of the message, had also gone to the stable and frisked the groom. How clever he was! He thought of everything. But neither was Sanford completely stupid, she acknowledged grudgingly. He had hidden the message somewhere well enough that it went undiscovered.

David went to the door and told the butler to notify Sanford his groom was unconscious, then walked back into the saloon. "So, what did you do with your night, Benson, if you wasn't at the Point and wasn't at Madame's?"

"I was searching *Seadog* for the gold. You half convinced me, David, that Sanford was our man, and I thought he might have the money there, but found nothing."

"Yes, but your mount wouldn't have been gone from the stable if you were only there," Marie said.

"What a clever pair you Boltwoods are!" he laughed fondly. "You don't miss a trick. The fact of the matter is, I have heard some few rumors about Sanford's servants. That groom of his is not the only Frenchman in his retinue. His valet likewise is French, and the pair of them spend a good deal of time in Plymouth, scraping acquaintance with the roughnecks that inhabit the wharf—the French element, I refer to. However, I could discover nothing against them."

David nodded. "So we still haven't got a lead on the gold. Have to keep after that."

"We'll never find it," Benson said. "I think we waste our time and energy searching for it."

This defeatist attitude disappointed both the Boltwoods.

David even thought the master was not confiding in him to the extent the equal partnership called for. He was beginning to take the notion the pupil had outpaced the teacher, and he must get cracking and find the gold himself. He was pretty certain he knew where to look for it, too. If the officer in command at the naval station had such high suspicions of Madame Monet that he was trying to court her into confidence, it was pretty clear she was sitting on the gold. He would have to stifle all his repugnance for the woman, and try his hand at making up to her himself. He was more than willing to take on this task for the good of the country.

13

It was late that night before the household settled down. There was the unconscious groom to be attended to. He had suffered such a cruel blow that Miss Biddy's help was required to rouse him. He had a purple welt on his temple, which she half hoped would grow into a concussion. His ramblings, all in French, led her to believe he was delirious, but Sanford informed her through clenched jaws that he was making perfectly good sense to him.

"What happened to him?" she asked, her hand shaking with the excitement of being roused from sleep to tend a patient.

"He ran into a beam in the stable in the dark," he told her.

"A very nasty blow," she tch'd tch'd, but it proved not to be too nasty for her curative powers.

"Extremely hard hit," Sanford agreed, with just a flicker of a glance to Marie, who was still down and in attendance. Benson and David had retired to the latter's room to discuss plans.

It did seem a harder blow than was necessary to knock the poor man out for three seconds to search him. But then the proper force must be hard to determine. Marie harbored no thought that there had been intent to do real harm. She began to see that there was a good deal of violence in Mr. Benson's job—almost more than a sensitive man like himself would like handling. She wondered for the first time why he did it. For altruistic purposes of course, but still to so discommode himself that he lost even his own patrimony bordered on the foolishly altruistic.

"That beam just at the corner of the first stall hangs too low," Biddy ran on, unaware of any undertones in the talk. "I've mentioned having it raised before. I'll speak to Henry about it again. How awful that a servant of one of our guests should be so severely wounded."

And here was another thing to give a little pause. Mr. Benson, who disliked to inconvenience Lord Sanford to the extent of mentioning the mortgage, had hit his servant a blow strong enough to leave him unconscious for half an hour, without even mentioning going to the man's help. He had sat with herself chatting while a man he had knocked out stone cold lay untended. He might have seen the man was attended to in some secret way, by his own groom, for instance, who was surely not in the dark regarding his master's work. Lord Sanford, on the other hand, who treated the family with something approaching contempt, showed a real concern for his servant. He spoke to the man in French, but any well-reared young lady spoke enough of the language to follow the gist of it. He asked the man, Belhomme was his name, how he felt, and told him to stay in bed the next day. He showed very proper feelings throughout, and when Biddy was wrapped up in her chore, she ventured a little apology on behalf of Mr. Benson. It was of course no secret to either of them who had done this.

"I'm sure he didn't mean to hit him so hard," she said in a low tone.

"You have no idea what he's like. Be very careful of him, Miss Boltwood," he answered, also in a low tone, but with strong feeling.

It was impossible to say more. Biddy called her to help with the plaster, and when it was done, Sanford thanked them both and went with the servant to see him got into bed. "I hope the poor man doesn't suffer a concussion," Biddy said as she packed up her stores. "What a hard knock he suffered. I never saw such a welt."

It was with a heavy heart that Marie went up to her bed. The hour was well advanced, and as she had had a trying night, she was fagged enough to sleep without interruption. She was dreaming of being on an island not bigger than six feet square, with dozens of yachts all around it trying to lure her off into perilous waters when a dark form slipped silently past her door, down the stairs, out the front door and around to the garrison, where he carefully lit a lamp and went down the two flights of stairs into the empty room that housed the winch and chain. He checked the mechanism silently, wondering how best to sabotage it without leaving any traces, then he turned to the heavy chest, pulled out the unused spare chain and began extricating leather bags full of sovereigns that were concealed beneath it. They were no longer safe in this spot, but he knew where they would be pretty safe, and he took them there before returning silently to the sleeping house and to bed.

There was a strained atmosphere over the breakfast table when Sanford announced blandly that he meant to sail his yacht to Sinclair's dock that morning.

"It will be no use to anyone there," Sir Henry told him, scowling from under his beetle brows. All pleas to Sinclair to prohibit the move had been in vain..

Sanford did no more than look. The reason was too well known to require restating. "Would you like to come with me to try her out, David?"

David said he thought not, thank you, in his coldest voice.

"You, Miss Boltwood?" he continued his invitation to Marie.

She had not anticipated the invitation, and thus had not sought instructions from Mr. Benson. "How long will you be gone?" Biddy asked. "We were to make up the menu for the ball this morning you remember, Marie."

"It will take a while," Sanford answered. "Mr. Sinclair has offered to show me over his place. I won't be back for lunch."

"You'd better not go then," Biddy said to her niece, not without regret. But then there could be no courting done aboard a windy, lurching schooner she thought.

Marie felt definitely piqued to be done out of the trip. She liked sailing, would have liked very much to try out Sanford's yacht, but there was more disappointment than that in her feelings. She felt a strong inclination to prove a point; to make Lord Sanford see that she, Marie Boltwood, could be as attractive and entertaining as an aging French hussy, and as she was a good sailor, she had never found the sea impossible of romance.

"*I* am not busy this morning, Sanford," Sir Henry spoke up, to everyone's surprise. "I'll run along with you. I would like to see *Seadog* in action." Despite their bouts of altercation, the host and Bathurst's godson continued on intermittent terms of amiability.

"Excellent," Sanford said. He made no offer to Benson to accompany them. However, as Benson fared so ill on a ship it was not necessarily an intentional slight.

While Biddy and Marie worked over the menu, deciding between lobster patties and oysters on the half shell, and finally going whole hog and having both, along with a wax basket of prawns, Benson said he would finish up his scientific drawing of the winch mechanism.

"I'll toddle along with you," David offered.

"Maybe you should go up to the telescope with your book of signals," Benson suggested. David had had more than enough of sitting up on the hill like a demmed sheep, while more exciting things occurred elsewhere, and said no, he'd given the guard the book, and he'd go along with Benson, as there were certain matters he wished to discuss.

Benson was not happy for his company, but could hardly forbid him access to his own home, and the two went off together. The drawing proved to be next to finished; Benson did no more than check it against the winch itself before putting it away. He then looked around the room, empty but for the heavy chest storing the spare chain. "Maybe we should just check out the spare," David said, noticing that Mr. Benson regarded the chest from time to time.

"That cannot be necessary. Sir Henry said it is in good repair."

"Sanford may have been working on it," David mentioned, to show he was as wide awake as anyone, and he lifted the lid.

Mr. Benson looked at the chain, his eyes widening in surprise. He dashed to the chest and lifted the end of the chain up.

"Looks all right," David said. "Shall we haul her out and see he hasn't lopped six feet off it, to make it useless?"

"An excellent idea," Benson agreed, and they both began pulling it out.

"The way you tell is to feed it around the edge of the room," David told him. "The chain ought to go around twice exactly. That's how we measure it."

They did this, and soon determined that the chain was of the proper length and in good repair. David was hard put to account for Benson's condition. The chain was safe and sound, but still he was upset about something. It was easily evident by his jerky movements, his lack of attention, by the angry tinge of his face. "What do you think we should do now?" David asked, perplexed. He knew full well his mentor was keeping something from him.

"It's time we got busy looking for that message Sanford received last night," Benson said, his face rigid with anger.

"Left it a bit late," David pointed out. "If you couldn't find it last night, I don't suppose you're likely to do it today. Had hours to get rid of it. Might have taken it to Sinclair's with him for that matter. Probably did."

"That's a possibility," Benson said, looking interested. "Still, we'll have a good look about here while he's gone."

The first look was in Lord Sanford's own room, while his valet was belowstairs polishing his master's boots. The door was locked, which filled them with hope, but when he got the housekeeper's key and went in, he found nothing of the message. He was diverted by many other splendors—silver-backed brushes and crested notepaper were examined for clues, but without success. The valet's room was similarly searched, after which Benson, whose intelligence was cast into serious doubt, insisted on rummaging through the entire house. From attics to cellars they searched. That's how they spent their morning. David was wishing he'd gone out on the *Seadog*, instead. A fool could see he had the message with him, anyway. She looked a proper fancy craft, and one he was eager to get his hands on quite apart from hidden messages. A good sailing breeze in the air today, too. He plodded obediently on with the task, however, through trunks and chests, all of which had recently been searched for gold, with a similar result. Nothing but moths and dust.

By the time lunch was over, he had had more than enough of routing uselessly through old lumber, and hit on the capital notion of driving the carriage over to Sinclair's to pick up his father and Sanford, to save Sinclair the bother of driving them home. Mr. Benson made not an effort to detain him, but had his own curricle called out the minute he left and nipped into Plymouth.

"I wonder where he is going," Marie said to her aunt, just a little offended that Mr. Benson had not told her, nor invited her to accompany him.

"To find another family to stay with I hope," Biddy said firmly. "I cannot think why Henry lets him stay on, now that he knows the fellow is only out for your fortune. He as well as agreed to be rid of him three days ago, but something changed his mind."

The something, so unexplainable to Biddy, was crystal clear to the younger lady. The Admiralty had asked her father to let him stay, and of course he would do as they asked. "If he's going to Plymouth, he might have mentioned it to us. I need some supplies. My basilicum is running low, though the pharmacist puts too much pine resin in his. I prefer to make my own, but with all the rash of wounds here of late I need a quick supply. And I wanted to order extra cream and eggs too for the ball. It's a nice day, Marie. Shall we go in? David has taken the closed carriage, but the gig is free. I wouldn't mind the open carriage on a fine day like this."

A trip to Plymouth was seldom spurned by Marie at any time, and with the expectation that Mr. Benson would be on the quay hanging out for information, she agreed immediately. To get to Plymouth, it was not necessary but possible to pass the cottage hired for Madame Monet, if one were willing to take a little jog north, only a mile out of the way. It had become the preferred route of all the Boltwoods of late. What was seen on this trip made all the former futile looklugs well worth while. Madame was there at the doorway admitting a caller, and the caller was none other than Mr. Benson.

"There's a good pair then," Biddy said, looking as hard as she could in past the privet hedge.

The quay was as busy as ever, the commoners and hedgebirds in as great abundance. There was the usual number of scarlet and blue tunics. Even the tunics were more observant of a young lady accompanied by only the requisite chaperone than of one guarded by a clutch of males, but all this, which would have pleased Marie a week ago, was hardly noticed. A very handsome officer tried for two minutes to catch her eye, without being even noticed. She did no more than look once out to Billy Ruffian, and as soon as Biddy began berating the jostling her arms received, the niece turned to go. What was Mr. Benson doing at Madame Monet's? It must of course be in the line of unpleasant duty that he went, but Rawlins was already pursuing that particular lead, and naturally Rawlins would pass on to the government agent what he discovered. The trip was not so pleasant an outing as Marie had hoped for. When she returned to Bolt Hall, there was nothing to do. The men were still not back from Sinclair's. It was an interminable, dull, stupid day.

They did not return, in fact, till nearly dinner time. David entered smiling to tell her, "Sanford took us out for a spin on his *Seadog*. By God, she's a lovely craft, Marie. You should have been there. Could outdistance the *Fury* easily. We must convince him to bring her back here. What a boon she'd be to our fleet."

"Benson went to see Madame Monet," she told him.

"Did he, by Jove? So that's where he was off to, and not breathing a word of it to me. He's too close by half. Sanford has got the cleverest setup on his yacht. Luxurious as any saloon I've ever been in. Even a fireplace in it, sort of a blue-looking marble or something. Imagine! She sleeps a dozen."

"I don't see why he should have gone there. Rawlins is already making up to her to find out what she knows."

"No harm for Ev to get to know her as well. I think it was lapis something or other, the fireplace. Very valuable. Sanford was saying he means to sail her to Wight after Boney is sent away, and asked me to go along with him. Now that was downright civil of him, considering that I've hardly said more than good day to him since he got here."

"It seems to me everyone is making a great deal too much of Madame Monet. I can't think *she* has anything to do with the affair at all. She's only here to find a husband."

"Best not to take any chances. He let me crew on the main sail, and says I have a good knack for it. I've never handled such a big ship before. Jove, but I wish Papa would set up a rig like that."

There was clearly no consolation to be gained from David, and in a snit Marie said, "You are getting on mighty close terms with Cicero!"

"Eh? Oh, you're talking about the brass buttons. All a hum. It was a uniform I saw, and not a lounging jacket. That's what he calls it, a lounging jacket. He is giving me a pattern for it. All the crack, but I think I'll have mine made up in dark green. Sanford is sorry he didn't get green. Sanford didn't get here till after three the night he arrived, and it was at one I heard the men talking below my window, so it must have been an officer, all right. Sanford is only here to try to stop anyone from freeing Boney, same as we are doing ourselves. Said so. He's really not so toplofty once you get to know him a little. *I* think we ought to join forces with him. The more heads we can get together, the better. Only he don't like Benson much, and didn't think it such a hot idea for us to include him. Clever of him to get to work on Monet. He beat us all out in figuring how to get around her. Took Rawlins a week to tumble to it. Sanford saw right off the bat the likes of her was to be cozened by a spot of romance. He says she . . . Oh, but I wasn't supposed to mention that."

"What?" she demanded sharply.

"Nothing to the point. It's only about her lovemaking. We're inviting her to the ball. Sanford thinks it's a good idea. I may have a go at her myself."

"We are not inviting that hussy to Bolt Hall!" she shouted, so incensed that she was sidetracked from discovering Madame's secrets in the arts of dalliance.

"Sanford's already done it, and she's accepted, too."

"Without asking me and Biddy if he might!"

"He told Papa."

"*Told* him!"

"Asked him, I mean."

The ball, so looked forward to as a social triumph by Marie, withered to dust before her eyes. "I suppose she will open the ball, too!" she demanded.

"No, how should she? She has no social standing here. It will be Sanford who opens it, be stuck to stand up with you, very likely. Only fitting. Well, I must wash up for dinner. Gad, but I'm starved. There is nothing like a good sail to whet the appetite. Sanford says before he leaves we'll go out for a whole day, and he's got a chef aboard, and a whole galley that can serve a hot meal, and even a bit of a wine cellar, with champagne."

Marie's spirits sank to see how David's reason had been perverted by a schooner larger than *Fury*, and a wine cellar. But it was not only Sanford's yacht that had won him. Benson was not confiding in him as he ought. To be sitting up at the Point reading the signal flags, that often didn't change once in three or four hours, was no fitting work for a spy. Benson had bungled the retrieving of the message the night before, while Sanford, wide awake, had got it and turned it over to the proper authorities. Not an inch of headway had Benson made in finding the all-important gold. David was toying with the idea of telling Sanford about the gold, and seeing what he suggested. Of course, he must let Benson know what they found out, but really Benson was not at all as wide-awake as a spy ought to be.

He asked Benson, when he returned just before dinner, "Anything turn up today?"

Benson said vaguely that he had heard some rumors at the quay about some aborted attempt to save Boney, but in the end it had been only the local moonling, with his lobster boat and a rope three yards long, and it was just a joke. Not a word about his having visited Madame Monet! No confidences shared. Benson had wasted his afternoon discussing Jed Sykes, the town's moonling, who had been bragging from Day One that he meant to rescue Boney, as he was his half brother. He was so disgusted he didn't tell Benson about Sanford turning the message over to the authorities, though he *did* wonder when he had done it, as he hadn't left Bolt Hall except to go to Sinclair's place. Must have mailed it off to London, he supposed.

14

Immediately dinner was over David began looking from Benson to Sanford, wondering which to approach with regard to looking for gold. "I have to run over and see Mr. Hazy," Sanford said. "I am anxious to hear what he thinks of public reaction to Capell Lofft's letter. The *Chronicle* announces it has had more than a hundred letters supporting it."

"That's not many out of the whole population," Sir Henry pointed out. "I had three hundred petition signers for his execution."

"True, but then Capell Lofft did not petition—his supporters are voluntary," Sanford parried.

Almost any other visit mentioned would have elicited an offer from David to accompany him, but the Hazy residence was off limits to him. Papa had let Marie go, but a girl on the catch for a title could not be expected to let mere principles stand in her way. He turned his attention to Benson instead. Ev was wearing a nice cagey expression on his face. Obviously he had some interesting plans.

"What are you doing, Ev?" he asked.

"I, too, must go out. I am meeting with Rawlins tonight."

"I'll run along with you," David offered at once.

"I'm afraid not tonight, David. He will be more communicative if I go alone. He is a little military in that respect—will only tell me if I am alone. I must find out if he had any luck in questioning Madame Monet, and inform him of that business about the message Sanford intercepted."

David eyed him askance. To have waited nearly twenty-four hours to tell Rawlins about the message, and to have done so little to find it, was already evidence of mediocrity. To omit mentioning that he had been to Madame Monet himself showed a lack of confidence. Benson was playing a close hand, and with his eyes narrowing suspiciously, David replied, "Very well, I'll keep an eye on things here while you're gone."

"I would appreciate that."

Benson was gone, and David Boltwood, spy-in-training, foresaw an evening doing nothing more exciting than listening to Biddy and Marie natter on about prawns in wax baskets and flowers and punch. It was infamous. He sat nibbling his thumb, turning over in his mind paying a call on Madame Monet. All the competition was safely accounted for. Sanford with Hazy, Benson and Rawlins together at the naval station. He wasn't likely to find such an opportunity again. He went upstairs to make a fresh toilette, lavishly sprinkling himself with Steek's lavender water, brushing his brown hair down over his forehead and before going out the door, giving his boots a final polish with the edge of a bed cover. He walked down the stairs to say good night to the ladies, but found Marie alone, moping in front of the cold grate.

"Where's Biddy?" he asked.

"Gone to bed. She didn't sleep well last night because of having to tend to Sanford's groom. Where are you going, David? Ugh—what is that *awful* smell?"

"Awful? It's my new scent. All the chaps are using it. I'm going out."

"Yes, I can smell that, but where are you going *to?*"

He was reluctant to confess his destination, but she had soon weaseled it out of him. "You're going to make up to her!" she charged at once, knowing her brother as only a sister can.

"No such a thing. Just want to see if I can find out where the gold is hidden."

"She won't be apt to tell you."

"She might let it slip out. No saying."

137

"Don't think the hussy will be alone. She'll have some man in her saloon."

"I'll peek in the windows first, and if she has, I'll just cock my ear to the window and spy."

Marie had spent an utterly boring day. No company but Biddy, and now even that companion was gone from her. To have to sit for hours waiting for the return of the gentlemen was too dreary to contemplate. "Let me go with you," she said. "Certainly Madame will not be alone. You won't be going in, and I can listen at the window as well as you."

"How can you go? Father will be looking for you. With Biddy gone to bed, he'll want someone to tell about his parish business."

"He never tells *me*. Did you hear the name of the latest mother, by the way?"

"Effie Muldoon, down at the inn."

"I thought so. But Father has gone out somewhere and probably won't be back till all hours. Let me go with you, Dave," she implored. His heart, as soft as a sponge, was persuaded. The nature of the call would necessarily change from romance to spying, but he was about equally keen on both. Marie was a good spy, too. It was she who had followed Sanford to the telescope and discovered about the message. Benson likely wouldn't have told him a thing if Marie hadn't been there. He was so secretive and evasive David half thought it might have been Benson himself at the Point.

"Oh, very well then, but mind you wear a dark outfit. We'll go on horseback—quieter, and faster to get away. I can't take my curricle if I ain't going to the door like a gentleman."

Within ten minutes they were headed down the road towards Madame's cottage. They tethered their horses across the road in an orchard and proceeded on silent feet to the window, familiar to David now from his work the preceding evening. The curtains were drawn this evening, however, and drawn so closely that no view at all was possible. It began to seem their evening was a total loss, or Marie's in any case, as David rather thought the thing to do was to make a social call. "Come around to the back," Marie suggested before he could voice his change of plans.

The house was small, only a cottage, and the main saloon took up the whole side of the house, with a window giving on to the rear as well as the west side. The curtain at the back was not drawn, but neither was the window placed low enough to allow easy viewing. David, taller than his sister by six inches, could get a peek only and the sister could see nothing. "There's somebody there with her, all right," David announced. "I can see a black head. Can't be Rawlins. He's grizzled."

"Rawlins is meeting with Benson. It might be Sanford, *letting on* he's gone to Hazy, but really come here."

"Could be," David agreed, stretching his legs and neck to try to confirm it. It was no good. He could see no more than the very tip of the black head. They began looking around the yard for something to stand on. The only likely object was a wheelbarrow. Not stable, and hardly large enough for two, but stability was achieved by turning it upside down with the wheel facing the sky, and height by their standing one behind the other, Marie right against the window, David peering over her shoulder. They distinguished the caller's identity at the same moment.

"Benson!" they said in unison, marveling a moment over his duplicity in coming here. They were soon marveling over greater marvels. He was not behaving at all like a spy trying to inveigle information out of a pretty foreigner. He was jawing at her, even shaking his finger under her nose, much as Papa did when he was in a pelter.

"Gudgeon!" David muttered. "That ain't the way to get it out of her. He ought to be making up to her."

Marie thought it as good a way as any other. Benson was too fastidious to pretend to *like* her; he was threatening, instead. Madame was not cowed by his bullying, however. She was soon shouting back at him, gesticulating in the French manner, throwing her hands about, hunching her shoulders. Benson, in his turn, replied, the anger seeming to lessen. Oh, if only they could hear! She seemed to have Benson on the run—his expression was apologetic, his hands and shoulders going up in a way that said as clear as words that he was at a loss—he didn't know—couldn't explain something or other. She was firing questions at him, receiving short answers. The Boltwoods were so entranced they weren't aware of another person approaching till the horse was a yard from the corner of the building. Had barely time to crouch down from the light of the window into the concealing shade of the wall. They stared after the back of the newcomer, not recognizing him, but both realizing it was not Sanford. The nag was not spirited enough, the man's shoulders sloping a little forward—an older man. For a whole minute David thought it was his father, and felt betrayed. The horse proceeded to the stable, and David was hit with inspiration. "We'll nip around to the front door and watch him go in. Might learn something."

This was done, and though they were unable to *see* the man, they would learn his identity as soon as they got back to the wheelbarrow at the window. Their trip around was worth their while. "Come in—he's already here," Madame said in an excited voice. "The worst news, George." Not Papa, thank God! Then the door was heard to close, and it was back to the wheelbarrow, to discover the newcomer was none other than Rear Admiral Rawlins. Again there was something like an argument enacted silently before their fascinated eyes. They said nothing, knowing they would have ample time to talk it all over later. Now was the time to look and wish they could listen. Rawlins flung angry statements at Benson, who returned with angry gestures and expressions of his own. Madame was the peacemaker, pacifying both, later going for drinks. Then the three sat on the sofa with their heads together for a long time, talking more peaceably. At length, after the Boltwoods' eyes were stinging from strain and their necks, arms and legs stiff from craning, the party broke up. Rawlins went out the door first, Benson a step behind him, after first placing a kiss on Madame's cheek. They exchanged a meaningful, familiar smile. It was dangerous to risk being at the window when the men went for their mounts, so they slipped away into the nearby field, holding back the million conjectures and questions that were eager to come out.

The two male callers parted at the roadside with no more than a wave, to go their separate ways. Benson would get back to the Hall before them and be wondering where they were, but this detail was only mentioned. Of much graver importance was to figure out what they had seen.

"What can it mean?" Marie asked.

"Benson didn't actually say he was going to the naval station. Maybe it was fixed for him to meet Rawlins at Monet's place. Well, it was—'He's already here,' she said."

"How could Rawlins tell him anything, or vice versa, in front of *her,* when he wouldn't discuss it before *you?* No, they were not discussing the message last night at all. It was something else."

"Unless Madame's working with them," David thought

140

aloud. "She says often enough she hates Bonaparte. Maybe she does."

"The navy would never trust a Frenchwoman in such a critical case," Marie thought. "And Benson *kissed* her."

"Pooh, a peck on the cheek. She's French—she'd expect it," he said, and stored this French custom up for future use.

"It seems to me there is something very irregular going on here, David. Benson shouldn't have been making such a fuss in front of Madame, jawing at her as if he were her father, such a familiar way he had with her."

"Rawlins welcomed as 'George.' What could the 'worst news' be? Must be the message Sanford got away with, don't you think?"

"I suppose it must be. but I'm surprised Benson should tell Madame. And I'm sure it was Benson at the Point last night too, though he denied it."

"I fancy it was. He don't trust us, Marie. There's the sum and total of it. They were both giving him the deuce for losing the message. We're left out of it because we're only amateurs. It's pretty clear to me Madame is his assistant, in the thing with Rawlins all the way. A professional spy. Nothing else makes any sense. Benson was too familiar by half with her for it to mean anything else. All his letting on to hate her is just part of his cover. And the reason he's sore at Sanford setting her up in the love nest is because he doesn't want another amateur horning in on the case."

"Or on his girl friend. He kissed her. Rawlins didn't, so don't bother letting on it is the custom." She found herself wondering if Sanford, too, kissed Madame.

"Well, you can be sure ther's nothing fishy in it when Rear Admiral Rawlins was right there. It's official business, right enough, and Benson don't see fit to tell *me* what's going on, after the *hours* I've sat up at the curst telescope. I'm sorry I ever thought of it. He's just trying to be rid of me so he can get on with his own business. But I'll tell you this: he ain't half as wide awake as Sanford. Who was it got the message last night? Sanford. Who was it knew in a flash Madame was right at the heart of it? Sanford. I begin to wonder if it ain't a poor idea having the chain sitting at home waiting for somebody to raise it at just the crucial minute, too. Sanford is up to anything. I mean to take him into my confidence. Only thing to do."

All Sanford's evil activities and views were beginning to be seen in a different light since Benson would not accept any

141

help from amateurs. The brass buttons were innocent of being anything but stylish; the association with Madame an act of deep cunning; the views on the chain a wise precaution (though not one to be heeded). There remained only his friendship with Hazy and his lenient views on Napoleon to be dealt with, and these were by no means impossible of overcoming. He wasn't vengeful, that was all. Bathurst himself used the word vengeful with regard to Papa's petition, and while David had happily put his signature to that petition in good faith, he would as readily at that moment have signed one requesting Napoleon's internment on the Isle of Wight. He was not so old as to be quite immovably set in his views.

"Next you will be saying it was well done of Sanford to have stolen Oakhurst."

"It ain't *stealing* to foreclose a mortgage that's come due. How do you think we come to own Hecker's little farm? Papa foreclosed the mortgage three years ago. It's just sharp business. Imagine Benson being such a clunch as to not pay up his mortgage. He could have raised the wind, too. The fellow ain't as bright as he should be, no denying."

"He's bright enough to ask where we have been when we get home," Marie reminded him. "I'll go up the back stairs and you can pretend you've been into town. Since *he* hasn't been he won't know the difference."

"Ah—that explains it!" David said. "The first night Ben was here he went out and let on he'd gone to Plymouth, to the inn, but I was there myself and there wasn't a sign of him. He was making his contact with Madame, way back then. He *was* at the inn, but up in Madame's room. That's why I didn't see him."

Marie went immediately to her room, letting David stable her mare. Shortly afterwards David came tapping at her door. "Funny thing, Benson ain't back. Horse ain't in the stable, and he ain't about downstairs. Now where the deuce could he be? He headed this way, right enough."

"Gone to the Point to get another message, maybe?"

"Very likely. I suppose I'd better go along and give him a hand. I won't bother though," he thought. "He won't let me see it, and I can't very well cosh him and take it, like Sanford did. Come to think of it, Marie, it can't have been Benson at the Point last night. Sanford would never have hit *him*."

"I think he's been wanting to hit Benson for ages. Maybe he doesn't know about his being a government agent. How should he know?"

"I dropped him the hint, but I hadn't done so then, come to think of it, so that explains it. Unless—good God!" David's eyes widened and his ruddy cheeks paled.

"What is it?" Marie asked in alarm.

"Nothing. Nothing at all."

"Don't *you* turn into a mute on me, too. What are you thinking?"

"It's impossible," David answered, and turned away to walk down the hall in a trance, to consider alone in his room with his now habitual quarter glass of brandy and three-quarters of water (his preferred ratio) the impossible idea that had occurred to him. Was it conceivable that it was Lord Sanford and not Mr. Benson that had been sent down from London as a special agent? The thought shook him to the marrow of his bones. Sanford's arrogance in pointing out all the dangers inherent in his father's preparations—that would account for it. But then, who was Benson? They weren't *both* government agents. Hated the sight of each other. Both had arrived the same time, give or take a few hours—arrived at a time that made it possible either one might be the government spy. So if Sanford was the real spy, who the deuce was Benson, and what was he up to? Might he not be a dangerous force working to free Boney, and himself and Marie giving him every aid? And here was he, muddling his brains with brandy *urged on him by Benson!* The man was out to corrupt him. With a sneer and a great heave of relief, he pushed the glass aside. He'd need all his wits to untangle this skein. What to do?

He was out the door and up to the telescope so fast his ears hummed with the wind whistling past them, to be confronted with utter desolation. Not a soul, not a horse, nor even much of a view of Billy Ruffian, though there were a few dim lights out on the water that must be it, well enough. He glanced at the sky, where the waning moon was nearing its vanishing point. He felt a tingle in his breast. The time could not be far off now. The thing to do was to get back home and put it to Sanford direct. Or Papa. But Sanford was still not back, and his father, just returned, stared at him as though he had run mad.

"That Whig, an agent from London? You're mad. Where did you get such a notion?"

"Why is he here then?"

"He's Bathurst's godson, and Biddy has taken the idea Marie might get him. His asking them to Wight looks like it.

143

A very eligible *parti* in every way, barring his politics. You mustn't fall under his influence, Son, to be setting up any plan to cut my chain."

"Oh no!" David assured him at once. No more than his father would he touch a link of its length. The chain of Bolt Hall was inviolable.

He returned to his room, half convinced he ought to resume drinking the brandy, if Benson were the real agent after all. Reviewing the confusing events of the past days, he decided it would take a wizard to figure them out. *One* of the two men was an agent, and the other might be anyone from a suitor for Marie's hand to an out-and-out anarchist.

He began to see his position was an extremely tricky one. He must craftily play the two of them along, being as silent and sly as they both were themselves, and give away none of his suspicions. For the first time in his life, he didn't quite trust even his own father. A command from Bathurst for secrecy might prevent him from opening his budget to his son and heir. It was clearly his bounden duty to get to know Madame Monet better too—there was a vital piece in the puzzle. *Cherchez la femme.* She was soon the only piece being thought of at all. As he crawled into bed and blew out his candle, his future plans centered around Madame exclusively, around getting her alone and making love to her, while she broke down and told him all her terrible confusion and doubt. How she was being used by the enemy, forced to take a hand in this business against her will, and hoping against hope that *someone* would rescue her. Some *younger* man she could trust.

Marie Boltwood's mind was not much more gainfully employed. They finally had two single gentlemen staying at Bolt Hall, neither of whom was at all satisfactory to her. The one who had always had a large edge was slipping back into the same rear position as the other. His lack of a fortune she could forgive, considering what had occasioned its loss, but for him to be making up to Madame was less easily forgivable. No point pretending he was sweet-talking Madame for the cause. That shaking finger under her nose bespoke familiarity. No, he *liked* her, like all the other men—there was jealousy in that look. His duplicity in liking her was worse than the others, for he pretended he hated her, called her vulgar and so on. Sanford had at least come right out and said she was charming from the start.

Then, too, while Sanford was certainly suspected of making love to her, he had not been caught doing it. She hardly bothered her head about their relative positions in the campaign of guarding the General. If David thought Sanford was innocent, then probably he was innocent of anything worse than admiring Napoleon. His judgment she already knew to be impaired, so that didn't surprise her. What did occasion surprise was that she felt so little sensation of loss at Mr. Benson's defection as a lover. Her pride was a little stung, but she sustained only a mild bout of anger, no wrenching heartbreak. Before her eyes closed, she had directed her thoughts to the approaching ball. David thought she must open it with Lord Sanford. She found herself wondering if he were a good dancer, and suspecting that he was.

15

David Boltwood realized as soon as he opened his eyes the next morning that he must leave off brandy. Due to its pernicious influence he had been grossly negligent in going to sleep without waiting to clock in Benson and Sanford. He dashed downstairs to discover what they had been doing, to find neither one of them at the table. A message had reached them earlier in the morning that Lord Sanford had spent the night with Mr. Hazy and would not be back till noon, but of Mr. Benson nothing was said. When still he had not come down at ten o'clock, David went up to his room to see what was keeping him. The man's appearance did much to return him to his former eminence. He had a black eye and a red bruise on his cheek. He had obviously been out fighting with wrongdoers all night long, and if only he had included David in his scrape, there wouldn't have been a thread of rancor felt for any mediocrity in other areas.

"There must have been a dozen of them," David said, smiling with envy at the various marks of valor. "Where did it happen?"

"A little tussle arose in Plymouth," Benson replied, making little of it.

Unless Benson had made a very late return to Plymouth he

was lying, for he had turned his mount towards Bolt Hall when he left Madame's. David remembered his resolution to play a close hand, and pretended to accept this.

"What happened exactly?"

"Nothing of much interest. After I left Rawlins I went down to the Hoo, and fell into an argument with an officer about whether Bonaparte should be sent to Saint Helena. There are some who think Scotland is far enough away. Such nonsense. The fellow was a Whig like Sanford, and our words soon turned to blows. He had a few friends with him," Benson finished up, implying that had it been one to one, the outcome would have been different.

Not even a good liar, David thought. As though officers, who were gentlemen, would gang up on a fellow! He did not indicate by any more than a narrowing of his eyes, an incredulous stare and a skeptical voice that he disbelieved this tale. "Ah, yes, what had Rawlins to say?" he asked.

"He feels the message Sanford got ahold of is about the masquerade, but we are alerted to it, and will keep our eyes open. I do feel, David, that you ought to go up to the telescope and . . ."

"Impossible," David answered firmly. No *Ev's* today. He would keep his distance and work his way into confidence by being as stiff as a rod and as unhelpful as possible. Why, wasn't it Sanford himself who had stood right there and ordered Rawlins to send Maitland the message about the masquerade? Benson took him for a fool.

"Have you other plans?" Benson asked.

"Yes, I must help Father today," he answered, not choosing to reveal to Benson his real activities, which to be sure he didn't know himself yet.

"Rawlins was saying last night that as a number of the officers have been invited to the ball, they might all come aboard one of the smaller navy vessels. A sort of semi-official show of support for your father's excellent work in the cause," Benson said. "The *Phoebe,* he mentioned bringing. I shall speak to Sir Henry about it, but first I must tend to these little wounds."

"I'll send Biddy right up," David promised happily, finding it impossible to treat the bearer of such good news with the scorn he merited. An official navy vessel sitting right at Bolt's Dock, cheek by jowl with *Fury.*

"I'll go down," Benson said, "but I would appreciate a plaster for this grazed cheek."

"Need a patch for that mouse, too," David informed him, looking once more with envy at the black eye.

Biddy was pleased to have a patient; Sir Henry delighted to have official recognition of his volunteer service, and Miss Marie Boltwood not entirely unhappy that Benson had got what was coming to him. The plasters and basilicum were brought out, and before Benson got away there was also an eye patch under construction, made of black felt from an old hat, and held on by an elastic band. Soon there would be an order sent off for proper eye patches. How had she come not to think of it?

The day was going well for all the residents of Bolt Hall, with the exception perhaps of Mr. Benson, till Mrs. Hazy dropped by. She sometimes called on her visits to Plymouth. The woman had not been five minutes in the saloon till she inquired after Lord Sanford.

"What, is he not with you?" Biddy asked, startled. "He went to see your husband yesterday afternoon, and we received a note this morning that he had decided to stay overnight. Odd, he didn't let us know in advance, not that we were worried about a fully grown man, of course."

"We have not seen him for three days," she answered. This told them what some of them had been wondering—whether he was in touch with Hazy on the sly—but did not inform them where he had gone yesterday, nor where he had spent the night.

Marie, who sat with them, had her own views regarding where he had spent the night, but the evening she knew he had not passed in Madame Monet's company, and she too was curious to know what he was up to.

Biddy mentioned that he had his yacht at Sinclair's, and had likely been there. This was of course said only to lend a hue of respectability to their guest's actions. Certainly he had not gone back there. Unaware of Monet's true activities, Biddy supposed he had been dallying with the French hussy. Better he than Henry. She neatly switched the conversation to recipes and gowns, and before too long Mrs. Hazy was off.

It was another few hours before Lord Sanford returned, and when he did, it turned out he had been not at Mr. Hazy's at all. He had changed his mind and gone back to Sinclair's, wading for leeches. He drove round to the stables with a large kettle of brackish water holding a couple of dozen leeches, and asked for Biddy to come to him. She went, full of curiosity, and Marie accompanied her, full of disbelief.

"Your leeches here in Plymouth are so much finer than ours in Devon I have decided to collect up a bunch of them for Mama," he told her. "I wish you will look these over, Biddy, and tell me if I have chosen well."

"Where did you get them?"

"In Sinclair's pond. We made a raft and used liver for bait."

She shook her head in satisfaction that wore the guise of sorrow at his ignorance. "Summer is a poor time for gathering leeches, and using liver or decayed vegetable matter is the wrong way to set about it. It is harmful to the leeches' health—infects them. No, leeches must be gathered in spring in shallow water, before they go out into the deep. That deep brackish water produces a perfectly useless leech."

"The shallow water looked more brackish," Sanford pointed out.

"This time of the year it is! August—*much* too late. Catch them by hand—never use bait. If they are frolicsome and plump in the water, you have a good leech."

"These fellows look mighty plump to me," he said, holding one up by the tail, a huge fellow.

"A *horse* leech, Lord Sanford," she smiled condescendingly. "They will not take blood at all. They feed on worms. Let us see what else you have."

Those of his specimens that were not worm-eating horse leeches were languorous infected fellows from brackish water. She consigned the lot of them to the burial ground, to prevent their causing harm in the stables.

"I have wasted my morning then," Sanford said. "And here I had hoped I had a surprise for Mama."

"Come along to my reservoir, Sanford, and I'll show you my little setup. I'll send a dozen to your mother, and show you how I get them to propagate."

She was never happier than when she had an admirer of her reservoir. Marie had seen it a dozen times, and went indoors, while Sanford was taken out behind the stable to see a large natural pond that had been heavily improved upon by Biddy. "I have had clay sides put in—for the cocoons to be deposited on, you see. And the bottom must be of turf and rushes. The pond had to be pumped out first to do the job properly. Make sure you give yourself a goodish area, for a leech won't survive in a little tank. Mine is eighteen feet square."

148

"How deep would it be?" Sanford asked, observing all this with the keenest interest, real or well simulated.

"Not more than three feet. Deepness is not a necessity. Indeed it is very hard to get them out if you make it too deep. I get them when they are young and raise them here. That is how I started, I mean. Till a leech is mature—five years—he is a poor drawer."

"Tell me, Biddy, about this propagating—ah, how do I know I am getting the proper ratio of the sexes? I hope you won't take the question amiss, but unless I have males and females . . ." He tossed up his hands and hunched his shoulders.

"There is no need to be embarrassed with me, Lord Sanford. It is an excellent point. In medicine, you know, mating is as common as eating or sleeping, but it is no problem in the least. Leeches are hermaphroditic. They look after all that messy business of sex all by themselves—each one by *itself*, I mean. The only thing to watch for is that you don't take out a leech that has its young clinging to its underside. When first they hatch from the cocoons, they do that."

"Now isn't that interesting!" he said, pretending not to notice that she was as red as a beet, despite her injunction to him not to be embarrassed.

She looked to her reservoir to avoid looking at him. The water was by no means clear. No leeches could actually be seen, but she discerned the telltale ripple on the surface, put in her hand and swept up an ugly leech, its convex, segmented back a drab olive green, with six red long stripes, dotted with black. "I'll send some of these with you when you go."

"When *we* go. You have not forgotten you are to come with me to Wight."

"Wight—I wonder how the leeches are there. It would be interesting to gather a few and compare," she said, musing.

"Don't let me detain you, Biddy," he said. "I want to take a good long look at your setup here. I'll have those horse leeches buried as you suggested."

Biddy went off reluctantly while Sanford had his groom get a shovel and bury his useless catch. But when she had been inside no more than fifteen minutes, she found she could spare another while to Lord Sanford to explain the turf and rush bottom—best interwoven loosely and held down by rocks so that it not break free and float to the surface. She heard a muted splash as she rounded the corner of the barn.

"You never threw your horse leeches into my reservoir!" she exclaimed in horror.

"No, certainly not! They have been buried."

"I thought I heard a splash." She looked around for his pail, but it was nowhere in view.

"You did," he said at once. "I wanted to gauge the depth, and threw in a rock. It won't harm your leeches, will it?"

"No, but the depth I told you is about three feet."

"I wasn't sure whether you had said feet or yards," he confessed. "What I would like, if you wouldn't mind too terribly, is to get a little drawing of it from you. With the scale marked, you know, and the best shape. I wonder if a circular reservoir wouldn't be better, Biddy. It would cut out the corners that must be useless for the cocoons."

She was distracted by the hastily posed question from asking Sanford where he had got such a large rock to throw in the reservoir. There was nothing but little stones in this area, and the splash had seemed to be caused by a much larger object. "The corners are the best place. I usually find half the cocoons in the corners," she said. "But you mustn't disturb them!" She went on to reveal other arcane matters in the care and breeding of leeches.

They were still at this unappetizing subject when lunch was called. After lunch, Sanford's interest had waned, and he said he was off to Plymouth, inviting no one to go with him. Benson's condition had to be explained to Sanford, who had a dozen questions to put to him, and a good deal of rallying jokes on the eye. David dropped hints, becoming less discreet as they failed to be recognized for hints, that he would have no objection to a rattle into Plymouth. Sanford failed him. He had a very odd kick in his gallop, that one. To be talking up a leech reservoir with half the nation out to free Bonaparte was equally as bad as Benson's getting seasick.

"They are mowing in the west pasture today, David," Sir Henry told him. "That is *your* pasture. The income of it goes all to you. Will you not want to oversee it? You want to see it is mowed short enough to give you the maximum yield, without taking her too close and pulling up the roots. You mind the mess they made of it last year."

David was thus saddled with the irksome, unglamorous and unnecessary chore of being a farmer, when his whole being craved danger, but the respite would give him a chance to think, to try to sort out events, particularly future events.

Marie, bored from her recent inactivity and the total disinterest shown her by the two gentlemen visitors, had her mare saddled up and went up to Bolt's Point. The guard was there by day, a helter-skelter boy of fourteen years who was more interested in the mutt he had brought along for company than in the telescope, though he did occasionally go and put his eye to it. A good fieldhand could not be wasted with the harvest coming in. She looked for a long time out at Billy Ruffian, and once even saw a dark form that she imagined to be Bonaparte himself. Her mind was half occupied with other matters, wondering where Lord Sanford had gone, and how Benson had really got his black eye. She thought Sanford had been happy to see it.

Weary of looking at the ship, she decided to return home the long way, down the far side of the slope, which would take her through the flock of sheep, around the circle at the bottom to the spinney, thus home via the fruit orchard. It was a very good day, weather-wise. She always enjoyed to see the sheep and lambs frisking on the stony incline, but today they held no pleasure for her. A sheep was really a very stupid looking creature, she thought. The spinney too was void of charm, despite the sighting of some wild daisies that grew near the path, inviting gathering. She went on, hardly noticing a hare that darted in front of her, till she came to the orchard, where the early apples were far enough advanced to entice her. She dismounted to look on the ground for a recent windfall not yet bruised into brownness. Finding none, she progressed into the orchard to have a look at the rennets for Biddy. It was from the rennets her aunt obtained malic acid that formed an ingredient of one of her herbal remedies. The apples were not to reach too ripe a condition before gathering. She pulled one from a low-hanging branch to take home for inspection. She thought it was about right—firm, without being hard.

As she stood looking and testing the fruit with her finger, she heard a low, throaty laugh coming from some little distance in the orchard. It was a feminine laugh, and a few shreds of conversation soon told her the female speaker had a French accent. *"Comme tu es méchant!"* the woman said.

That Madame Monet was *tutoying* her companion told Marie it was a lover, but then providing the person were a male, *naturally* he would be a lover. Benson, she first thought, and looked around the trunk of the rennet tree to confirm it. She saw a garish red, bright red elbow, and assumed Madame was seducing an army officer, till the elbow was flung out to show a dainty white hand, holding a parasol folded down. It was the blonde herself, wearing red like a lady of pleasure. Marie stood stockstill, craning forward to catch a glimpse of her companion. He had a low-pitched, undistinguishable voice. He was speaking French, and his accents sounded loverlike, but then French had a way of sounding either angry or intimate she had often noticed. When the two emerged from behind the trees, there was no doubt as to their mutual status. The man's arm was wrapped around Madame's waist, holding her tightly to his side. They hadn't gone two steps before, after a piece of bantering, Madame was pulled right into his arms and kissed in an expert, thorough fashion. The experienced lover was observed to be Lord Sanford.

A tide of anger swept over Marie, engulfing her. She told herself she was angry that their guest dared bring that French hussy on to Papa's property to make love to her, told herself she was angry he should so hoodwink Biddy as to think he was a suitable husband for herself, that it was Madame's *nationality* that vexed her, and a dozen other lies. That she was jealous as a green cow was not allowed to occur to her at all. It was only the indecency of the behavior and the location that so incensed her. She turned to take a step after her mare, for she had no intention of staying here to have her common decency assaulted by such a disgusting scene. Her mare ambled forward, her harness jingling, but the lovers a few yards away were too well wrapped up in each other to hear a thing. Till the mare whinnied in pleasure to discover the apple in Marie's hand, she remained unseen. The two lovers heard the sound at once, and drew hastily apart to look to the cause of interruption.

Madame's outfit drew Marie's attention. She looked like some clownish cross between an officer of the army and the navy. The scarlet dress had a navy weskit with brass buttons, and on her head she wore a sort of modified shako with ostrich feathers. Madame's face was nearly as red as her gown, but Sanford maintained his usual sangfroid. It was Madame who came forward first, in confusion, extending her hand. "Ah, it is Miss Boltwood," she said.

Marie took up her mount's bridle to avoid touching that infamous set of fingers, and busied herself with checking the buckling of a saddle that required no checking. Biddy's rennet was gulped down by the mare without a thought to malic acid.

152

"Quel verger charmant," Madame ran on, looking with admiration at the apple trees surrounding her, forgetting her English with the strain of pretending nothing unusual was going on.

"I am happy you admire it," Marie said, her nostrils pinched with displeasure.

"Oh, *il n'y a rien* . . . nothing so glorious as an orchard."

Marie said not a word, nor did Sanford. Madame turned back to him, "Don't you think it charming, Adrian?"

"I did," he answered, looking around and seeming to find not a tree to please him, from the expression he wore.

"When I leave, as I am about to do, I think its charm will return to you, *Adrian*," Marie said, fixing him with a glaring eye, and adding an awful emphasis on his Christian name to show him what she thought of his familiarity with the trollop.

"I have some hopes that it will, Marie," he answered pleasantly enough. He offered her his hand to speed her ascent and departure. She disregarded the offer of help, scrabbled up unaided and ungracefully, to give her mount the signal to leave at her fastest gallop. She thought after just a little peek from the corner of her eye, that a clump of earth had flown up and hit Madame's uniform. She hoped so.

Marie had succeeded in falling completely out of love with Benson. With a patch on his eye and a plaster on his cheek, he looked to her not like a daring spy, as he did to David, but like a brawling, unprincipled ne'er-do-well. Still he had only pecked Madame's cheek, whereas Sanford had embraced her passionately, so it was Benson who was favored to take Marie into dinner, and receive any smiles she could muster over the meal. The talk at table was of the navy's kindness in sending the *Phoebe* over to honor their dock the night of the ball. Sir Henry recounted former occasions when not one small vessel but half a dozen ships, once even the flagship, had been docked there. The depth of the water in the harbor was mentioned—enough draught for a man of war, should the need arise. Biddy asked how many officers were coming, along with a list of their names.

"Does Rawlins himself come?" Sanford asked.

"We asked Admiral Lord Keith," Sir Henry said, "but if he is out, as I suppose he will be, Rawlins will have to stay at the station. We sent him a card for the looks of it, but I doubt he will come."

"If Keith gets back, he will come and Rawlins will still

153

have to stay at the station. Either way, Rawlins won't be here, I expect," Sanford said.

"He is not at the station around the clock," Benson told them. Marie and David exchanged a look. How well they knew what he did with his evenings! "Rawlins plans to attend. Says he wouldn't miss it for the world. He would leave Wingert on duty, or one of the older officers. He will allow only a small number of officers to come—ten or a dozen. Certainly Rawlins said he will come. The commanding officer in Keith's absence—you may be sure he will be here to honor the occasion."

Sir Henry nodded his head in satisfaction that whoever was in command, Keith or Rawlins, he would be at Boltwood's ball, to do it honor, and never mind about who was guarding the station for one night. What were a dozen frigates compared with Bolt Hall's fleet? Huge, lumbering ships with no maneuvering ability.

"I just missed seeing Rawlins today myself," Sanford mentioned in an innocent fashion.

Benson looked at him sharply, thus alerting David that there was something of significance being said, though he couldn't for the life of him see what it was. Sanford had already said he'd been in town.

"Yes," Sanford went on," "shortly after I left Sinclair's today, after gathering my leeches, Rawlins dropped over for the specific purpose of seeing my yacht. I was sorry I wasn't there to point out to him its features. But Mrs. Sinclair, who told me of the visit in the village this afternoon, says he took a very thorough look at it, all the same."

"Sinclair accompanied him, I expect?" Benson asked.

"No, he was busy. Rawlins went over it by himself."

"Your deckhands would be on board?" Benson asked.

"I didn't think to inquire," Sanford answered casually. "They may possibly have taken the opportunity to stretch their legs on terra firma. Knowing the boat is safe at a private dock, I do not insist anyone remain aboard twenty-four hours a day. If I were docked at the wharf at Plymouth, say, it would have been guarded. The crowd there would be apt to board and take away a chip of my lapis lazuli fireplace, or help themselves to my wine." He went on to relate a tale of having his ship burgled when docked at Ireland, and David listened, but in the end could make nothing of it.

"If there had been anything of real value aboard, of course, I would remove it and have Sinclair keep it in the house for me, but my jewelry, my money and so on, I carry with me and my valet looks after them."

"Your groom, he is due for a new plaster tonight, Sanford," Biddy reminded him. "Have him come to me before he goes to bed, and I'll see how that wound is coming along."

"He would appreciate it," Sanford said. "Somehow or other my valet has managed to wound himself, too. Such an accident-prone bunch as we are—myself, Benson, John Groom, and now Jean Valet—he is French, my valet, as is my groom, too, actually. He managed to bruise his hand rather badly. I told him he ought to go to you at once, Biddy, but a swelling has set in, and I think your ice pack, or possibly a splint, would be a comfort to him."

"How did it happen?" Biddy asked at once.

"He was helping some fellow stop a runaway jackass, and got bruised in the process."

David, still observing, noticed that Benson turned an angry shade darker at this, but he didn't look at Sanford at all, so there was no telling if Sanford and Benson, too, had been involved with the runaway jackass.

"That'd by Tony Parkins. That ass of his is the most obstinate beast there ever was. Will never go when you want him to, and won't stop once he gets started," David told them.

"I believe Parkins was the name my valet mentioned," Sanford answered. Then he began complimenting Biddy on the meal, and got stuck to hear a recipe for plum cake.

Benson disappeared the minute the meal was over. He didn't even stay to take port, but dashed out at once, to go into Plymouth he said. Some friends of his had arrived during the day, and he was having a purely social evening out with them. David checked to the extent of seeing Benson's nag headed not into Plymouth (nor to Madame Monet's, for that matter), but west towards Sinclair's, Hazy's, or somewhere. Any of them might be his destination, but David had nearly switched all his allegiance to Sanford. He returned to the dining room to take port and said to Sanford, "Benson going into Plymouth, all a hum, you know. He ain't headed that way at all, and wasn't there last night, either. What do you figure he's up to, Sanford?"

"I don't know. MacKenroth is on his way to town. He is the fellow who means to deliver the subpoena to Admiral Keith. Possibly Benson is involved in some scheme to do with that." The whole habeas corpus business was public knowledge now, and often discussed.

"How do you know he's coming?"

"Hazy told me."

"Thought you hadn't gone to see Hazy," David said, forgetting momentarily his intention of playing a close hand. Demmed near impossible to find out anything if you sat with your lips closed, in any case.

"I was talking to him in town today."

"Oh. How will MacKenroth proceed, do you suppose?"

"He'll try to reach either Napoleon or Admiral Keith. It should be an interesting scene tomorrow. I mean to spend the day at sea, aboard *Seadog*. Will you come with me, David?"

"By Jove—*will I*?" David answered. Had he a tail, and such an adoring pair of puppy's eyes ought to have had a tail attached to them, he would surely have wagged it.

"I hope you will," Sanford replied, with a lazy smile. "And I *wish* you will help me crew, as I am short one hand."

"Oh I'd be glad to give you a hand, Lord Sanford."

"My friends call me Adrian. Now that we are friends, I wish you will do the same."

Sir Henry chose this infelicitous moment to inform Lord Sanford of his dealings with the parish board. His real aim was to reach a chummy first-name basis with Bathurst's godson as David had done, but it was not achieved. As he might have known, Sanford said it probably evened out in the end, with other parishes getting stuck with the work of the men of Plymouth.

"Shall we join the ladies?" Sanford asked later, with a light of anticipation in his eyes. The gentlemen, none of them great drinkers, put down their glasses and went into the saloon.

16

Marie sat rehearsing what insults she would offer to Sanford when he entered, but she had no opportunity to deliver any of them. He went straight to Biddy without glancing at herself, and began talking about leeches. "What temperature do you keep the reservoir at?" he asked.

"It is at its natural temperature. I don't alter it, though I have slipped out on occasion when we get an unusually cold night during the breeding season and covered it with a tarpaulin. I don't think it is necessary, but I have done it once or twice."

"What temperature would it be now, for instance? What I am thinking is that Wight has a warmer temperature than Plymouth, and when I take your leeches to Mama, I should perhaps modify the temperature by degrees, till they are used to it. I could add a little chipped ice to cool it, for instance."

"I doubt there would be much difference in temperatures," Biddy said, considering this innovation, and disliking to think of ice.

"Still, I'll run out and check it. Would there be a thermometer around the house?"

There were half a dozen of them right in Biddy's medical kit, and she was soon hopping off to select the best one for Sanford. While she was in the mood, she also requested the valet sent down for a bandage. There was no hope of getting the vacuum hood over such a small area as a hand, and the heat was no cure for a bruise, in any case. Really there wasn't much of anything she could do for the bruised knuckles, only slightly swollen, and in the end she gave the unfortunate man one of her possets and sent him off upstairs.

"It doesn't look so very bad, but it bothered him so he couldn't sleep last night," Sanford told her after the valet left.

"You should have let me know. I would have given him a few drops of laudanum. I don't often prescribe it, but losing a night's sleep is worse than anything, and a few drops wouldn't hurt him."

"I wonder if I might have a little in case he can't sleep tonight," Sanford asked. "I have been disturbing your rest shamelessly, you know, and wouldn't want to pester you after you have retired."

"Take it. I have plenty. Use what you need and give the bottle back tomorrow," Biddy told him. He put the bottle in his pocket, and went out to take the temperature of the reservoir.

When he returned, Biddy asked him, "What was it? I am curious to know. Truth to tell, I never took the temperature." She was coming to see that Sanford was even keener on the subject than she was herself.

"Seventy-two," he told her.

"That high? I would have thought it would be much lower. But August—perhaps it gets that high in August," she said, storing the useless bit of information up.

Sir Henry, who had been signalling Biddy with his eyes for some minutes, succeeded in gaining her attention to inform her of a new infamy. The Watkins girl was suspected of being in an interesting condition. They discussed together the prospect of unbridled digging into the parish coffers nine months hence as a result of the staggering number of hedge-birds courting the local wenches. Sir Henry went to his office to sit amidst his trophies and draft up a petition requesting government aid for the future crop of bastards, as they could hardly be considered a strictly local liability with the whole of England making merry at Plymouth.

"You going out at all tonight, Sanford?" David asked hopefully.

Sanford stretched back comfortably against the sofa and said, "No, I am a bit fagged after gathering leeches and having a particularly active afternoon." He just flickered an eye in Marie's direction as he said this. She glared mutinously, then turned her head away. "I'll just stay in and relax, and go to bed early to prepare for our day at sea tomorrow."

David was disappointed at such dull goings on. He decided he'd take a nip into Madame Monet's and check out who she was entertaining this evening. He didn't bother with his Steek's lavender water or polishing his boots, and was disappointed when he saw her all alone that he was too shabby to go in and make love to her. But he enjoyed watching her sit at a clavichord with the lamplight falling on her profile, where the second chin was nearly obliterated by the shadows and the dirty windows. Later she took out some papers, maps he thought, and studied them carefully. There was clearly nothing in this. A foreigner in the country, likely she was checking out just how far she was from London, or Devon, as Sanford had invited her there for a visit.

Sanford turned to Marie and said, "Your lover becomes every day more cavalier in his treatment of you. Abandoned entirely the last few days. I haven't seen him making up to you since I interrupted him in the rose garden. Is he so easily scared off?"

"Yes, he's not quite so brazen as some gentlemen," she answered sharply.

158

"We don't much care for an audience ourselves, if it is us you refer to by the term 'some gentlemen.' "

"It is somewhat of a misnomer, to be sure."

"Certainly it is. I am only one gentleman, and have no right to the royal plural."

"Very little right to the name 'gentleman,' either, bringing your mistress onto Papa's property to make love to her. Could you not confine your lovemaking to the house you set her up in?"

"I'm very sorry about that," he answered readily. "I had no thought of making love to her when I took her to the orchard. Madame adores nature, the countryside. Merely we wanted to go out and take a little air, but she is so irresistible." He finished up with a deep sigh, words beyond him to describe her attractions.

Marie could scarcely believe her ears. His only excuse was that he found the plump matron irresistible. "Rear Admiral Rawlins and Mr. Benson share your view. They, too, are unable to resist her," she said, the angry, jealous words out before she thought how to account for her knowledge.

"Rawlins?" he asked, interested.

It was odd he should pick out Rawlins. Benson was younger, more attractive. "Has Rawlins been making up to her?" he asked.

"So David tells me," she answered, happy to be able to tell the truth without involving her own part in the affair.

"Has he, by God!" Sanford said, with a look that was hard to interpret. Then his long face broke into a smile that was pure mischief. "Marvelous! I thank you for that piece of news, Marie. I wonder what else you could tell me, if you weren't always in the boughs."

"I expect I could tell you plenty, and no one said you could call me Marie."

"That is your name, is it not? I took for granted when you were kind enough to call me Adrian, without also being asked to, that I was expected to return the familiarity. You shouldn't be leading me on if you wish to be treated with full propriety."

"I'm not leading you on!" she said at once, furious that *his* lack of manners was being turned against *her*. "I don't expect to be treated with any propriety by you, either."

"I'll remember that, and try to fulfil your expectations. Are you quite sure David said Rawlins?"

"Of course I'm sure. And if you really cared for Madame, you should be angry instead of laughing like an hyena."

"Oh, the poor maligned hyena! Why is it only the creature's so-called laugh that is remembered? It cries and barks and growls, but it is always the insane laugh emitted upon discovering a carcass that is mentioned. Let us say I have just stumbled on an interesting carcass. But enough chatter about hyenas. Do you come out with David and myself tomorrow to watch MacKenroth try to deliver the writ to Admiral Keith? It should be an interesting spectacle."

She was strongly inclined to go. She had not yet got onto *Seadog* to see for herself the lapis lazuli fireplace and other refinements. If she stayed home, Biddy would keep her busy with preparations for the ball, only two days away now. On the other hand, she wished to show her displeasure to Sanford, and accepting an invitation was a poor way to go about it.

"You won't want me on board, getting in your way," she said, hoping for some insistence that he would.

"True, if you are the sort of female who flies into vapors and is afraid of every wave that washes over the deck, you would be in the way. We may have some interesting chases to follow."

"I don't take vapors, and have been sailing since I was four years old."

"Why are you afraid of being in our way then? Madame does not come, so you will not be in *my* way on that head, if that is what makes you hesitate."

It had not so much as occurred to her that Madame might be aboard. The very mention of the woman's name threw her into a pelter, and in a rush of bad temper she said, "No, I sha'n't go. Thank you very much. Mr. Benson does not like sailing, and I shall stay home to bear him company."

"You're whistling down the wind if you think you'll have his company. Mr. Benson will be otherwise occupied tomorrow," he said, with a smile that was not far from gloating.

"With Madame?"

"Possibly, but probably not. No, I think not, all things considered. Madame will have problems of her own to deal with."

"I sincerely hope they include a trip to a dressmaker, for since *you* have seen fit to ask her to *our* ball, she will need something other than her scarlet tunic to wear."

160

"I noticed you admiring her ensemble. Quite a get-up, don't you think?"

"Stunning!" she answered, the word laden with irony.

"She is a stunning woman. She can wear anything."

"She looked like a pudgy little general!" Marie was forced to point out, as he appeared not to realize she had been joking.

"She is pleasingly plump, in the style of Rubens' nudes, you know. Or probably *don't* know."

"I don't claim to know as much about blond nudes as you do."

"Nor about art, surely. The masters of the seventeenth century are a bit of a specialty of mine, with Rubens my favorite in painting women. That luminous quality he manages to get on the skin, glowing like a pearl, and dimples in all the most *unexpected* places. Sir Joshua Reynolds, no slouch himself in painting a woman, says Rubens' nudes look as if they had 'fed upon roses.' I often think of that quotation when I am with Madame."

It was too much to be borne in silence. "She looks to me as if she had fed upon a great deal too much of fatted pork!"

"That, too," he allowed, with frowning consideration. "Yes, there is a certain earthy, animalesque quality in Rubens' women. One would not be likely to mistake them for a madonna. They are too sensuous, too erotic for that."

"They are fat and ugly!" she declared, basing her decision more on Madame than the work of Rubens.

"We never did agree on matters of taste, so it is pointless continuing the discussion. So, do you come or not tomorrow? My servants will want to know whether a lady will be aboard, that they may make their arrangements accordingly."

"What difference will that make?" she asked, curious to hear what extravagances awaited her, as she was ready to be talked into going.

"They will prepare the ladies' withdrawing room, and see to your comfort," he answered vaguely. "You might as well come," was his only urging.

"I suppose I might as well," she agreed, putting the utmost indifference she could simulate into her acquiescence.

"You will be perfectly safe with your brother there to protect you. Your invitation to me to behave with impropriety will have to await another occasion."

"It was what I expected from you, not what I invited," she pointed out.

161

"What's the difference? We are treated as we expect to be treated. And I fully expect you are readying your poor little wits to give me a setdown, so I shall escape while I can." He arose and went to the table to peruse a recent newspaper for letters in reply to Capell Lofft's letter. Very unhappy with his lack of manners and lack of making up to her, Marie went upstairs to her room to examine her face in the mirror for luminosity and dimples, without finding very much of either.

17

Biddy, unaware of the galley, the chef and the general high tone of life aboard *Seadog*, was up early to have a lunch packed for the sea-bound. David told her how unnecessary was the hamper-preparing in the kitchen, and she sat nodding, impressed with the manner in which she would make the trip to Wight. It was pretty well decided now that she would go, along with both David and Marie.

"I'll just run out to the reservoir and check that temperature once more before we leave," Sanford said. "Will you come with me, Biddy?"

David clamped his lips in disapproval. If it weren't for the day at sea pending, he would have been in a very bad humor with Sanford. This interest in leeches was highly suspect in a spy.

Biddy never needed any coaxing to go to her reservoir, and arose with a half-eaten bun on her plate to accompany him. David took advantage of their absence to try to discover what Benson had been up to the preceding night.

"Anything new happening?" he asked.

Benson, in a foul mood the last few days said sharply, "No, nothing new." Marie was happy she had not elected to remain behind with him. Really he was become remarkably incivil.

At the reservoir, the temperature was seen to be sixty-seven, not seventy-two. "I'm surprised it would fall five degrees in one night," she said.

"I may have misread it last night. The light was poor. It

was why I wanted to check this morning," Sanford said. Then looking at the murky water he went on, "The leeches seem particularly quiet this morning, do they not? I don't see a single ripple."

Biddy regarded her pond critically, and even as she looked, one leech floated to the top, in much the manner of a dead fish. "Good gracious, I think this one is dead!" she exclaimed, lifting it out.

"It certainly isn't frisky," Sanford agreed. "But it is moving a little—not quite dead."

"I'll be rid of it, all the same. If it is in poor health I don't want to risk its infecting the others."

"If it hasn't already," Sanford said ominously. "Maybe you ought to pull out another and just see."

"It wouldn't have had time to spread. There was no sickness in the reservoir yesterday. Here, you see," she said, sticking her arm in up to the elbow, to fish around for another, but when at last she got ahold of one, it too appeared unduly torpid. "Mercy! What's happened to them!" she asked in rising alarm. She held it to her arm, and it didn't even bother grabbing on. She fished again, and again came up with a sluggard that barely wiggled between her fingers. "I can't think what is the matter. I must get my book and see if it mentions this. Dr. Heywood's excellent treatise on diseases in the English leech."

"How I wish I could stay here with you," Sanford said, "but the children are looking forward to this little expedition we've been talking up."

"Don't think of it, Sanford. I'll look after my leeches. I'll get my book this minute."

"You will want to keep a close eye on them. We don't want you losing the whole tankful of them. Take good care of them, Biddy. I'll curtail our sail and get back early to see how they go on."

"No, no—you will want to stay and see the excitement of MacKenroth trying to deliver the summons. I'll carry on here. You may be sure I'll save them. Whatever ails them, it has not had time to kill many of them." She was half pleased to have come up with a unique case, for while she spoke of reading her book, she had in fact got the thing nearly by heart, and knew she would find no explanation for such torpor in the warm summer season. In winter, of course, a leech was inactive, but here confronting her was sluggishness on a scale that suggested a whole new chapter to Dr. Heywood's treatise. Boltwood's Disease, it might be called, named after the discoverer in the usual way. Of primary importance was to have a cure included in the chapter, and she set her mind to restoratives.

With a dozen regrets, Sanford was off, urging her again and again to take care of them, keep a sharp eye on them, and save them if at all possible. Once he left the reservoir, the matter seemed to fall from his mind like magic. *Seadog* had been sailed down from Sinclair's dock for the trip and was waiting for them, its sails fluttering in a way that promised a good day. While they got under sail, David showed Marie around the glories of *Seadog*—an actual dining room with furniture in the delicate style of Louis XIV, the saloon with lapis lazuli fireplace, and over a velvet sofa a framed, scantily draped female nude with glowing skin, looking strikingly like Madame Monet. There were sleeping quarters for a dozen, two of the beds canopied. All the promised treats were there for inspection and praise, and as Sanford was not along to curb her tongue, Marie expressed every astonishment and a good deal of laughter at the extravagances.

As they approached Plymouth, they sailed within shouting distance of another ship, and were told that Admiral Keith, aboard the flagship *Tonnant,* had been in the harbor, and was sailing out towards *Bellerophon.* Yes, MacKenroth was not only already in Plymouth, but had learned from James Meek, Keith's private secretary, that Keith was in the harbor, but not which ship he was on.

"The chase is on!" Sanford said with excitement, and from that moment on the glories of *Seadog* were forgotten. All eyes, excitement and comment were for the water ballet about to be enacted before them. The harbor was full of hundreds of craft of all kinds. It was a regular picnic. A move in the chase would no sooner be made than it was being discussed across the water from ship to ship, along with every unlikely conjecture that occurred to anyone. Keith had given *Bellerophon* orders to sail farther out to sea, as MacKenroth's boat was small and not able to go far from shore. Why did not *Bellerophon* leave then? The wind was down, it was awaiting a wind to get to safety. Meanwhile MacKenroth rowed towards Billy Ruffian, waving the writ. The *Tonnant* drew closer to *Bellerophon.*

"You see what Keith's up to!" David laughed. "No ships but official ones are allowed within a hundred yards of Billy Ruffian. By going so close, Keith has got beyond reach of

MacKenroth. There, the Officer of the Watch is ordering MacKenroth off, threatening to blast him out of the sea. He can't very well do it with so many boats all around, though. By God, I wouldn't have missed this for worlds."

A good deal of figuring was necessary to discover what was going on, for with the racket made by hundreds of boats and thousands of excited passengers, the sea was a babel of noise. The center of the show was Billy Ruffian, the *Tonnant* and the little vessel holding MacKenroth and his writ. MacKenroth learned from an unwary officer aboard *Bellerophon* that Keith was aboard the *Tonnant*. So Keith could accept the writ, MacKenroth began rowing to the portside, while the Officer of the Watch continued shouting and threatening, but not shooting. With a head on view, the occupants of *Seadog* saw Keith, the admiral, being lowered on the starboard side and escaping in a pinnace that outpaced MacKenroth's little boat. The crowds let the pursuer know what had happened and MacKenroth, waving an angry fist in frustration, made for the harbor and disappeared for a while.

The watchers at sea felt more action would occur, and waited patiently for MacKenroth's return. Sanford's chef was as good as his reputation, serving a sumptuous meal in the dining room while they awaited the next move. When they returned to deck, a small boat was delivering a crouched form to the *Tonnant*. The telescope discovered under the uniform of an ordinary seaman huddled the form of the admiral. His pointed head was concealed, but the black slanted brows, long nose and square jaw of the Scottish admiral were recognized as he was smuggled back aboard the *Tonnant*. MacKenroth's spies were not long in learning of the deception, and soon MacKenroth reappeared in a somewhat larger boat with twelve oarsmen, again in pursuit, again waving his writ. The wind was rising. Both *Bellerophon* and the *Tonnant* were preparing to go out to sea, while their pursuer urged his men on to reach the flagship before it could get under sail.

He was within shouting distance when once again Keith was down the side and slipped into yet another naval vessel, the *Eurotas*. Eager for sport, the crowds informed MacKenroth of this sly trick, and he was hot off after *Eurotas*. The *Eurotas* was a smaller, faster vessel than the flagship, and with all sails billowing, took off at an alarming speed for Cawsand Bay, while MacKenroth fell ever farther behind. Disgusted, he returned once more to Billy Ruffian to try to serve his writ on the General himself. The General was not on deck, of course. Maitland knew too much to allow that. MacKenroth's shouts of "urgent business" and "in the name of the King" went unheeded. A warning shot was fired off over the tops of all the assembled vessels, at which point MacKenroth conceded defeat and rowed to shore to begin writing up letters of complaint in the most virulent tones to the newspapers and influential supporters.

The afternoon was well advanced, and *Seadog* turned for home, working its way with difficulty through the welter of smaller craft littering the water.

"I think that's the end of the game," Sanford said with an air of satisfaction.

"You sound happy with the outcome," Marie mentioned.

"I am. I have said before I don't think any plan for Bonaparte's well-being that rests on the goodwill of the English people has much chance of success."

"What I'm wondering is why Admiral Keith chose today of all days to come to Plymouth at all," David said. "Rawlins must have told him MacKenroth was coming."

"He ought to have," Sanford agreed. "It almost makes one question his integrity."

"Or his sobriety," Marie added.

"Probably drunk as a skunk," David said. "Must have been tightly screwed to have slipped up on that. It'll be another demotion for the poor fellow."

"What do you think will happen now, Ade?" David asked.

"Bonaparte will be whisked off to Saint Helena so fast his head will spin. It is the business of needing the approval of the Allies that has delayed it so long. It has been given now."

"If someone don't get cracking and rescue him soon, they'll be too late," David said, worried that he would miss his chance for action, *real* action. This bit of spying he had done so far was tame to what he secretly longed for. A chase on the high seas, gunfire, a medal and national heroism to be the natural outcome.

"They'll have to make their move within the next few days," Sanford said. "It won't take longer than that to make the arrangements for transferring Boney to another ship for the voyage." There was a certain look of anticipation on his face that belied his oft-repeated hope that nothing of the sort would be tried.

"Do you really think they'll try it?" David asked hopefully.

"I know it," he answered with satisfaction. "As you are all

166

good seamen, have you any objection to a tour along the coast a bit to the west?"

They had no objection. Thus far they had done very little actual sailing, spending the better part of their time bobbing at rest amidst all the other craft. With the strong breeze now blowing, they made quick time westward. David had the ultimate pleasure of being completely in command. Sanford took a seat with Marie astern, where they sipped champagne and occasionally Sanford lifted the telescope, examining the coastline.

"You are selecting the spot where Napoleon will be taken ashore, are you?" she asked.

"Just so. What is your opinion?"

"Bolt Hall," she answered instantly.

"No way. I'm not sure he'll be landed in England at all."

"Of course you are! A dozen times you have told us it will be a rope slung over the cliff some dark night."

"They don't get much darker than they are these nights. Still, they might make directly around the tip of Land's End to Ireland. The fleet is mainly concentrated in the Channel between England and France. With a good fast ship they might make it to Youghal Bay on the south coast of Ireland. It would require a good head start, of course."

"Napoleon will not be rescued without the navy learning of it in a hurry."

"Best to be prepared, however. Who is to say the navy won't take a hand in rescuing him?"

"You forget Admiral Keith is back at the station. You can no longer count on Rawlins to get roaring drunk and oblige the rescuers."

"No, I don't count on Rawlins to be drunk at all at the time. Nor can I count on you to imbibe enough of my excellent champagne to make you tipsy before we have to go back home. Charming as you are, I have other creatures to see to." He arose and set aside his glass.

"A French creature, I fancy?"

"No, English leeches. They are feeling sorely pulled today, poor things. Excuse me."

He went to ask David to turn around and go back to the Hall.

"Do you plan to sail her back to Sinclair's today?" David asked.

"No, I'll leave her at your place for the time being."

They climbed up the steep cliff to the Hall, to regale Sir

Henry with the day's activities. He was loud in his praise of Admiral Lord Keith, the British navy, the townspeople in general who had turned out in such abundance to watch the show. He was also satisfied but silent that *Seadog* had at last found its proper place, at his dock.

"How do the leeches go on?" Sanford asked Biddy.

"The strangest thing in the world, Sanford. They are reviving nicely. About four this afternoon they became active again. In fact, I was inadvertently leeched of half an ounce of my blood. They had been so dull all day that I put my arm in up to the elbow without a thought of it, and at four o'clock one of them attached on to me. There is no pulling them off, of course. They'll leave in their teeth—not really teeth but a plait of hard skin, and cause a painful inflammation, along with being unable to bite again. I have an excellent poultice, by the way, if your mother should ever accidentally find herself with the teeth left in. I was so happy to see them back to normal I didn't regret the loss of blood in the least. In fact, I feel better after it. I can't think what can have caused their lassitude this morning. They were all as stupid as if they'd been doped. But there is no harm done. The fellow that grabbed on to me gave up a good bit of blood when I stripped him between my thumb and finger. That is the way to do it, you must know. Better than applying salt or vinegar to its mouth. Then I put it in successive fresh water, and it is surviving, and will be usable again in four or five months."

Sanford listened to all this lore with not only interest but enthusiasm. "Should we not check the temperature again?" he asked.

"If it dropped from seventy-two to sixty-seven overnight, that might account for their torpor. They might think it was winter coming on. Let us just run out and check it," she agreed.

Together they hastened out to the reservoir, to see that the temperature still read sixty-seven. Biddy was hard pressed to think how it had reached seventy-two the evening before. She concluded someone had dumped hot water into her pond, and went to chide the stablehands, and warn them against repeating this practice. They stared to hear they had done anything of the sort, or that they might have had hot water in the stable, but she felt she had discovered the cause of the lassitude of the leeches. She would have no disease named after her, but she had at least saved her crop.

"What has Benson been doing with himself today?" Sanford asked as they walked arm-in-arm back to the house.

"He hasn't been here at all, but plans to return for dinner I believe, as he didn't leave word otherwise. I cannot like his being here. I wish he would leave."

"He won't go now before your ball."

"Very likely that's why he hangs on, to see what other unsuspecting girl he might make up to, now that Marie is through with him."

"You think she is over her brief infatuation?"

"Certainly she is. And as *I* have given him the hint no offer from him will be welcome here, he has stopped showing her the least partiality. Really, I cannot think why he hangs around."

"I bet he'll be gone the day after the ball," Sanford comforted her, then they went upstairs to change for dinner.

There was little enough to complain of in Benson's being with them. He appeared at the table for breakfast and dinner, but for the rest of the day and the entire evening he absented himself. If only he had been a little pleasant during his brief hours with them, no one would have begrudged him the bed and board, but he had become downright surly, particularly to Sanford, which was very odd and rude as Sanford had become as pleasant as may be with Benson. He would often relate to him some little joke Madame Monet had cracked, which angered Marie almost as much as it maddened Benson. Dinner was no sooner over than Benson was off again. David, having switched allegiance to Adrian, let him go without even observing which direction he took. He was eager to have some activity for the night, however, and turned to Sanford.

"Are you calling on Madame tonight?" he asked.

"No, I'm giving Benson a turn."

"Well if that ain't a low trick! *Your* chick, and he there making up to her every time your back's turned."

"Truth to tell, I am becoming a little bored with Madame," Sanford said.

Marie sat two yards from the gentlemen, ostensibly sorting through cards of acceptance for the ball, but in truth listening as hard as she could to every word spoken. She peered up when Sanford made this statement, to find his blue eyes resting on her in a quizzical way. Her attention, or at least her eyes, went back to the cards.

"Shall we jog up to the Point and have a look through the telescope?" David tried next.

"My groom is there. He will let us know if anything happens. I don't think the telescope features prominently in the case any longer, David—if it ever did."

"My own opinion as well," David agreed knowledgeably, wondering why this should be so. "What do you say to a dash into Plymouth, to hear what's being said at the inn. See if MacKenroth managed to get his writ served."

"He didn't. Keith has been smuggled aboard the *Prometheus* and will hide out there a while," Sanford told him.

Here was a spy who knew what he was about! "How the deuce did you find out that, Ade?"

"I asked his wife. Sent her a note asking her to let me know and she sent an answer back with my man. She is a good friend of my mama. Keith will take to the sea and await orders to transfer Napoleon to the *Northumberland*. Sir George Cockburn, its captain, has been standing off the Isle of Wight, and is en route here now for the trip to Saint Helena. Of course you realize this is told in confidence, David," he added, to give an air of importance to his words, though they were no secret to anyone really interested in the case.

"Oh, certainly! Secrets of this sort are not to be spoken of in front of just anyone." He lowered his voice, deeming it time to return tit for tat with his favorite spy. There were whispered words regarding Cicero, ten thousand pounds, a set of brass buttons, accompanied by many knowing nods, narrowed eyes, and sharp looks around the room, lest he be overheard by Marie, who knew the whole.

Sanford didn't turn a hair. "I've taken care of all that," he said. "The only matter that bears watching now is your winch and chain. Shall we go and see it hasn't been tampered with?"

"What—you mean all along you have *wanted* it left intact, and have just let on otherwise to fool the enemy into leaving it alone?" David asked, a smile of approval at such chicanery as this.

"Exactly," Sanford agreed, and went with David to the winch room, to raise the chain to the surface, then lower it, just to make sure it was all right, and in good operating condition.

"You'll leave *Seadog* here, won't you, Ade?"

"Yes, I see no reason to move her. She'll be required very soon."

"Why did you take her to Sinclair's then?"

"To make sure our enemy was convinced I was serious

170

about wanting the chain cut. That I wouldn't trust my own yacht here was good evidence of my seriousness. And you see how well it worked. The chain is intact. If only we could be sure no one sabotages it tonight. I think we should have a guard set on it. Which of your men do you trust implicitly? A good, sharp, wide-awake lad."

"I'll guard it myself!" David volunteered obligingly, thus ridding Sanford of his dogged presence. He hinted strongly to know where the chest of gold was, but was fobbed off by being told that "just in case he was captured and tortured" it was better for him not to know. This thrilled him to the core. He bitterly resented the days spent in ignorance of Sanford's doings. Of course, Sanford was the London agent, despite Papa's protest to the contrary. Still he cheered up to consider himself a year hence, his face bearing a scar, by no means disfiguring, but rather an enhancement of his phiz—a line on the left cheekbone he thought might be effective, or possibly just at the upper corner of the eye. It provided just that little dash, that air of mystery a face a fraction too round demanded. People would whisper about duels and intrigues, but no one would ever quite know the truth—that he had been tortured. Actually being cut across the face, or even bumped on the head, never once entered his mind as he sat, rapidly falling to sleep, in the dark, silent winch room. It had been a tiring day, spent on the water, and a good bit of wine had been consumed, too. Champagne—so much more elegant than brandy. He ought to have known a real spy would drink champagne. How could you court a lady like Madame Monet with brandy? You'd be flat on your face in half an hour. Some pleasant reveries of courting her with champagne followed.

Sanford returned to the saloon to find Marie alone, awaiting him. That it was his return she awaited must not be suspected for a moment, so she made a great show of counting up cards, and wondering whether Aunt Biddy realized the Stantons had accepted, and the deVignes declined, due to a bout of flu in the family.

"Certainly she knows it. You heard her say she was sending over some medication. Did Madame Monet send in an acceptance?" he asked, thus bringing up the real matter of concern between them.

"Yes, you must not fear you will be deprived of her company," Marie snipped.

"Good."

This sent her reaching for a book, which he summarily lifted from her fingers and laid beyond reach. "No looking at Latin for you tonight. We must talk."

"I can't think what we have to talk about."

"I'll give you a little hint. Monique Monet."

"Your favored subject of conversation is of little interest to me, you must know."

"I disagree. You never look half so animated as when she is under discussion. It was business between us yesterday in the orchard. I was only trying to discover if she knows of any plans to rescue Napoleon."

"Was it indeed business you spoke of? What a strange way you go about it. Your solicitor will be amazed if you try conducting your other business affairs in that way."

"He certainly would. He don't speak French."

"The language presents no barrier to you, obviously."

"Nor to any educated person. I like to be able to say what I think."

"And do what you please. You mustn't let *me* stop you."

"Thank you, I won't," he said, and reaching across the sofa, he put both his arms around her.

"How dare you, sir!" she cried in alarm.

"Shades of Mrs. Radcliffe!" he laughed. "Where outside of a bad novel would you have come across such a missish expression?"

This, laughing at her, was no way to conduct a romance, and she pokered up in mingled embarrassment and anger. Her alarm was chiefly lest they be discovered, and she glanced fearfully towards the doorway.

Sanford did the same. "The dragoons didn't hear you. I expect they are the standard rescue team." With no rescue in sight, she went in hope of further indignities, that were not long in forthcoming. He tightened his grip and went on to embrace her, a surprisingly gentle embrace considering what she had witnessed in the orchard. She had hoped for worse from him. She was obliged to make a good show of disliking even this light kiss, however, and pushed him off. With a disheartening swiftness, he allowed himself to be disengaged.

"You have just told me I must not let you stop me from doing what I liked, and I would like to kiss you without having my jacket torn from my back," he pointed out reasonably. "Now, did you mean what you said, or do you really want me to stop?"

"Yes!" she said angrily.

172

"Yes what, you meant what you said?"

"Yes—no! Oh, don't be so stupid!" she said in vexation.

"I deserved that," he answered, but as there was some ambiguity in the matter, he chose the answer he wanted, and went on to embrace her in a much more accomplished way, fondling her neck and back with his fingers, while his lips burned on hers. For a long moment she submitted to this outrage, then felt impelled to object.

She disentangled herself and pulled away primly. "You will please remember I am not Madame Monet," she said.

"You don't have to remind me. The lack of reciprocation makes it obvious."

"I don't have the French flair for it, is that what you're telling me?"

"I wouldn't say that, love," he answered, patting her chin with a finger in such a manner that she found if difficult to go on being angry. "Lack of reciprocation was the phrase I used."

"When I have a small fraction of Madame's infinite experience I shall do better."

"Very likely, but I haven't got twenty years to wait. You'll have to start reciprocating faster than that."

Into the arena stepped Sir Henry, to request a private word with Lord Sanford. Marie could have killed him. She refused to be caught twice sitting waiting for Sanford, and went with the greatest reluctance to her room.

It was much later, about one a.m., when Benson returned, and he began a scouting about that took him to the winch room, where David was discovered fast asleep, rolled up in a blanket. Benson nudged him awake.

"Oh, Ev, what are you doing here? I am guarding the chain. It as safe as can be. Not a soul has been near it all night."

"It is not the chain I wish to talk about, David," Benson said in a significant tone. "It is the money. You know I have been looking for it. I thought I had a line on it, but it came to nothing. I have discovered in town Sanford may have been influential in raising that money. It is he who has it, hidden somewhere. We must discover where he has it."

Just what part Benson played in this whole affair was by no means clear to David. At one point he even thought he might be Cicero, but in any case he was no longer the favorite. He played his close game, giving away nothing. "What do you suggest we do?"

"He has taken you a little into his confidence. Has he said anything about the money? Do you think he knows where it is?"

He hesitated, pondering a cunning reply, but in the end answered truthfully enough, "He didn't tell me where it is."

Benson sighed wearily, and put his face in his hands. "I have a dozen things to do tomorrow, David. I want you to dog his every step. Try if you can find out where it is, and let me know *at once*. It is extremely urgent."

"How will I let you know? Where will you be?" he asked, thinking to discover the man's whereabouts in this tricky way.

"I have various things to do, but I'll check back with you from time to time."

"I could leave a coded message in your room," David suggested.

"Yes, an excellent idea. Just say you want to see me, and I'll know what it means, and find you."

David was disappointed that the code should be so simple. He had thought to be let in on secret combinations of letters and numbers whose figuring out would require a secret code book, of which only two copies—three at the outside—existed anywhere in the world. Benson left and David returned to his sleepy vigil, pondering just what Benson's game was. He had very little intention of looking for the money, none of telling Benson if he should find it, but dogging Adrian's steps he had already determined on, and would have been happy to find the gold for his own satisfaction. Couldn't think where in the dickens it could be.

18

The fifth of August, the day of Boltwood's ball, dawned cool and cloudy. It was no more than anyone expected. Biddy was prophesying howling wind and lashing rain by nightfall. A mere squall would not put off the ball, however, and soon she was busy working out her list of preparations for rooms and food, greenery for the ballroom, mentioning to Marie those areas where she could be useful. Benson sat silent at the table, looking surreptitiously to Sanford to hear what he planned.

"I ought to have a look at my leeches, too," Biddy said, as she set down her cup.

"Let me do it for you, Biddy. You have too much to do today to burden yourself with that," Sanford said, "whereas *I* have not a thing planned. I have left my day free to be of help to you."

A visitor under her feet promised little help, but in this one matter he proved useful. To the disappointment of David and astonishment of Benson, Sanford meant just what he said. He spent a quarter of an hour at the leech reservoir, then entered the house and took up a book—Dr. Heywood's excellent treatise on leeches, it was. Later in the morning he also condescended to give advice on the arrangement of ferns and flowers in the ballroom. Lunch had come and gone, with every one of the young males still cluttering up the house, waiting and watching each other, but when Lord Sanford then took the idea of having his seafaring chef in to mix up a batch of rack punch to regale the guests, Benson and David gave up on him, and found more amusing pursuits. The storm had blown out to sea, and with the weather improved, Benson went into Plymouth, while David went down to the dock to have all the neighbors' yachts moved about to make space for the naval vessel, *Phoebe*. So busy was he in giving commands and personally taking over the helm when the actual move of six or eight yards was to be negotiated that he failed to observe a figure, clad all in gray much the color of the rocks, clambering along the cliff across the bay where the Bolt Hall chain ended. He was in a little perplexity as to which vessel ought to be given the best position. It was necessary that his father's yacht be in the lead, anchored seaward of all others, ready for the chase. Yet Sanford's *Seadog* was the larger, faster yacht.

All these movings and decisions took over an hour. He was still on the dock wondering what to do about his dilemma when Sanford strolled towards him. "Oh, got your punch all made up, have you, Ade?" he asked.

"Yes, I have come to ask you up to try a glass and see what you think."

"Excellent. Just before you go, though, where shall I put *Seadog*? For tonight, I mean. I'm moving all the yachts to make room for the ship Rawlins is sending over."

"Which do you plan to take in case of trouble, mine or your father's?"

"Which do *I* plan to take?" David asked, staring.

"It is only right that a Boltwood be captain of the ship. Your father will want to take his own, so why don't you captain mine? You got the hang of it yesterday, I think?"

"Yes but . . . Do you really mean it, Ade?"

"Certainly I do."

The dilemma was solved in the wagging of a tail. *Fury* was hauled back and *Seadog* was pulled out to the fore. The vision of a chase called to mind that the winch and chain had been unguarded since morning, and before they went to try the rack punch, David said he thought he'd just take a nip down and have a gander. Sanford offered to do this for him, and David took the opportunity to take up a stand at the helm of *Seadog*, looking out to sea with a hand shading his eyes, seeing a mirage of a hundred ships, with the *Bellerophon* at their center, the General climbing down its side while bullets flew and smoke belched. He had *Seadog* just within ames-ace of sideswiping Billy Ruffian, and a rope at the ready to bind Napoleon when Sanford shouted from the dock. "She's all right and tight. Let's go."

Napoleon was left hanging off the side of the ship while David scampered up to the dock to join Sanford. With a hand thrown over Adrian's shoulder in a way to tell any chance observer what easy terms they were on, the two went into Bolt Hall. "What is this brew called?" David asked, tasting the potent drink judiciously.

"It's really rack punch quickened with gin and—other things. I call it a Devon Mule. It has a bit of a kick. Not too sweet for your taste?"

David took a more liberal swallow. Finding it not too sweet, he quaffed off his glass. "What's in it?"

"An alcohol distilled from coco sap is the base. I added a little sugar to please the ladies, and the gin of course." He also added a good dash of brandy, but didn't mention this ingredient.

"I believe I get the taste of brandy," David said, measuring out another glass. Sanford accompanied him.

"Yes, a little brandy for taste."

They discussed the recipe, adding a dash of wine, a soupçon of brandy, and tasting it at each addition till David got a little woozy. As his eyes began to wander just a little, Sanford said, "You and Benson are still on good terms, I see.

He has been much in your company today. What is he doing? Anything of interest?"

"Trying to find out where you've got the gold stashed, Ade. I didn't tell him a thing."

"Good lad. I knew I could depend on you. He didn't mention any endeavors for the evening? Whether he thinks anyone will take a stab at freeing Boney while we all make merry?"

"He don't think it'll be tonight. Truth to tell, Benson ain't up to all the rigs at all, Ade. A bit of a slow top, letting *you* make off with the message and gold and Madame." He poured out another glass of punch as he spoke, but Sanford put a hand on the ladle and modified it to a trickle.

"This is strong stuff. Remember the kick."

"Yes, by Jove, jolly good stuff."

"Does Benson ever speak of Rawlins at all?"

"Sees him all the time, but he don't like me to go along. A regular Tartar, old Rawlins. Martinet for discipline. After the ladies for all that, though. I've been keeping a weather eye lifted on the pair of them. A regular set-to they had one night at Madame's place. The night of the day you and Papa went to Sinclair's, it was. But they all settled down to harmony in the end. Tell me, Ade, about Madame—she's a spy too, ain't she? I mean, hand in glove with Rawlins and Benson. Why should she be for Napoleon when he stole her château and slept in her tapestries? That woman's been treated hard."

"Madame is involved, of course."

"I knew it! Seems to me us spies ought all to get together, instead of working each on our own. You and Benson going off your separate ways—me and Madame never acknowledging we're both in on it. What's the point of so much secrecy, just between ourselves?"

"But then if one of us is captured, you know, he might be forced to give away the whole. It is often done in this way—each member of the team doing his own little bit."

"And you at the head of it all, pulling the strings. I knew how it was. How do you get to be the *chief* spy, Ade?"

"It is necessary to work your way up the ladder, like anything else."

"I hope you'll put in a good word with me—*for* me, I mean, with Liverpool and Bathurst. Tell me, Ade, what should we be doing till the ball starts? To uncover the plot I mean."

Feeling that David required fresh air to clear his head before dinner, Adrian sent him off to check the spinney, orchard, gazebo and stables for any signs of desperate enemy activity. He feared he had let him indulge too heavily in the Devon Mule when he came running up to him not forty minutes later reporting have found a clue of vital importance.

"What's that, David?"

"Uniforms. A whole crate of 'em."

"What kind of uniforms?"

"Navy officers' uniforms."

"Where did you discover this clue?"

"In one of our spare rooms. I decided to start looking inside the house first. A lucky chance I did."

"They would be for the sailors—officers coming to the ball tonight, I expect. They will change into their dress uniforms here after they arrive."

"Oh—very likely Biddy has set the blue room off for the purpose," David said.

Sanford next got rid of him by sending him to perform his first assigned mission outdoors. It seemed a little curious to him that the officers should change at Bolt Hall. Why not just wear their uniforms? David had imagined. He went up to the blue room to see for himself, and found no sign of uniforms. There was a carton on the floor, but it held only blankets and winter wear. There were some blue blankets—that must be what had led David astray. Benson was coming along the hall from his own room when Sanford came out. He looked at Sanford with his habitual dislike and suspicion.

"All set for the big do, Benson?" Sanford asked.

"Big do? Oh, you refer to the ball. I was just in to see if my valet has my formal clothes laid out. He didn't have my shoes polished, come to think of it. I'd better go back and remind him."

"I should do the same," Sanford said, and went to his room to do it. But he noticed over his shoulder as he closed the door that Benson lingered at the top of the stairs, looking towards the blue room. A moment later he checked, and Benson was not in sight, therefore had not gone to his own room, which was past Sanford's. Was wasting his time looking in the blue room for a chest of gold he supposed. With a chuckle, Sanford went to his valet's door.

"Everything set for tonight, Belhomme?"

"*Oui, milor'. Tout*, she is *prêt*."

"All our rag, tag and bobtail forces assembled? You have spoken to my chef and his assistants?"

178

"*Moi*, Belhomme, I look after all the detail. The suit, he is ready *aussi*." He indicated with a pointing finger the black satin breeches and jacket hung ready for donning.

"Yes, you are also a good valet. But *Seadog*, is he ready, too? You have prepared a comfortable cabin for the admiral?"

"*Le chef*, he chills the champagne and prepares the hors d'oeuvre as you command."

"Excellent, then you leave me time for a spot of *amour* before dinner."

"There is not time to visit the Monet," Belhomme told him sternly.

"The Monet has been superseded by an *anglaise*. Sorry about that."

"Me, I prefer the ingénue for us."

"That makes it unanimous."

Marie was in the ballroom adding a few end tables to the collection of chairs along the room's edge for the dowagers and chaperones. "Looks very nice," Sanford complimented her.

As he had himself supervised the placement of greenery and blooms, there was little praise in this statement, and little response to it. "I expect you are looking forward to the dance," he tried next.

"I always enjoy a ball."

"I notice you enjoy the company of the officers. With Rawlins bringing down a dozen, you should be happily occupied. I expect Biddy has set aside a room for them to change in."

"Nothing was said of changing. They will come in dress uniform. They are not invited to dinner, but only the dance afterwards."

"David mentioned something about the blue room being used for them to change in."

"No, we never use the blue room at all. It hasn't been aired, and is in fact full of boxes of blankets that are about to be aired before being put back on the beds."

"I see. I must have misunderstood him. Did Biddy mention to you we are to open the dance?"

"I suppose we must."

"I am flattered at your enthusiasm. I am not at all a bad dancer, however, and you will have the rest of the evening free for the officers. And Benson, if *he* still figures in your daydreams."

"He doesn't. He'll look a sight with that eye patch and a bruise on his cheek."

"To say nothing of his mole, as large as a pea."

She was about to make some pejorative remark on his mentioning the afflictions of another when the word "pea" struck her as significant. "Sanford, do you mean to say *he* is Cicero?" she asked, her eyes enlarged with the idea.

"Cicero?" he asked. "Oh, you refer to our discussion of Cicero being named after a wart. But what . . ."

"Don't treat me like an idiot. I know all about it. I know very well what is going on here. Is Benson Cicero?"

"No, but I wish you will be careful of him, for all that. In fact, there will be as much cause for worry as enjoyment at this ball tonight. Be very careful at all times."

"What do you mean?"

"I wish I knew exactly what to warn you of, but I don't. Just be careful of Benson and Madame, and any of the officers with whom you are not familiar."

She felt a quick rush of excitement. "You can't mean *Benson* . . ."

"But I do. He is dangerous. I wouldn't want anything to happen to you." He regarded her for a long minute with an expression more tender than ever seen before on his face. Then he reached for her hand, and began to walk from the room.

Her head was awhirl. That Benson was involved in anything worse than dangling after her fortune had not previously occurred to her. Still the shift in his status came easily to her. For some days now she had been finding him unlikable. He was easy to transform into a villain. In the case of Madame, the transformation was an improvement. She was more acceptable as a villain than as Sanford's lover. "What will *you* be doing?" she asked.

"Making up to Madame," he answered in a teasing tone. "But it is all business, and you must not be jealous. Well, perhaps a *little* jealous, now that you are aware of the manner in which business is conducted between us."

"If I took into my head to be jealous of all her flirts, I wouldn't have a moment's peace."

"You needn't be jealous of the others. Only me."

"Oh, jealous! I am more apt to pity you, having to waltz with an overstuffed doll."

"That is by no means the least agreeable of my coming activities. She waltzes superbly."

180

"When have you been waltzing with her?"

"My dear goose, we don't spend *all* our evenings making love. I am not a rabbit, after all."

"Oh! You're impossible," she said angrily.

"What happened to the pity?"

They were in the hallway at the bottom of the stairs, and soon were interrupted by a servant, so that the dalliance was ruined.

19

By late afternoon the tension around Bolt Hall was increasing. On top of the normal bustling of servants to set the final touches on food and house for the ball, there were certain amongst the inhabitants who expected more than a feast and a spot of dancing to occur. Sir Henry knew the *Phoebe* was not to dock till eight and hit on the idea of setting up a row of torches, not so much for the convenience of Rawlins in landing from the vessel as for his own greater glory in allowing his neighbors to see it, anchored at Bolt Hall. Biddy, having observed some lessening in the thaw between Marie and Sanford, held to her theory that no two young persons of opposite sex and mutual eligibility could remain unattached throughout such a romantic evening. Care had been taken to see that Marie was irresistibly arrayed in a gown of white, the color that had lured Captain Monro into proposing to Biddy all those years ago. David too was outfitted in style in his black jacket and breeches, with a pistol cunningly hidden in his pocket, with only three inches of the handle sticking out. As the family and some select guests (those who had volunteered a yacht to the cause in fact) met for dinner, the currents of emotion in the air were almost visible.

Sir Henry took everyone out to the top of the cliff to admire his dock and torches. There were sundry slighted yacht owners, who thought their vessel merited a better position than being pushed to the rear, with another ship hitting against their sides and likely giving cause for a new paint job. Those who had not already stopped around to admire *Seadog*

181

had to make a few comments on it. Sir Henry, till that moment unaware that *Seadog* had been put in advance of *Fury*, gave his son a killing stare, and told him to "get those yachts arranged properly at once." David meekly said, "Yes, sir," but as the arrangement that existed seemed proper to him, he did nothing about it, knowing the matter would soon slip his father's mind, as indeed it did, as soon as he remembered his petition regarding the "situation" in Plymouth, and brought it out for signatures. The guests became quite merry after a few kicks from the Devon Mule. They sat long over a repast of several courses, till Biddy began to fear the guests invited for dancing would find the family still at table when they began arriving.

Marie's eyes continued to fly toward Sanford and Benson. She could not like to see Benson so patched up and with his little mole assuming an awful significance, growing to the size of not only a pea but a radish. Sanford had said he was not Cicero, but she felt sure he was. And while the mole grew, Sanford's chin shortened, for *he*, obviously, was the government agent sent down from London. That much she had worked out to her satisfaction. When he smiled warmly at her a couple of times, the chin was no longer any other length than the optimum one. A man wanted a good strong chin. There was nothing worse than a chinless, weak-looking man. She noticed there was some tension between the two gentlemen. Not that they behaved in any way markedly different from formerly, but she could sense something going on. As surely as one would glance at the other, the other's head would turn quickly away. They didn't exchange a word as far as she could see, yet each was alert to the other's presence and every move.

She took her place in the welcoming line with her family, so that for a while with the guests coming in she lost track of her two gentlemen. She waited most eagerly for the arrival of Madame, wondering whom she would come with. She was very much surprised when she entered hanging on Sanford's arm. He had gone to town to deliver her! Her evening took a little turn for the worse as this realization dawned on her. The other item of interest regarding Madame was to see what outfit she had chosen. She was in black, a new twist as she usually favored highly-colored gowns. With the Monet sapphires, Marie had been expecting blue, while hoping for pink to make her look as common as possible. The black was too sophisticated, too flattering to Madame to please Marie. As

Madame shook Marie's hand, uttering some pleasantry about the ball, Miss Boltwood looked to have her first view of the necklace. The Monet sapphires were not being worn. Around Madame's neck hung a set of imitation pearls, purchased as any local resident knew at a glance from the everything store in the village for a crown. The rhineglass clasp holding them on gave it away. It was all a faradiddle that Madame had any jewels at all, and if she had a château either it would be a wonder. Madame was positively effulgent, radiating joy and goodwill. She noticed how Marie stared at her poor fish-paste pearls, and explained her wearing them.

"You have heard the dreadful news, Miss Boltwood? The sapphires stolen!"

"No, I hadn't heard," Marie replied. "How horrid for you." But Madame would not be glowing like a new mother if she had just sustained the loss of the fabulous Monet sapphires. Marie took care that she not lend enough pity to her tone that she gave any impression of believing this tale.

. ."*Ah oui, quel dommage!*"

"Stolen right from your cottage, were they?" Marie asked, somewhat indifferently.

"Yes, incredible, is it not? And the constable, he does nothing. Some of the riffraff visiting town have stolen them."

"Or it could be one of your many callers, Madame. With so many of them, it would be difficult for the constable to know where to begin questioning," Marie consoled sweetly.

Sanford held his lips steady, his eyes not quite following suit. He said as he led Madame away, "Madame does not think any of her *guests* to be the culprit, however." Then it was time to say good evening to Biddy, who proffered all the proper consolation the theft of the sapphires demanded, while her mind contemplated the good a regular leeching would do to one of Madame's size.

Others came along for greeting in quick succession, and the little incident passed from Marie's mind. There was some commotion in the hallway. The word was quickly going around that the *Phoebe* was pulling in. Everyone, even including the reception line, made a dash for the platform to see this wonderful sight. The host of the party made such an undignified exit that he jostled Mrs. Sinclair's side against a table and knocked over a vase of flowers, whose cleaning up caused Biddy to miss the landing. David was the recipient of a hard stare as *Seadog* was seen to be still to the fore, but Sir Henry was too gratified to be very angry. To see the *Phoebe* coasting in, her white ensign flapping, and the ship manned not by a crew of ordinary seamen, but by officers, everyone in his brass buttons, was too unique a view.

"Rawlins has had the officers who are invited man the ship while the other chaps remain at the station in case of trouble from Bonaparte," Sir Henry explained, pulling the true explanation out of the air quite by chance. "This is not the first time Bolt Hall has been host to an official vessel, of course. During the Civil War we had a host of them stationed here. Well, well, we had better get back into the reception line to make them welcome." He did this, gathering a reluctant Marie and David to go with him, but as the crowd of onlookers were more interested in seeing the complete landing, Sir Henry, too, returned. He was back at his post in good time to make Rear Admiral Rawlins welcome. "Admiral Lord Keith is still out, is he?" was his warm greeting.

"No, sir, he is at the station, but lying low to prevent that upstart MacKenroth getting to him with his writ."

"Ah, yes," he said, regretting the admiral's loss to his ball, but taking some compensation from the dozen tall officers standing in line to be presented.

Out in the throng, David elbowed his way to Sanford's side while Madame was bestowing her pelisse and said, "I didn't think the officers would come in their dress uniform. What can that box of uniforms have been doing in the blue room?"

Sanford frowned. "You're quite sure it wasn't blankets?"

"Blankets? What would brass buttons be doing on blankets? And a box of shakoes, too. It was uniforms. This wants looking into, Sanford."

A blanket might have been mistaken for a jacket after a few glasses of the Devon Mule, but David had not had enough to imagine brass buttons and shakoes. Yet these items had not been in the blue room a short while later. And Benson had been hanging around that area. "There's been a change of plans then. I have to dash upstairs. Nothing will happen for a while. Listen, David, I want you to keep an eye on Benson. Don't let him out of your sight. I'll take care of Rawlins. If Benson does anything suspicious, let me know at once."

"Suspicious in what way? Why don't he just tell us what he means to do?"

Sanford looked on the verge of a disclosure. He directed a long, penetrating regard on David, and saw an eager, guileless face that couldn't hold a secret for ten seconds. "He will, in good time. Watch him. Do as I say."

Sanford dashed up for a fast conversation with his versatile Belhomme, and David did exactly as he was told for nearly an hour. A dozen times he smiled and winked at Benson in a conspiratorial way, lifting his brows, pointing to his watch and generally behaving in a way that led Benson to believe he was completely foxed. Of course he didn't devote every second to the chore of watching Benson. As the junior host, it was necessary that he disburse some gallantry amidst the female guests, and he did so in any spare minute he got from watching Benson and admiring Madame. Gad, but she cut a classy figure in the black gown, all glittering with shiny bugle beads, and the white pearls, almost invisible against her creamy throat. She was easy to keep an eye on, due to a pair of black ostrich plumes that towered above the throng, and were in some little danger of being ignited by a low-hanging chandelier.

Marie and Sanford opened the ball, but she was so miffed at his having brought Madame personally that she couldn't be civil to him. No leading comments about business or anything else could stir her into a smile. Nor was Sanford's whole attention on providing her an amusing partner. Marie found much to say on the attractiveness of a naval uniform, and some few comments on the pusillanimity of a full-grown, able-bodied man who spent his time buying forged masterpieces while a war raged about his head. They parted as soon as the minuet ended, to become involved with other guests. The dancing, drinking and merrymaking continued unabated for several hours. Marie had her fill of officers, every one of whom seemed young, gauche and poor partners this evening. She took it as a matter of course she would be joined by Lord Sanford for dinner, but dinner-time found him at Madame's side, showing her every gallantry. Biddy disliked this as much as the younger lady, but hid her displeasure more successfully. Was it possible this ball, designed to secure Sanford for Marie and herself, was to benefit the French widow?

When Sanford looked to Marie just as the dancers were going to the dining room, she lifted her head in the air and quickly turned away. He shrugged, and looked around to see David was keeping a guard on Benson. Rawlins was with Biddy and Sir Henry, and with all the protagonists accounted for, it was felt that any interesting events would wait for the meal to be over.

Before returning to the ballroom, some of the guests strolled out to the stone platform for another look at the yachts, but the torches had been extinguished and the lights from the Hall itself hardly stretched so far as to illuminate the flotilla. The general outlines of the yachts were visible, with *Phoebe* in her place of honor. *Phoebe* was the vessel of greatest interest, of course, and there were a few lights, small lanterns only, seen bobbing about. Some skeleton crew left on board, it was assumed. With no moon nor stars to aid romance, the company soon straggled back in for more lively entertainment.

Sanford, standing up for a dance with Madame, temporarily lost sight of Rawlins. Benson was present and accounted for, however, and he expected no important move that would exclude Benson. Madame was flattering, amusing and light-footed during the waltz, but as it drew to an end and she requested a glass of wine, he began to become worried about Rawlins. He got her the wine, then excused himself on some excuse and went to seek the rear admiral. A careful search of the ballroom told him he was not there. Thinking Sir Henry might have cornered him to show him Bathurst's inkwell, he went to the office, with no success. He began to be seriously alarmed, but before flying off half cocked, he went to David.

"Are you ready, partner? This is it!" he said, his voice tense with excitement.

David gulped. "You mean *now*, right in the middle of our ball?"

"That's the idea. Your job is to keep an eye on Madame and Benson."

"I'll let them know. Er—just what is it they're to do exactly, Ade?"

Sanford put an arm around David's shoulder and turned him to such a position that the goggling eyes soon to be seen in his head would be hidden from Madame, who was glancing nervously toward them. "The fact is, they are the enemy. You understand me?"

"No—you mean they're the ones going to free Boney?"

"With Rawlins' help."

"But he's a rear admiral!" The eyes were not goggling, but unbelieving, even suspicious. David didn't believe him, an unseen complication.

"He is a tool of Cicero."

186

"Oh—I see. And Madame is, too, you mean."

"No, Madame *is* Cicero."

"You mean she ain't a woman at all?"

"Oh, she's a woman all right! You have to take my word for it, Dave. Now I depend on you *utterly*, Boltwood, and I trust you can follow instructions. Here is your assignment." He threw in these important sounding words to trim David quickly into line, and they worked marvelously. He snapped to attention—would have saluted if he hadn't been holding a glass of wine.

"Aye, aye, sir," he said instead.

"Here's what you're to do. Keep an eye on Cicero and Benson. Don't let them know you're watching them; don't for God's sake give it away you know what they're planning. Just watch them. I have to leave for a minute. If they leave the room, dash right down to the dock, and make sure you have your pistol with you. Are you ready to put on your captain's hat?"

"I'm ready! Oh, hadn't I better tell Papa?"

One Boltwood was already proving enough of a handicap that Sanford squelched this suggestion at once. "Remember your orders. Benson and Madame. I fancy they'll be together. Watch them!"

Sanford was off, and David, his heart hammering in his ears turned back to the saloon, searching for the two black ostrich plumes. He found them, but Madame was doing no more than tell a sympathetic neighbor about the loss of the Monet sapphires, so he began looking about for Benson. They were not together as Adrian had thought. Benson was on the far side of the room, and watching them both with the care the occasion demanded proved impossible. He garnered up Marie to assist him.

"All hell's about to break loose," he told her out of the side of his mouth. "You'll never guess what! It's Madame and Benson that's the sneaks planning to free Boney."

"David, you've had too much wine!"

"Damme, will you listen and hear your orders! I've got to keep an eye on Madame—she's the big fish, and you'll have to watch Benson for me."

"Did Sanford tell you so?"

"Of course he did. He depends on me completely. Now, I'll watch Madame and you don't let Benson out of your sight for a moment."

"Where's Sanford?" she asked, beginning to believe, but wishing to confirm it.

"He's attending to something else. I'm in charge here. Your assignment is to tail Benson. Tell me if you see him nip out."

With a memory of Sanford's warning regarding Benson, and with the eventual realization that David was drunk with importance and not wine, she was convinced.

The best way to keep an eye on Benson was to become his partner for the next dance, and she foresaw no difficulty in doing this. Trembling inside, but determined to carry it off with credit, she pinned a bright smile on her face and accosted him. "We have had only one dance, Mr. Benson. I hope you mean to stand up with me again."

"You do me too much honor, ma'am. But I have set my heart on enjoying your company for a waltz, and shan't be fobbed of with a mere cotillion. The next waltz will find me by your side, I promise you."

This answer was suspicious enough to convince her of his guilt. "Shall we treat ourselves to a rest and a glass of punch?" she suggested.

"Delightful, but would you excuse me for a moment first? My eye is bothering me. Your aunt has given me some drops to ease the itching. It does not actually pain, but only itches. I shall be back in two minutes."

His eagerness to get away from her was perfectly obvious. He was on the fidgets, as nervous as a kitten. And how she was to detain him by her side, when he claimed the need of medication, was an insolvable puzzle. She could do nothing but watch with a sinking heart as he left the room, to go and rescue Boney! She must make some excuse to go upstairs herself, say, if he saw her, that she had to pin up her ruffle. To reinforce her claim, she even pulled an inch of the flounce loose, and hastened after him. As she looked to the staircase, she saw no sign of Mr. Benson. He had not had time to reach the top—he was gone elsewhere.

She looked about wildly, and though she saw nothing, she heard the telltale squawking of the door that led to a flight of stairs descending to the next floor, and by a little used corrider to the stone steps to the winch room. Was the Emperor even now making for Bolt's Dock? She had to admit it was unlikely they had chosen such an inopportune moment as a ball to do it, and to be landing him at the actual scene of it. No, Benson was going to raise the chain so that none of the yachts nor the naval vessel could go after him. Sanford had been right to foresee this danger. She hurried after Benson, wondering how she should prevent him from doing what he obviously meant to do.

A weapon—she must provide herself with a weapon. She dashed into the nearest room and took up a poker from the grate. She figured Benson had had time to get down the first flight of stairs, and went cautiously after him. It was about at this time that she realized she had no desire to go into the dark hall alone. Benson was bigger than she, could overpower her in a minute, and a traitor bent on such a perilous task as freeing Napoleon Bonaparte would not hesitate to strike her down. It would take him a few minutes to get the winch moving—she must run quickly for help. She dashed back up the stairs, making no effort now to be silent—speed was the major consideration. Below, Benson heard the flying feet and slamming doors, and prepared himself for trouble.

The first person she encountered was her father, coming out of his office. He seemed to her a suitable person to appeal to. "Papa, Mr. Benson has gone to raise your chain and keep the boats all in while Bonaparte is escaping!" she said. He looked to the poker in her hand, the very real and strong consternation on her face, he recalled Sanford's many entreaties regarding the chain, and recalled, too, oblique hints, always denied, that Benson was not to be trusted. With only a second to consider that he ought to get other recruits, he went with her alone. Benson—he could handle that jackdaw of a fellow well enough with Marie's poker. His head full of the glory he would soon be reaping from the whole country, and heaven only knew what rewards besides, he took the poker from her fingers and bolted down the steps, not even feeling the twinges in his knees as he went.

There wasn't a single light as they got to the stone stairway. He sent Marie back for one, standing against the damp wall himself with the poker raised and trembling violently, but ready to be lowered forcefully at the first stirring of a sound. He rather thought then he should have had some men stationed here with a brace of lights—Sanford should have thought of it. He claimed to know it all. But in the middle of a ball, who was thinking of Bonaparte being rescued? Like David's, his heart was hammering—worse, he even feared a seizure. Marie was back with a single candle. He surprised her with a very strong oath at her foolishness. It was a lantern he had wanted. The candle, one hand to carry it, the other to shield the flickering flame, left him poorly able to wield his poker. He stepped forward slowly, frightened half to death, peering into the distance, but he couldn't see six feet beyond the weak illumination. Marie clutched at his arm, further impeding his advance. Still he didn't wish to be quite alone in the dark with Benson, so he let her stay. Both went on towards the winches, taking the smallest of shuffling steps, and praying as hard as they could it was all a false alarm.

20

When the attack came, it was not from the shadows ahead of them, but from behind. Silent, hard, expert blows, first to Sir Henry's temple, then across Marie's skull, with the butt of a pistol. They fell forward not a second apart. The candle was snatched up before it could be extinguished, and Benson set it on the stone floor. He looked with disgust at the pair of insensate bodies before him, calculating whether they would stay unconscious till he did what he had to do. There was a rattling of the chain at the opening where it came into the room. The signal—the time had come. Too late now to worry about securing this pair. He blew out the candle so that they could not positively identify him, if they should revive. The curst girl had seen him enter of course, but he could say he had followed someone else. He dashed to the winch and set his shoulder to the wheel, heaved his strength into it. The handle moved easily—more easily than formerly, but it had been oiled and worked much recently. He suspected nothing amiss. He turned and turned, waiting for the stopping of the wheel that would tell him the chain was taut at the surface. Nothing happened. He kept turning, and the chain kept reeling in, more and more easily instead of with more difficulty. When a greater quantity of chain than should have been there was wound in, he realized what had happened. With a curse he dropped the wheel and dashed from the room, stumbling over Sir Henry's ankles. He ran up the flight of stone stairs, back up the wooden stairs, along the corridor and into the part of the house where the ball was in progress.

He looked around for Madame, signalled her violently. She smiled to David, excused herself, and tore over to him.

"We're done for! Someone has cut the chain. Sanford has figured it all out, and will stop Rawlins," Benson said in a fierce whisper to Madame.

"Rawlins has had time to get well ahead of him. He has been gone ten minutes."

"Sanford was gone before I went below. He's going to block us, I tell you!"

"You panic too quickly, my dear. Let me consider," she said, her soft smile changing to a calculating expression. David, watching them across the room, was much struck at the change in her habitual charm. She *looked* like Cicero, or one of those old statues with a face as mean and cold as marble. She noticed him staring at her, and the smile was back on her face in a flash. "That *petit chien*, Boltwood, he suspects."

"The whole crew of them are on to us. The bitch and the old man followed me," he said in a frantic voice.

"*Mon Dieu*—this is serious."

"What shall we do, Monique? We must escape before they stop us."

"You may be right, for once. I have the grand headache, Monsieur. You must take me home, *tout de suite*. A dignified exit—all may not be lost. We'll head for London and await word."

"Thank God you unloaded the sapphires. How much do we have?"

"Enough for *two* to escape," she answered.

"Rawlins will talk. Spill the whole story."

"*Tant pis*. We haven't time to take care of him. We may have to dash for France. But first, I think, London. They won't be expecting us to stay in England. Yes, London will be safer for the present."

"Better we get out of the country while we can."

"But we *can't, mon chou*. Let *me* do the thinking. It was never your forte."

She sauntered forward, plumes waving playfully atop her head, smile beaming. David went forward to meet her. "*J'ai terriblement mal à la tête*," she told him, putting a set of white fingers to her brow. "It is the music, the dancing, the wine. You will excuse? Monsieur Benson has offered to take me home. Adorable party. You will come to me tomorrow, yes? I look forward to seeing you."

191

David stood uttering a number of incoherent "but's" while Cicero turned and walked from the room, Benson at her heels. He looked around in perplexity, but chanced to remember the latter part of his orders, "If they leave the room, dash right down to the dock." This was *really* it!

He tore out at such a high speed that Biddy took the notion the place was on fire, and went after him. But he was too far in advance for her to catch him, so while all the excitement was occuring, she sniffed about for smoke, and missed it all.

By the time he got to the dock, he saw the naval vessel sailing out beyond the harbor. Sanford was already aboard *Seadog,* with his crew at their positions. "She's all yours. Go after them," he said.

"Hadn't we better notify the other shipowners? We'll want the whole fleet."

"They'll be coming right along. We want a few witnesses. Sinclair and Hopkins are on their way." Even as he spoke, a few dark figures with white triangles at their throats indicating they wore formal clothing darted down the cliff to the dock and began leaping into their yachts. David took up his post, so thrilled he couldn't quite believe it was really happening.

"Just what am I to do, exactly, sir?" he asked. It distressed him to have to say it, but there must be no slip-up.

"Just follow *Phoebe* along to Billy Ruffian and watch."

"Is Rawlins aboard?"

"Yes, with a bunch of Frenchies he's hired and stuck into those uniforms you spotted this afternoon. That was a new twist in the plan. I understood they were to wear ordinary seamen's uniforms that had already been issued to them. Keith must have suggested sending the officers as crew, so that accounts for the change of plan. Lucky you tumbled to it. You've been a big help, Boltwood."

David thought his heart would burst with joy. To be standing at the helm of *Seadog,* commanding the ship, after having been the key to figuring out the whole plan! Practically—a few details were not quite clear to him. As he looked ahead to *Phoebe,* a good deal larger than *Seadog,* faster as well on the open seas, he began to wonder whether he shouldn't have been told all this sooner. It had apparently not occurred to Sanford, sharp as he was, that with a rear admiral giving orders to a mere captain to turn over the prisoner, a faster, larger ship in which to pilot him to safety, there was very little likelihood of stopping him. Not a gun on board but his own pistol, either.

"Not to worry. I have an ace in the hold," Sanford laughed. "Just go as fast as you can, and pull alongside when *Phoebe* gets to Billy Ruffian."

"Yes, but they won't listen to *us*, Sanford."

"They'll listen to Admiral Lord Keith," Sanford answered.

"You mean he's *here*? Aboard *Seadog*!"

"In full regalia, with ten pounds of medals and ribbons on his chest lest Maitland not recognize him in the dark."

"By Jove, *I* am captaining a ship that has Admiral Lord Keith aboard!" This was a little dab of glory never even worked into the daydreams.

"Your destination—don't lose sight of it—is Billy Ruffian. We are presently tacking east," Sanford pointed out. They corrected course, and flew ahead in the black night, with never a thought of Benson and Madame.

Rawlins was of course aware that he was followed, and wondered how *Seadog* had got past the chain, but there was only one ship at all close to him. The others straggled in the rear. Maitland would take his orders right enough. Soon *Phoebe* was approaching its target.

"Ahoy!" Rawlins shouted. Maitland stepped up to the deck and called down, asking what was happening.

"Change of plans," Rawlins called back. "I am to take General Bonaparte aboard. He's being moved back to Tor Bay. Doing it late at night, to fool that fellow MacKenroth."

"I received no notification of this," Maitland objected.

"You are receiving *orders* now, sir," Rawlins called back, huffy as may be.

They shouted back and forth for a few moments, till Sinclair too was alongside to hear the nature of the discussion. Maitland looked with curiosity at the other two yachts, mentioned to Rawlins he'd order them off first, in case of trouble.

"They're with me—escorts," Rawlins explained, the whole having to be said in loud shouts, audible aboard *Seadog*. Maitland looked in consternation, to see two young gentlemen doubled with laughter at this critical moment in history. What should he do? No naval manual gave a hint as to proper procedure in such an instance. Rawlins was known to like a drink pretty well. If he handed Napoleon over to him, and the General escaped . . . Still, Rawlins was a rear admiral. The manuals were clear enough on obedience to a superior officer. He stood, undecided.

"Snap to it, sir!" Rawlins called angrily. He didn't *seem* to be drunk. Maitland turned to follow orders, then cast one last worried look to *Seadog*.

As he looked, Admiral Lord Keith, wearing his hat and the chestful of ribbons, stepped up to the deck and hollered to him. What a blessed relief it was to hear that deep, authoritative voice, easily recognized by its Scottish burr. The same voice struck Rawlins' heart to ice. He stared, and in his confusion saluted.

"Don't bring Bonaparte to the deck. Keep him in his room, and see there's a double guard posted on it," Keith commanded. "Rear Admiral Rawlins, I place you under arrest!"

Maitland stood, stunned but happy. He soon recovered his senses and began issuing orders to man all guns. Lanterns were soon bobbing up along the decks and below in the cabins of Billy Ruffian as the men went into action.

Rawlins looked at the *Seadog*, unarmed, and with a practiced eye at Billy Ruffian, lying at anchor, and calculated his chances of escape. They were not good. Certainly, Maitland would order the men to fire, but it was at least a better bet than being hauled immediately into prison. He turned to begin issuing orders of his own, but found that while he had been staring at Admiral Keith, more than half of his crew had mutinied on him, and held the other half at gunpoint. The occupants of *Seadog* noticed this as well, of course, and Admiral Keith said aside to Sanford, "A wise precaution, milord."

"My chef would have been very angry with me if he had been left out of all the excitement. The others are the regular crew of *Seadog*. They all spent a few days on the Hoo ingratiating themselves with the French element there, letting it be known their loyalties lay with Bonaparte. Nothing came of it at first, but when my chef accosted Madame personally with a plan of his own devising—highly impractical, but it served to make a contact—she hired him and he arranged to include the others. An excellent fellow, my chef. You enjoyed his hors d'oeuvre, I hope, Admiral? Losing my crew has necessitated the use of my valet and groom here on *Seadog*, but it is not their first time to haul a rope."

He looked across to *Phoebe* to see his chief exceeding his usual enthusiasm. "Good God, he's lashing Rawlins to the mast. You'd better speak to him, Keith, or he'll nail up a plank and have him walking it. We want Rawlins alive, I take it?"

David was not totally inactive during this affair. He dove right into the sea in his evening clothes, and clambered dripping up on *Phoebe's* deck by the aid of a rope thrown down, and was soon in command of the ship, feeling he could perhaps trust Admiral Lord Keith to get *Seadog* back without too much trouble.

Keith had some last instructions to call up to Maitland, having to do with raising sail and going a few miles farther from the coast for safety, then *Seadog* and *Phoebe* sailed jauntily back to Bolt Hall, while the men on the smaller yachts, Sinclair's and Hopkins', looked and wondered what they had just seen.

There were no cheering crowds awaiting them, as David had been anticipating. Nor was he allowed to lead his prisoner in shackles on to the middle of the ballroom floor to receive the ovation of the multitude. That dull old dog of a Keith, trying to keep all the triumph for himself, of course, wanted to nip right over to the naval station with Rawlins and put him in the clink. He suggested that David go into the ballroom and round up the twelve officers as quickly and quietly as possible to accompany him to Plymouth aboard *Phoebe*.

This was done. However, it could not be done too quietly in the middle of a waltz, so that he had to ask the musicians to stop playing as he had a very important announcement to make. The nature of the announcement, that all officers were required *at once* for a very important mission having to do with the safety of Bonaparte, did just raise a little fuss. People *would* ask him what had happened, how he had fallen into the sea, and as it was all over and done with, he saw no harm in saying he had uncovered an infamous plan to free Napoleon Bonaparte, using an official navy vessel, the whole a wicked plan of Rear Admiral Rawlins. But there was not the least cause for alarm, he had all under control. Had personally gone after Rawlins and caught him, and Bonaparte was under guard, so they could just get on with the dance. Somehow, a waltz seemed dull stuff after this little story was told. David had nearly as much glory as he had so often foreseen. The crowds were all over him, slapping his wet back and saying they always knew he was a long head, and by God he should be knighted like his father for this.

It was at this point that David began looking around for his father, not without a few qualms that he had done wrong to go off and take care of everything without him. And in

195

Seadog, too, instead of *Fury*. Still he did not think of Marie, and Benson and Madame. It was not till Sanford got through the mob to him to tell him Keith and the officers had taken Rawlins away that he gave a single thought to Cicero and Benson. "Where did they go?" Sanford asked him.

"They went home. Madame had a headache."

"Home? I made sure they'd be smuggled aboard *Phoebe*. It was Ireland they were to head for. I had it of my chef. You're sure . . . But of course they weren't aboard. The officers went below. It must have been the plan for Madame and Benson to go separately and meet them there. They didn't tumble to it their plan had run amok?"

"Don't see how they could. Marie was with Benson. He tried to shab off on her, but she was after him fast enough."

"Oh, hell—the chain. Benson must have gone to cut the chain."

"Well you needn't worry. The chain ain't up. We got out and back in, too, with no hitch, so she stopped him. Probably shot him. No, she didn't though," David said frowning. "Benson was back talking to Madame after Marie followed him out."

"The chain was cut," Sanford said. "Otherwise I would have had to have a man on it."

"When was it cut? It was all right when you checked it this afternoon."

"No, I cut it before that. Benson went to raise it no doubt, but . . . And Marie followed him out, you say?"

"Out the door not three steps behind him, and I haven't seen hide nor hair of her since."

"She wasn't alone I hope!"

"Yes, all alone."

"Oh, my God!" Sanford dashed from the room, to meet Biddy in the hall, carrying her portable hospital.

"Ah, Sanford, so glad to see you. Would you mind giving me that bottle of laudanum I lent you the other night. Sir Henry has a dreadful headache," she said, not wishing to let him know there was madness in the family. Certainly, Henry had run stark, staring mad to be ranting about Mr. Benson being a spy and hitting him. He had stumbled in the dark while going to check out his winch and chain. She had as yet not run across Marie, and was becoming worried about her.

"I used it all. Biddy, where's . . ."

"The whole bottle! You never gave that poor valet of yours eight ounces of laudanum. You'll kill him!"

"I spilt it," he changed his story. "Biddy, where's Marie?"

"I haven't a notion. Haven't seen her for an hour. Which is very odd now you come to mention it. Henry said . . ." She stopped, not liking to confess Henry's condition, yet becoming very worried.

"What? What did he say?"

Sanford was deeply disturbed, and she began to tumble to it that something was very much amiss. Possibly even Sir Henry had been not crazy after all, but telling the truth. "He said she was with him in the winch room when Benson attacked him. Them—both. Hit them on the head."

"But where is Marie?" Sanford repeated, his voice rising.

"I don't know. Henry staggered into the study—muttering something about Benson being a spy, and Marie going to watch him. Just see what he was about."

"Oh, Lord!" Sanford bolted back to the ballroom, to make inquiries of the servants. He learned that Madame and Benson had left, but no one knew anything about Marie. She had not been seen to leave. Perhaps she had the headache, like Madame. Servants were sent scurrying upstairs to her room, all over the house, then finally it was clear she was gone. He wondered if she had been fool enough to go after Benson on horseback.

David was at his side when word came back from the stable that her mount was gone. "Oh well if she's gone to spy on them, I know where she is. Come, I'll take you, Ade," David offered. He still wore his wet suit. Sanford's shirt, too, was clinging to his back with perspiration. He had thought the worst of it was over, but began to understand that there might be much worse yet ahead, if she had fallen into the hands of Cicero.

21

By the time Marie returned to consciousness, her father was already sitting up and rubbing his aching head. "The devil has raised our chain!" Sir Henry railed. That was his major concern. They could see nothing, not even each other, but there was a feeling in the place of the culprit being gone. Sir Henry struggled to his feet, stumbled to the winches, and felt with his fingers the load of chain on the wheels. He turned the wheel, and it spun too freely.

"Cut! The chain has been sabotaged!" was his next announcement. He began to wonder whether this were a good or bad thing. If it meant the flotilla had been allowed to get out, it was good. On the other hand he had only Marie's word for it that the flotilla had been required. Likely Boney had been sneaked up the estuary, as Benson had cut the chain.

He must get to his lookout platform. Together he and Marie felt their way to the stairway, with the girl receiving an unjust tongue-lashing the whole way for her part in the affair. On the rampart they saw *Phoebe* making her way out to sea, with *Seadog* at her heels, and the other two yachts following hard.

"Now what can this mean? Humph. Sanford is on to them. He has had Rawlins give chase. Wouldn't you know it would be Sinclair he asked to go along! Never a sign of *Fury* having left the dock, you will notice. Where is David during all this? Well, Bonaparte will not break away with Rawlins on hand." He wished to take command at home, to let his guests know he was right at the thick of things, but was in such confusion that he succumbed to a migraine instead, planning to center his own heroics around the attack in the dark, guarding the Bolt chain. David was sent for, but could not be found, so he let Biddy cosset him while he tried to figure out his story.

David had informed Marie that Benson and Madame were evildoers, but the name Rawlins had not arisen in their brief talk, and she was as confused as her father. But she still had the job of watching Benson, and she told her father she would just tidy her hair and go to try to discover if he had left the house, and where he had gone. He'd have to leave Bolt Hall, but he might be packing his belongings.

She discovered easily enough he had gone with Madame. They had made no secret of their departure. Neither Sanford nor David could she find, and she knew that if she told her father what she had in mind to do he would prevent her, so she decided to go alone to follow Benson. She intended no more than following, just roll the wheelbarrow to the window to see if they were at Madame's cottage, waiting for Boney, then she would dash back to Bolt Hall to tell Sanford where to find them. She threw a dark pelisse over her white ballgown and went at a fast pace down the road, concealing her mount again at the orchard across the road. Lights were burning in every room of the place—either a clever ruse to pretend they were within, or else indicating frenzied activity. She slipped around to the rear, rolled the barrow to the window and crawled up. She saw through the window that Madame and Benson were there, alone, with a trunk in the middle of the floor, tossing things into it with haste, obviously preparing an instant departure. It was well she had come, but she felt she ought to do more than be able to say "They've left. They drove away," when she saw Sanford again. He would expect her to tell him where they had gone. For all she knew, Bonaparte might even now have got free, and it was of the utmost importance to know his destination. She was enough of a Boltwood to know there would be glory in this for herself, but it was not the glory that led her on. She wished to impress Lord Sanford. He admired Madame, a clever spy, and he would admire herself more if she outwitted Madame.

She strained her ears against the glass, but not so much as a single sound came through. Suddenly Madame threw up her hands and ran from the room, excited about something. When she returned, she carried a wooden box, a jewelry box possibly. The sapphires, not stolen at all, but hidden for some reason? Benson took the box from her fingers, and he was laughing, lifting up gold coins.

The money—the chest of ten thousand pounds! Was this it? Such a small chest? Impossible. Madame snatched it back, chatting all the while. Oh if only she could hear them! She leaned closer still to the window, the wheelbarrow jiggling precariously beneath her. She made a snatch at the window ledge, bumping her head lightly against the glass as she moved. It was not a loud noise, but it was enough. She was seen. Both heads turned towards her in alarm—the fingers pointed, then in a flash Benson was ordered out after her. She realized he was giving chase, and jumped down from her perch. Wearing a long, flounced gown, she caught her toe in its ruffle as she jumped, and went hurtling onto the ground. She was not hurt, but the delay in disentangling her feet took up the critical few seconds that allowed Benson to see the direction of her flight. He was dashing after her, into the night. She was young, long-limbed and hadn't far to go to reach her mount, but still she felt Benson gaining on her. Faster and faster she ran, her heart pounding dry in her

199

throat. She'd never get mounted and away before he got her. Have to untie the mare's rope looped around a tree.

It was soon over. He grabbed first ahold of her flying pelisse; that pulled her to a stop, then had her by the arms, twisting them cruelly behind her back. "You got in my way for the last time, bitch!" he said. "Walk!" He pushed her forward, towards Madame's cottage. His anger at losing out on the reward turned him to pure venom. "I suppose you've known all along what my game is. Been working hand in glove with that cold bastard, Sanford. I should have done you in proper when I had the chance. Well, you mǎy have cost me a hundred thousand pounds this night, but you'll pay dearly for it. And so will that crazy old coot of a father."

The change in his manner was so remarkable that she didn't know how to talk to this barbarian. But his words at least made sense. He meant to hurt her, possibly kill her. She was shoved across the road, around to the back of the cottage and into the saloon, where Madame stood with her pelisse and bonnet on, ready to leave.

"Everett, what is this? Why do you bring the girl here?" Madame asked in perplexity, but in a polite tone, still wearing the pose of a friend of Miss Boltwood. She had expected Benson to knock her out and leave her outside while they escaped.

"Shall I kill her or lock her up in the basement?" Benson asked, not bothering with any civility.

Madame glared at him, furious, but as he had bungled it, as usual, she soon directed her thoughts in a different direction. Her blue eyes narrowed, and an extremely crafty expression settled on her plump features. "We'll take her with us," she said.

"What, drag this noisy wench along to London!"

"*Tais-toi*!" Madame commanded sharply. Fool of a man! Why must he blurt out their destination. "We are not going to London, *chéri*."

"Where then?" Benson asked.

"We'll discuss it later. She won't be so noisy when you get through with her, Everett."

"Yes, but why do you—Oh! You mean to kid . . ."

"*Un enlèvement*," Madame interrupted.

"I speak French, Madame," Marie said. "You will have some difficulty carrying me against my will to France." She put on a greater show of courage than she was feeling, hoping to stall for time and perhaps discover their plans.

"We're not going to France yet," Benson said.

"*Ferme le bec!*" Madame shouted angrily, and Benson obediently closed his beak. "Sanford won't like it if we beat her. Better . . ."

"Hah *He* won't like it! How do you think I liked having him make up to my wife?"

"Your *wife!*" Marie gasped.

"You didn't think I really wanted *you*, you silly country bumpkin," he scorned. Madame preened, a hand to her blond curls and a supercilious smile on her cheeks.

"I think Mademoiselle wants a little something to *relax* her for the trip, *chéri*," Madame said in meaningful accents. "A glass of wine, *peut-être*, to calm her nerves."

"Excellent!" Benson said, and ran for the decanter, while Madame fumbled in her reticule for a bottle of colorless liquid. He poured a hefty wallop of the "relaxing" agent into the wine and gave it to Madame.

"Hold her hands," Madame said. Benson walked around behind her, again gripping her arms in a painful hold behind her back, while Madame held the glass to her lips. Marie closed her lips tightly and jerked her head away. She mustn't drink it. Unconscious, they could do anything to her. Take her to France, or kill her if it seemed easier. She was very frightened, praying for rescue. Surely she had been missed by now! Someone would come after her!

A hand, Madame's, came across her cheek with a hard smack. "Better do it the easy way, miss," she said. "A pity to have to mar that platter face of yours. It is bad enough as it is. Insipid! That is what Lord Sanford thinks of you. Did you know that. *La fermière insipide* he calls you."

"Jealous, Madame? Would you like to hear what he calls *you*?" Marie shot back.

"Never mind the cat fight. Get it into her," Benson said impatiently.

Marie held her lips clenched. Madame set aside the wine with an angry grunt, took her by the hair and pulled her head back, held her nose till she was forced to open her mouth for a gulp of air, then swiftly let go of the hair to reach for the wine. The edge of the glass was between her teeth, while she wriggled desperately to avoid swallowing it. At least half of it was running down her chin and neck. Then, with success so close, Benson put his arms around her body, holding her back taut against him to prevent her struggling, while Madame tried to finish the job. In the midst of this scene of kicking feet, writhing bodies and muffled grunts of outrage, the front knocker sounded.

"Dammit, who can that be?" Benson asked, alarmed.

Madame considered it for a split second, then took her decision. "I'll go and won't let anyone in if I can help it. It might be the puppy. He was concerned for my headache. I'll get rid of him."

"It might be the police," Benson cautioned her, his voice tense with worry.

"But what if it is, *mon cher*?" Madame asked. "What have *we* done? They cannot know the whole yet. It is no crime to have a headache, even at Sir Henry's ball. Better take her across the hall in case I have to let someone into the saloon. For God's sake, keep her quiet." As she spoke, she closed the lid of the trunk and pushed it behind the door, while Benson dragged Marie across the hall into a small room and closed the door behind him. Madame remembered in all the confusion to pick up her handkerchief, and with it trailing from her fingers, her other hand to her head, she walked to the front door.

It seemed Madame was correct in her guess. Voices trailing from the door reached Marie's eager ears. "Madame!" she heard David say, "the strangest thing has happened. Marie has vanished. Just disappeared out of the house. She wouldn't have said anything to you?"

"*Oh mon Dieu*! This is terrible," Madame replied. "Disappeared? But no, she said nothing to me. I have no idea . . . She was there when I left, I think? Yes, surely I remember seeing her, dancing with an officer."

"No, she was last seen with Benson," David pointed out.

"But Benson brought me home. Did he go back? Perhaps *he* could tell you."

"No, Benson's gone, too. That's the awful thing about it. We fear they've run away together," David said, sounding very worried.

Listening through the closed door, Marie knew that if she didn't act now, if Madame got David to believe her story, she was in for a very bad ordeal, worse than it had been thus far. She wondered that David had come alone. What had happened to Sanford? No matter, it was now or never. Benson held her against him in an iron grip, one hand firmly clamped against her mouth, the other holding her around the waist, with her back to him. She was nearly powerless, but if she could get free long enough for one loud shout it would be

202

enough. She took a deep breath, jerked her head away to get one of Benson's fingers between her teeth and bite down on it with all her strength, while simultaneously lifting one foot to give him a kick in the shins with her heel. The hand at the mouth came away, and she screamed, "David! David, I'm here!"

To her amazement, David seemed not to have heard. She heard him talking on, asking Madame more pointless questions. Before she had time to shout again, Benson had sworn off a stream of low curses and raised his hand to strike her a blow across the face. Madame's sharp slap was but a love tap compared to this. The full force of a grown man's strength was in it. It sent her reeling against a table. She had never been struck by a man before, hardly ever by a woman, though it was not unknown for Biddy to give her a cuff when she was younger. To see a man sink so low, and hit so hard, shocked her.

Before she recovered from her shock, a greater one occurred. The window exploded; with no warning whatsoever a black form came hurtling through it. Benson as well as herself was momentarily startled into immobility, but the man without an instant's hesitation took a leap at Benson. It was Sanford, with such a fierce expression on his face Marie was half afraid of him, even while she drooped with relief. Caught off guard, Benson was sent flying against the wall as a fist hit his jaw. He had soon recovered himself and raised his own fists for battle. Marie was as innocent of seeing grown men fight in earnest as she was of being struck. She stood mesmerized as they danced around, raining incredibly hard blows on each other. There was the ugly sound of flesh hitting flesh and bone—a dull *whuck* of a sound. It was both fascinating and revolting at once. They didn't say a word, either. Just glared as if they'd be happy to kill each other. She could feel the hatred between them in the air. The strangeness of it, combined with her fatigue and shock, robbed her of half her faculties. For full two minutes she didn't think to lend Sanford a hand. But really, it was not at all necessary. Had he been getting the worst of it, no doubt it would have occurred to her. At length she tore her eyes from the bloody spectacle long enough to discover a weapon—a rather ugly but large and heavy vase. Benson was already sinking to the floor, his face battered, but she hit him across the side of the head for good measure.

Sanford, panting and with a welt across his chin, stepped

over the body that was now on the floor between them, still looking fiercely murderous. "You bloody fool!" he shouted at her, just before he pulled her into his arms. She was ready to retaliate for this injustice, but the manner in which he clutched her to him, tightly and possessively, removed any odium from his description. After nearly squeezing the breath out of her, he held her back and looked at her, touching her red cheek with his finger. She knew from his eyes he was going to kiss her, but she didn't expect he would do it so forcefully. The half smile on his lips led her to expect a gentle, tender embrace. She awaited it breathlessly, but he was in no gentle mood. He kissed her very roughly, indeed, as though it were a penalty he was exacting for her being a bloody fool. He kissed her as hard as he had been hitting Benson, with the same hot blood and violence. The embrace left her as shocked as the blow. Then he pulled her head on to his shoulder and said in a shaking voice, "If I didn't love you so much I'd beat you. If I had the strength, I would, anyway. What possessed you to come charging into the lion's den all by yourself?"

"Oh," she answered, smiling and undismayed by his ill manners when she discovered their cause to be anxiety, "but if I had told Papa I was coming, he wouldn't have let me."

"Then he would have shown more sense than he usually does." He cocked an ear to the door, to hear Madame and David rushing towards it. He opened it and bowed formally. "Welcome to my parlor, et cetera. Do come in, Madame. You will want to try your hand at rallying Benson around to his senses. Don't be in any hurry, or I will have to knock him out again." Madame flew to Benson and knelt on the floor beside him, while David smiled broadly.

"I see everything went all right. How'd you get in, Ade? When I went around to the front door to distract them, you were still at the other window."

"I saw Benson dragging Marie out the door and ran to the other side of the house, to see where he was taking her. He was just beginning to manhandle her when I got here. I'm afraid I didn't wait to clamber down and go to the door. I came through the window. However, it is *my* house, in a manner of speaking."

"Drew his cork, eh?" David asked, stepping closer to the prostrate body to admire its condition. "What are we to do with them? Shall we take them into town, or send the constable after them?"

"You go into Plymouth and bring the constable. Marie and I will stay here and stand guard. I don't think Benson will be going anywhere for an hour or so. If he comes to, I'll stick him in a closet. Better hurry. Marie is eager to get home, I should think. She is likely missed already."

"He needs help," Madame told them, looking up.

"Give it to him then," Sanford replied. "We'll go into the next room and keep an eye on the luggage, to see you don't develop wanderlust and sheer off on us." He turned to Marie. "Did you happen to see through the window what they did with the loot?"

"There's a little wooden box of gold in the trunk."

"Fine. We'll guard it. We needn't fear Madame will dash off without her gold, whatever about her husband." He called to David, just leaving. "Turn the nags in the stable loose, just in case Madame becomes restless."

For a month, David had been wholeheartedly infatuated with Madame. He steeled his heart to do his painful duty, looking to where she leaned over Benson. Crouched over, worried and frowning, she looked like an ugly, old woman. "Good idea," he answered, and went off to do it. He felt disillusioned, a little sad, and infinitely wiser in the ways of designing women.

With a great air of offended dignity, Madame began rounding up supplies to tender care to her husband, while Sanford went with Marie across the hall, leaving both doors open to allow a view of the pair. He pulled a pistol out of his jacket and showed it to Madame Monet. "I don't particularly want to kill either of you, but then I don't feel like any more running tonight, either. Don't tempt me."

22

Madame's mind appeared to be not on escaping, but saving her husband's life. She scurried about, bringing bandages and medications, while the other two sat talking, keeping a close eye on the door. "We could use Biddy," Sanford said.

"She will have plenty to do patching you up when we get home. Your chin is purple."

"Your cheek is red. Did he do more than cuff your cheek?"

"No, and I bit him. I hope he catches hydrophobia."

"I hope he don't. I wouldn't want to discover you're rabid."

"What happened to Napoleon? He didn't get away?"

"No, David prevented it."

"Was it David who cut the chain then, and let Rawlins' ship get out? We made sure Benson had done it for some reason."

"No, I cut the chain myself this morning. It was Rawlins who went to free him, using the *Phoebe* and a bunch of Frenchies decked out in official naval uniforms. David went after them in *Seadog*."

"Rawlins! You mean he is one of *them!*"

"Afraid so. He has been disenchanted with the navy for some time. He did not advance so far nor so fast as he felt he should. He is a little prone to brandy, however, and after his demotion he was ready for any revenge. But you were aware of that—you gave me the clue the first day I met him. Inquiries indicated he was badly dipped, therefore open to bribery. Madame knew it, of course. She set herself on to him, to seduce him from the path of duty. I had hoped that might prove a weak link in their chain—jealousy, you know, if I could make Benson think there was an affair going on between them, but they were all too deep into it by then."

"I think he *did* know. One night when David and I were here, Benson was ragging the life out of the pair of them, shaking his finger under Madame's nose. I knew then there was something between those two."

He regarded her askance. "David told me he brought you here with him. Scatterbrained thing to do, but *not* so bad as your coming here *alone*, milady! That was downright foolish, and unnecessary as well."

"It was not! They would have got clean away if I hadn't wasted so much of their time, and have been gone by the time anyone came after them."

"They wouldn't have got far."

"There's gratitude for you! I, risking my neck. They were going to kidnap me, you know, and make you—Papa pay a fat ransom for me."

"Did they quote a price? I'd like to have an inkling what you're considered worth on the open market."

"There was talk of a hundred thousand pounds!" she answered grandly.

"Over-valued," was his damping reply. "One could pick up a deposed emperor for that sum."

"I realize I don't rate so high in your estimation as that fat French strumpet, but then I always had an *odd notion of your preference in females*."

"That one struck at the quick, I see. But I only prefer French strumpets for business. For a wife one must naturally select and appear to be content with a well-bred prude. A nice wholesome country wench will do as well as any."

"You omit one of my advantages. Do you not prefer your country wench insipid as well as wholesome?"

"It is a velleity, merely. I do not insist on insipidity. And don't think I am going to get it, either," he added, regarding her sparkling eyes with a lazy smile.

"Let us count the money while we wait," she suggested. "There is nothing like ten thousand pounds there. It is only a small box."

"Ten thousand? No, no, I have that at Bolt Hall. That money you speak of is from the sale of Madame's sapphires. Under five hundred—she got four-fifty for them." He arose and walked to the trunk, pulling it out from behind the door. "They were required to raise some emergency blunt when I got their big cache. It was the disposing of the sapphires that caused Madame to miss our little water party the other day."

"Where did you find the money? David and I looked all over for it."

"Under Benson's instructions. He was careful to lead you away from it. It was in the bottom of the big chain box in the winch room. Not even locked, but pretty safe for all that. No one was likely to haul out that great heavy chain. Sir Henry told me David's story about the money. I thought it was moonshine at first, but after scrutinizing Benson a while, I noticed he spent an inordinate amount of time in the winch room, and a good search one night told me why. Answered a few other questions that had been plaguing me, too. I had no reason to suspect Benson when I came. He was some connection of your mother's, and had a right to be there. I knew from London that Madame was in town, and she of course was my chief suspect. She had caused trouble before, in Vienna. Benson over-reacted to her from the start. The day we all lunched together at the inn he was at considerable pains to ignore her—not his customary reaction to ladies of her sort."

"Nor anyone else's, apparently."

"It was ordained on high that men be attracted to pretty women. I put it right in the Almighty's dish, you see, where you daren't disagree with me. Benson was a neighbor of mine, and I was extremely curious to hear why he had sold up Oakhurst, with no rumors of his being so deeply in debt. I got busy with my pen. Inquiries in Devonshire discovered that it was not even mortgaged, and the sum obtained for it was ten thousand. That interesting figure already featuring in the case, I then began to look at him with heightened suspicion. Then of course when I bumped into him at Bolt's Point pulling in a message from Billy Ruffian my little suspicions took on a stronger coloring. The message itself was uninteresting enough. I had hoped for a firm date or means of rescue, but it was only a request to know what chances MacKenroth's ploy had of succeeding. It was our old friend Hazy, of course, who warned me to be on the lookout for messages coming and going. It was obvious flags couldn't be used, and communications between Billy Ruffian and naval vessels were so well attended, with Boney carefully below-deck, that nothing could be done then. It was of course a written message coming ashore by a bribed seaman. The Point, with its telescope, seemed a nice private spot for it. Anyway, knowing that Benson had all his gold concealed on the premises induced me to nose around till I found it, and I put it away for safekeeping."

"Where?"

"I took it to Sinclair's aboard *Seadog*."

"So *that's* why you went back there, to watch it, and not to gather leeches. Do tell me, is that how Benson got his black eye, too, trying to get it back?"

"No, no, you will recall he was kicked by a jackass."

"A jackass named Lord Sanford?"

"I am not so hard on myself. It was Jean Valet who had the bruised knuckles, you will recall."

"And that's why Rawlins went down there the next day, snooping around *Seadog*. I suppose it was all a hum that you had no crewmen aboard your yacht guarding the gold."

"No, there was no gold there to guard by that time. Once I knew he had tumbled to where I had it, it had to be moved."

"What a well-traveled box of gold it is, to be sure! What was its next resting place?"

He opened his mouth to tell her, then shut it again, rather quickly. "Where I didn't think Benson would be likely to look for it."

"How clever of you not to hide it under your bed. *Obviously* you hid it where he wasn't likely to find it, but *where* exactly? It wasn't in your room or your valet's."

"No, it wasn't there. Er, tell me, when did you get around to checking Belhomme's towels?"

"David and Benson did it, but where was the money?"

"I might tell you someday, after we are safely away from Bolt Hall. I don't think my hiding place would have universal approval, though really it wasn't the *chest* that did the damage."

"What damage? Adrian, tell me at once! Was that how you broke the chain, hiding the money?"

"Certainly not! That was no accident. Took me half an hour of filing to get through that damned chain. I made sure David would see me, right across the bay at the dock, moving the yachts about."

"Much he would have cared. He would have helped you, for he had realized by then, I think, that you were the real spy. I don't see why you couldn't have *told* us, and let us help you."

"You were a better help not knowing. Oh, both full to the brim of good intentions, but not discreet, my dear. Not at all discreet." He waggled a finger under her nose. "You had already informed Benson indirectly that London had sent down an agent, and of course he knew I was it, but I fear my plans would have had a poor chance of remaining unknown had I divulged them to you and David. What puzzles *me* considerably is how you took the notion Benson was the one sent, when *he* had the reason of being family, and *I* came with no other excuse than being a godson of a business associate of Sir Henry."

"Benson came first—had already arrived when David overheard the men talking beneath his balcony, so we *assumed* . . . And once you get a notion like that in your head, you know, everything seems to support it."

"Benson was at pains to support it, of course."

"I wonder my father let him stay on once you told him he had lost Oakhurst."

"He was wanting to show him the door, but I told him—

209

asked him to keep him on. Easier to keep an eye on him when he was right under my nose."

"I suppose if the truth were known, you were afraid he'd move in with his wife and cut you out. Just what did you hope to gain from setting Madame up in a love nest, other than love, of course?"

"I had various reasons for doing it—none of which involved love, incidentally. I knew she was Cicero, and hoped to con her into thinking I would help her. I professed myself ankle-deep in admiration for Boney, but that was no good. She actually *does* hate him, I think, and is only in it for the money. Then, of course, there was the possibility my attentions would cause her to lose her head, and utter some revealing statements regarding her activities. Even knowing when she would *not* be home to receive my gallantries might have been useful, though in fact Benson got stuck with all the leg-work, and she was there with open arms, night and day. God, what a bore! And didn't give away a useful word, either. As sly as a diplomat."

"One marvels at your pertinacity in returning night and day, considering how futile and boring the job was."

"Mostly day. I had a number of little activities I had no wish to publicize chez Bolt Hall. I had the messages to check for at night, along with some shoulder-rubbing with what Biddy chooses to call hedgebirds in the city, to discover what groups my assistants—valet, groom, crew of *Seadog* et al—should make up to in order to make contact with Madame. All was not fun and games at the cottage."

"No, indeed, some of the fun and games occurred in the orchard, and don't let on you were bored there."

"I wasn't, once I perceived your arrival. That added a very welcome dash to the proceedings. You arrived just in time to save me the expense of replacing *les saphirs Monet*. She was hinting I might like to buy them, it being the plan that they would be a parting gift, of course, to herself."

"Hinting in *French*, I presume?"

"In every language but English. Later she confessed their loss, as she would have to sell them, and thus appear without them at the ball after all the wonderful talk about them. All useful information to have. There was just a little doubt that my getting their money away from them would bring proceedings to a halt. Not cheap, you know, to bribe a crew to man the ship for them, and arrange to conceal an easily-recognized General in Ireland for a month or so, till they

210

could get him smuggled out to America. Damned expensive, but their using a naval vessel free of expense helped in the bookkeeping. The four-fifty from the sapphires might have done it. When Benson sold up Oakhurst he had counted on having to buy a ship, I suppose. Bribing Rawlins must have been nearly as expensive. Rawlins was in it up to his ego by the time I got their loot, however, and must have agreed to wait and be paid out of the prize money."

"Was there actually such a sum offered?"

"Hazy said so, and he would certainly know. Probably put up some of the blunt himself. But I am not working on that end. The Admiralty has more than one agent."

"Did you really agree with Hazy that the habeas corpus was a good thing?"

"Now, love, you of all people, who entered and searched my room, must know I dashed off no letters to the *Morning Chronicle*. It would be a wretched thing. But I am a Whig, with just a narrow stripe of Tory, picked up from my godfather no doubt, on the subject of Napoleon Bonaparte. I want him stashed away good and safe. I had to express some admiration for him to make myself acceptable to Hazy and find out what he was up to. All part of my orders. Holland, a friend, was kind enough to drop him a line I was coming and would call on him."

"But then did you know all along Rawlins meant to steal a naval vessel and go out to Billy Ruffian?"

"No, not at first. Well, Cicero herself didn't know it at that point. The idea first came up the day I introduced Benson to Rawlins. Of course they were already known to each other— had met at Bolt Hall the night David saw those much-discussed brass buttons, I should think. Madame must have sent Rawlins along. She would have been chummying up to him sooner. Wide awake on all suits, Cicero. David mentioned that damnable idea of Boney masquerading as a seaman and I foolishly said it was either that or a whole crew of Frenchies masquerading as British sailors. I believe that's when the idea first occurred to them. I think it would have been easier to have just one person pose as Boney, but I made Rawlins pass along that item to Maitland. He didn't want to do it, either. That was their first plan, certainly. My valet and groom were busy snooping around, and let me know Rawlins was on close terms with Madame. I didn't realize there was love-making in it till you and David told me."

"Certainly that is what Benson was shaking his finger under her nose about. I knew he was jealous."

"No doubt, but they patched it up and that is when the new plan began to emerge. With their ten thousand gone, their alternatives were severely limited. I think Rawlins was originally sucked in to do no more than resign his commission and captain a bought or hired ship for them. In for a penny, in for a pound, however. It was either the extremely bold scheme of using *Phoebe*, or stealing another ten thousand, which is not done in the batting of an eyelash. Now it would not be easy in the normal course of proceedings for Rawlins to get an excuse to take a ship out and dock it in some out-of-the-way spot to allow a change of crew to take place. When we heard that he was to bring a ship to Bolt Hall for the ball, that was obviously when the thing was to be done. Time was running very short."

"Well you are a great deal more stupid than I ever thought!" Marie told him bluntly. "You had only to leave the chain in one piece, and raise it when Rawlins left the ball to go to *Phoebe*."

"So I had, wizard, but it is not against the law for a rear admiral to go onto a ship under his command, or even to take it out in the harbor. No, we had to catch him actually making the attempt to free Bonaparte. We had to let him out and it was to be the job of one of them, Benson, as it turned out, to then raise the chain to keep the rest of us in."

"How did David stop him, with only your *Seadog*—a smaller ship, and with no official status? Maitland must have taken orders from Rawlins."

"No, he preferred to take his orders from Admiral Lord Keith, who happened to be aboard *Seadog* tonight."

"How convenient!" she said with a knowing look.

"He was happy to have such a good hiding place, with MacKenroth beating the bushes looking for him."

"And that's why Benson professed such interest in keeping the chain preserved."

"He was in favor of it even before the plan was devised. But I think he only said so at that point to ingratiate himself with your father. He knew once *I* turned up that his losing Oakhurst was bound to arise, and wished to be on the old boy's good side."

"I wonder why he decided to come to us at all. Why did he not just go to the inn, like Madame?"

"The rooms were full. Unless he was ready to announce

his marriage, he could not very well have bunked in with her. She must have known she would be watched. A scarlet past, you must know. Her chase of Sir Henry precedes Benson's arrival by some time. Likely she had an eye on *Fury* from the start, or one of the yachts there. In any case, Bolt Hall was certainly *the* place to be—plans, news, and ships—all of interest to Madame. When she failed to gain entry, she put Benson up to it. His coming as a suitor to your hand was a ruse. I didn't actually know about the marriage till I had written London he was here, and asked them to check him out for me. But I had begun taking objection to his courting you even before that time."

"When did you begin taking objection?" she asked with interest.

"Along about the time you knocked me off the door at Steele's barn—very early on in the game, you see. Nothing attracts a perverse gentleman like poor treatment. Or maybe it was when you so generously offered to run for the makings of the posset. No, really I think upon reconsidering that it was the evening I saw you two in the rose garden, all oblivious to the storm gathering, but very much aware of each other. Jealousy is another strong inducement, of course. It is at that point the attraction became bothersome, in any case."

She blushed at the memory, but rushed in to defend herself. "I didn't know he was married!"

"*He* knew it. I'm not blaming you. He is not at all a bad looking chap, and as a connection—tenuous I hope?—of your family, there was no reason you should mistrust him."

"He is bad looking," Marie decided. "With that ugly old mole. You're sure he's not the one who is Cicero? Why should she call herself Cicero? She has no wart or mole."

"She's Cicero. She has a wart actually, but not on her nose."

"Where is it?" Marie asked, instantly suspicious.

"On her—ankle. I happened to see it once she was climbing into my carriage.

"You're lying!" she charged, looking at him closely.

"Maybe it was her wrist."

"Adrian! Tell me the truth."

"You won't like it," he cautioned.

"Tell me *at once!*"

"Oh, very well then, she *said* she has one on her knee. Naturally, I haven't seen it."

"You're still lying!" she declared, but was not quite ready

to push the wart any higher. "And another thing, why were you so *unpleasant* to everyone when you first arrived?"

"Unpleasant?" he asked, offended. "No, merely I had to show Sir Henry who was boss. He proved incapable of learning, however."

"That was no excuse for being on your high ropes with David and me."

"I refrained from exerting my dangerous charms so I wouldn't have David tagging at my heels, getting in my way. I could see Benson wished him at Jericho, and I was afraid you'd go throwing your cap at me."

"You have the gall to sit there and tell me you thought yourself so irresistible I'd be running after you! You needn't have worried."

"I know. You have very bad taste. As soon as I saw you preferred Benson, I felt it permissible to let some small measure of my natural . . ." He intercepted a look of animosity and came to a halt. "My natural character emerge," he finished humbly.

"Let me tell you, your natural character is such that no woman with a pittance of mind would wipe her feet on you."

"Nor on anyone else, surely? But you mean just the opposite from what you say, very likely. Women so often do."

David was soon back with the constable, and the others were free to leave. As they went to retrieve their mounts, David said, "I must cook up some story to Papa about the chain, Ade. He won't like your having cut it."

"Let me handle it. There are many things about this night's proceedings he won't like, but he'll like Boney's not being rescued well enough, and if we can lay it at his door, he'll swallow the rest."

"How can we do that? He was knocked cold through it all."

"We shall contrive. Fear not."

"The thing *I* can't understand," David went on, "is why Papa lied to me. And why didn't he let you cut the chain, anyway, knowing you was an official spy?"

"Agent is actually the word we use," Adrian said with a smile that went undetected in the darkness. "As to not telling you and not allowing me to cut the chain, it all amounts to the same thing. Had he told you who I was, you would have put pressure to bear on him to give in, and that was the one thing he would not allow. The Bolt Hall chain has stood since 1380, guarding . . ."

"Yes, I know the lecture by heart," David reminded him, to avoid hearing it again, "but I still think he should have told me. I suspected, of course, right from the start. Asked him outright once, and he said no. Said I shouldn't help you . . . Well, I daresay that's what he was afraid of, all right," David admitted.

"I shall undo the damage as soon as possible. Make sure the chain's back in working order to withstand the next invasion before I leave."

"Dash it, you ain't going to be leaving soon, are you, Ade?" David asked. He felt there was still much glory to be wrung from having an agent friend. He looked forward to long talks, preferably late at night, when he would be introduced, over champagne, to the arcana of becoming an agent, which ordinary Johnnie Trots would be calling a spy. He was eager to try his hand at this métier.

"Are you not looking forward to coming to Wight with us?" Sanford asked, to remind him of this treat.

"Yes, certainly, but we'll be heroes here for a week or so. No point in passing up all the fun, now we've had the work and danger of it all."

"We'll wait a few days till the cream of the glory runs thin, but people soon forget, David. I am eager to get to Wight. Mama is waiting for those leeches."

23

By the time they got back to Bolt Hall, refreshed their toilettes and went belowstairs, the ball had turned from a dance to a general state of pandemonium. There was no pretense at music or dancing, but clusters of guests standing in circles asking questions of each other, with some of the more inventive fabricating answers out of thin air. There was not a single Boltwood in the room at this most prestigious ball ever tossed. David was known to be the real source of information, and his arrival was treated with all the yelling, shouting and questions he could wish.

With an air of bestowing a favor on loyal subjects, he

raised his hands, requesting silence, that he might explain the state of affairs to everyone. One of the servants ran to Biddy and Sir Henry to report that the family and Sanford were back, and Sir Henry, leaning on Biddy's arm and on the blackthorn stick hobbled to the ballroom to learn like the others what had happened. He was pleased to see it was David, a Boltwood, who was the center of attention, and not Lord Sanford, as he had feared. He was even more charmed when David was led to the bandstand to allow one and all to hear and see him. What a fine figure the lad had, shoulders like the Tower of London, and how modestly he conducted himself in all his glory. A very modest smile on his face.

"Now, I know you're all curious to hear what happened, and I'll tell you all about it," he began. "The thing is, there was a plan to free Bonaparte tonight, and it was thwarted." Sir Henry felt there was just a little more modesty than he could like in this speech. "It was thwarted" should better have been "I" or at least "we" thwarted it. Then, too, it was *Seadog* and not *Fury* that had done the thwarting. David's next speech threw him into complete frustration. "Lord Sanford discovered . . ." he began.

Sir Henry elbowed his way forward, using the blackthorn stick without concern for protruding hips or limbs. "Make way. Make way!" he commanded in a peremptory voice. Way was made, and soon he stood beside his son on the platform, without a single word to say. What had happened? He had no idea, but whatever it was, it was over and done. "There is no need to alarm yourselves. Bolt Hall has once again served its duty in defending England. Napoleon has not been got off *Bellerophon*, and you may go on with the dance," he finished up, to forestall bothersome questions. Still, it did not serve the purpose. People would inquire who had tried to rescue Napoleon, and who had discovered it, and how it had been prevented.

"It was this way," Sir Henry said, improvising wildly. "I discovered the plan, and went to the winch room to protect the Bolt chain from sabotage. I was attacked by one of the plotters, and this bandage I wear on my head gives you an idea what occurred."

Ripples of still unanswered questions ran through the room, swelling in volume as they circulated. The word "who" was most often heard. "Rawlins. Rear Admiral Rawlins is your traitor," Sir Henry announced. He had learned this much from Sinclair and Hopkins.

Then he walked away and left his son to fill in the few omitted details. David made such a mishmash of this, turning so often to Lord Sanford, that eventually Sanford arose and spoke very briefly.

"As I understand it, Sir Henry and Mr. David Boltwood, working with the Admiralty from London, discovered a plan to free Bonaparte. In order to outwit the plotters, Sir Henry Boltwood gave the order that the chain be cut. It was a hard decision to take, the Bolt chain having stood guard on England's shore since 1380, but a safeguard can operate in more than one way. Sir Henry wished the *Phoebe* to be allowed to leave the harbor and make its attempt, that the plotters be caught actually pursuing their aim. It was the plan of the outlaws that the Bolt chain be raised to prevent any rescue operation being launched, and with this fact known to him, Sir Henry had his chain cut, to outwit them. David Boltwood, with the help of his neighbors, gave chase and prevented the rescue. Shall we give three cheers for the Boltwoods?"

Amidst the lusty ringing of "hip hip hooray," Sir Henry smiled in satisfaction. Not a word of Admiral Lord Keith, not a word of *Seadog*, and discreetly, no mention of Mr. Benson, Sir Henry's wife's connection. He was near to being in perfect charity with Sanford. There was but one link missing in the chain to prevent it, and he was fast coming to accept that broken link.

The question period that followed was sufficiently confusing that no real addition of fact was necessary. Sir Henry described in detail how he had been attacked in the dark in the winch room, but did not feel it necessary to reveal Marie had been so foolish as to expose herself. A woman, after all, she wouldn't want the scandal of being a heroine attached to herself. When some pesky person, Sinclair, to be sure, asked why he had gone to the chain, knowing it was already cut, he said wisely, "They didn't know that, and it was a chance to eliminate one of them." The impertinent question, "Which one of them was it?" was fobbed off with the answer, "One of the ringleaders." Then he had the inspiration of serving more food, to put a stop to conjecture till he had had a good nose with Sanford.

Biddy was desperate to provide yet another meal, with every dish and glass in the house dirty, and the food reduced to crumbs. It was a very indifferent repast, but gave Sir Henry an opportunity to learn from Sanford that Madame and Benson had been arrested. He heard with equanimity as well that the agent preferred always to remain in the background as much as possible. David heard it with less equanimity, but as he was already so well to the fore in this story, he accepted stoically there was no avoiding it this time. Nor would it hamper his future secret career, as the whole desperate affair had taken place on his own doorstep, where he had every right to be, apart from being a secret agent.

After dinner Madame Monet's part in the plot was let out, which proved so diverting that it kept dancing pretty well to a minimum while all the guests, particularly the males who had been grinning at her for weeks, assured each other they had suspected as much all along. The crowd had to go out to the rampart to see the heroic yachts dancing quietly at anchor. A few daring bucks took the notion of luring some intrepid ladies into the winch room, with a good many candelabra, of course, while the more sedate chaperones and squires were led to Sir Henry's office to hear the inside story, and be shown a peek at the original letter informing Sir Henry of the whole. Mr. Hopkins, who made the error of taking up a chair, heard as well the history of the inkwell, the Prince's miniature and the Peninsular campaign.

During the mêlée, Sanford and Marie were tended by Biddy in the morning parlor, where some approximation of the truth was disseminated. "I never did like Benson above half," Biddy reminded her niece. "To be using one's family connections so shabbily is not what a gentleman would do. And as to dangling after Marie when he was already married!"

"It was not the dangling I minded so much as the slap," Marie pointed out.

"A bruise! Certainly you will have a discoloration on that cheek," Biddy prophesied, sending off for chipped ice to lessen this ill effect.

"And that French hussy, trying to get into the house," Biddy continued her tirade.

"She'd have been easier to keep an eye on if you'd let her," Sanford mentioned.

"Cheaper, too," Biddy added practically. "But then I suppose you will be repaid for any expense you had in the matter. With a prize of ten thousand pounds to be dealt with, the Admiralty will not be clutch-fisted. Where did you hide the gold, Sanford?"

Marie turned to regard his answer with interest. "It's

218

buried outdoors," he replied. "I'll dig it up tomorrow and turn it over to the authorities."

"Where did you bury it?" Biddy asked.

"Out in the stables."

"What a good idea! Always stablehands there to prevent Benson getting at it."

"Yes, I had my own groom bury it late one night."

Marie could not see that any damage would have been done by this means of hiding, and doubted she had heard the truth yet.

"Benson won't get his money back, will he?" Biddy asked. "Will they give it back to him? He should buy Oakhurst back if they do."

"The price of Oakhurst has risen considerably since he sold it, has it not, Sanford?" Marie asked with a knowing smile.

"It has had considerable repairs made to it. It is worth more now. But in any case, the Aldridges would not be interested in selling it back. They are very happy there."

"The Aldridges?" Marie asked. "It was yourself who bought Oakhurst, was it not?"

"I? What the devil would I want with it?" Sanford replied. "Aldridge did sell me ten acres for pasture at the back of his lot. He is retired and keeps no cattle. It was from him I learned Benson had sold out. I knew nothing about it till the deal was closed."

"That's not what Benson told us. He said you had bought up his mortgage while he was in Vienna and wouldn't sell it back."

"The place wasn't mortgaged. He sold it to finance Bonaparte's rescue. Madame must have been the first woman in Europe to know what was coming. Oakhurst was sold before Boney handed himself over. But he was eager to turn you against me, and a lie would be nothing to him."

"He'd lie as fast as a dog would trot," Biddy agreed. "Well," she said, looking at her two patients, "it's nearly three o'clock, and as you will both have a busy day tomorrow with journalists and government men here asking questions, I suggest we all turn in. You won't go back to the ball looking like this."

"I'm not up to it," Sanford admitted. He did feel up to a few moments private conversation with Marie, however, and to gain it, asked Biddy what she meant to do about Benson's effects, still in his room, hoping she would make some move to go and leave them alone.

"I'll lock the door and leave all the evidence there for the police tomorrow. I'll make sure to lock it when I go up to bed."

"Better do it now, in case he sends that valet of his back to get rid of any incriminating objects—maps, routes, that sort of thing," Sanford suggested.

"An excellent idea!" She went in such haste to do it that she left all her medical paraphernalia behind her, thus ensuring she would soon be back with them.

"You mentioned it was Ireland they meant to go to," Marie said. "How did you find that out?"

"My chef from *Seadog* and a couple of the crew were hired to run *Phoebe*. But we can find something more interesting than Benson to talk about." He arose and joined her on the sofa.

"Indeed we can! Would you like to discuss Madame's wart, the true location of it I mean, or for that matter the real location of the buried gold? Or that faradiddle you announced at the ball about Papa giving the order to have his chain cut?"

"I was thinking rather of us."

"Oh, *us*! We are as dull as ditch water. Who wants to talk about an insipid country wench, or a fashionable fribble?"

"The combination, being so unlikely, provides some interest. I had to tell Madame something to put her off the track. She already suspected from the dilatory manner in which I pursued her after setting her up in that cottage that I was not half keen on herself. She expected more gallantry from me and must have suspected you were the fly in the ointment."

"Such a flattering image you find for me! And the manner in which you were pursuing her was not so dilatory, either. You were kissing her in the orchard."

"Dilatorily, and only in the line of duty," he pointed out. "I wasn't kissing her like this." He swept Marie into his arms and kissed her in very much the same way, but as it was no longer a duty he enjoyed it considerably more. Inexperienced as she was, she was more impressed with it, too. She hardly minded the pain as he bruised her sore jaw, nor did he pay the slightest heed to his stinging chin. Still, even a blissful pain cannot be endured for long, and he soon released her. "You just wait till we're both healed!" he was threatening her when Biddy re-entered.

"What is that you mean to do when you're both healed?" she asked with lively interest.

220

"We're going to take up studying French, Biddy," he answered blandly.

"Why, I thought you already spoke French pretty well," she answered, surprised.

"Yes, I am going to teach your niece while we are at Wight," he said. "We even may have a few lessons before we go, if we can find some nice quiet spot around the house where we won't be disturbed."

"That can easily be arranged. My, I don't like the looks of those bruises on the pair of you. The ice packs did no good at all. They seem to be aggravated. I think I must leech you both tomorrow," she said happily. "I'll go out to my reservoir bright and early and select half a dozen plump ones."

Sanford glanced at her, startled. He soon made his excuses and left, to rout Belhomme out of his chair and advise him he must be awakened not later than six in the morning.

24

Despite the late night and despite the nearly total lack of sleep by anyone under the roof of Bolt Hall, Biddy Boltwood was at her reservoir at seven in the morning fishing out likely suckers, and Sanford was up an hour earlier to retrieve the chest of gold and have it ready for the authorities. By the time Marie got downstairs at a tardy eight o'clock, the chest was open to the elements and the excited eyes of her family. She noticed puddles of water at the chest's corners, and doubted they had got there from its being buried in dry earth.

"You washed the chest down, did you?" she asked Sanford.

"Yes, it was covered in dirt from being buried. You can go to the stable and see where it was buried," he offered. Sir Henry made a mental note to honor this corner in some suitable manner—a stone or a brass marker were compared for suitability, and Sanford hoped Belhomme had had the sense to make a hole of a proper depth.

Marie walked around to the rear of the chest, glancing down as she did so. She saw, sticking to a leather thong that bound the wooden slats together, a choice leech. Sanford saw her expression of surprise, and hastily walked around to join her. His eyes followed hers to the incriminating evidence. He talked on unconcernedly as he pulled a handkerchief from his pocket. "I seem to have got my boots muddied in the stable," he finished up, and reached down to whisk the offending leech into the folds of muslin, under the pretext of wiping his toes.

"That versatile Belhomme of yours, does he ever act as a valet at all?" Marie asked in a low voice.

"When he is not busy with more demanding chores. Well, shall we have some more coffee?" They walked together to the morning parlor.

"Do tell me, was it the chest of gold that made the leeches so torpid? Is that the damage you referred to?" Marie asked him.

"My dear girl, gold always excites living animal matter; it does not depress it. It was the bottle of laudanum I borrowed for my groom's sore hand that did the trick. But don't for God's sake tell Biddy so. I wanted to give them symptoms interesting enough to insure her hanging around the reservoir, just in case Benson tumbled to the hiding place. He didn't, as it turned out, but that is hindsight."

"I bet you didn't need the vacuum hood for your liver, either, nor all those headache drops. You only did it to bring Biddy round your thumb, didn't you?"

"It was necessary to be on terms with one of the family. You youngsters had both taken me in such aversion that I required any ally I could summon. One never knows when some request of a bizarre nature will be necessary, and it helps to have unquestioning friends. Sir Henry, of course, was wishing I would get myself killed. Is he still, by the by, or do you think he has taken to approving of me since I let him decide to cut the Bolt chain himself?"

"He referred to you as Bathurst's godson this morning, and not as 'that demmed Sanford,' so I *think* he is reassessing you."

"Good. Then it remains only for him to reassess *your* worth—a hundred thousand is a little steep for a country wench—and I shall speak to him."

"A little judicious puffing up of his part in last night's intrigue should lower my value," she suggested.

"Throw in the coronet and he'll be paying me to take you off his hands. I wonder if that isn't an idea!" he said, with a considering look on his face.

"Sanford! How can you be so cheap!"

"How can you be so cork-brained! We negotiated the deal days ago."

To reestablish goodwill with his fiancée, Sanford flattered Sir Henry with all the skill at his command when the gentlemen of the press and government arrived not much later. Before the morning was over, Sir Henry had hit on the exact moment when he had come to the fateful decision of cutting the chain. It was just when his son pointed out that the rescue would be done by means of Rawlins masquerading a bunch of renegades as British seamen. But David was always up to anything, and had got a pack of his own friends on to the ship.

"It is my opinion that Prince George ought to have the chain repaired at the government's expense," Sanford said. At this point he actually received one of Sir Henry's beetle-browed smiles, that looked so terribly like a frown. "As it was maintained by Edward VI in the old days," Sanford mentioned.

When Admiral Keith arrived a little later to add his august presence to the assembly, he diverted a good deal of interest to himself, by announcing that Captain Cockburne was arrived aboard the *Northumberland* to carry Bonaparte off to Saint Helena, and was only awaiting official word from London, and a stout breeze, to do it.

There was no question of Sanford's leaving before this interesting event had occurred. He had plenty of time to have the chain repaired at his own expense, and make up a story to Sir Henry that the Prince Regent had asked him to do it, and he would be reimbursed. He had more figuring to decide how he would get a letter from Prinney attesting to this agreement; Sir Henry wanted it for his files. A series of hasty urgings to his godfather culminated in the raising of Sir Henry Boltwood, K.B.E. to Sir Henry Boltwood, Bart. He and his successors were henceforth to be styled baronets, within easy grasp even of a barony the next time the Bolt Chain was required.

Before *Seadog* left for the Isle of Wight, bearing in Sanford's cabin two dozen green speckled leeches, and on its deck all the Boltwood ménage except Sir Henry, there was a gratifying announcement in the local papers that Sir Henry Boltwood, Bart., was happy to announce the betrothal of his daughter, Marie, to Lord Sanford, the wedding to take place

223

soon at Bolt Hall, which led inexorably to a lengthy recounting of the history of Bolt Hall.

As *Seadog* lifted anchor and caught the prevailing wind in her sails to drift out over the chain to the sea, Sir Henry stood on the rampart, waving a white handkerchief, and formulating plans for a slightly larger yacht, a schooner, actually. Something to do justice to a baronet. A schooner that would sleep a dozen was what he had in mind, with a fancy fireplace and a bit of a wine cellar. Davey, good lad, would like to have it.

This plan dropped from his mind as he went to his study, to smile at all his trophies, and lastly to let his eyes linger on the patent outlining all details of his new eminence, the baronetcy. As he got down to business, drawing up the letter disclaiming the municipality's liability in forthcoming "delicate matters," he was a happy man.